THE PENITENT ONE

BRIAN SHEA

Severn River
PUBLISHING

ALSO BY BRIAN SHEA

The Nick Lawrence Series

Kill List

Pursuit of Justice

Burning Truth

Targeted Violence

Murder 8

The Boston Crime Thriller Series

Murder Board

Bleeding Blue

The Penitent One

Sign of the Maker

Never miss a new release! Sign up to receive exclusive updates from author Brian Shea.

BrianChristopherShea.com/Boston

Sign up and receive a free copy of

Unkillable: A Nick Lawrence Short Story

This one goes out to my father-in-law, Burt, or better known to my girls who absolutely adore him, Pop Pop. Your newfound love of reading is contagious! Thank you for being you and all the tireless support you've shown for all of my endeavors.

1

Donovan O'Brien, or Father Donny as he was known to his parishioners, looked out on the congregation spread out amidst the pews. He remembered a time when the bench seats were packed with people. His Masses seemed to fill the rows more than the much older Father Winslow's services. Father Tomlin, who was closer in age, had not been with the parish long and wasn't from the neighborhood. His support was growing but he hadn't garnered much of a following yet. Not that O'Brien was keeping track. More obvious was the disparity in age for the ones he presided over. This morning, the crowd was a good two decades younger than those who attended Father Winslow's Masses.

Debbie Shoemaker sat in the front row. He'd known Deb for years. And in a very personal way. That was before his calling. But there she was next to Joslyn Roswell. The two couldn't have been more different in outward appearances.

Even though it was only twenty-seven degrees outside, Deb felt the compulsion to wear a low-cut silk blouse accentuating her ample cleavage. She intentionally leaned forward to read her missalette, allowing the soft curvature of her flesh to push against her shirt, testing the strength of the light pink bra. Any onlooker trying to avoid temptation best look elsewhere. Even for a man of the cloth, it was a test of willpower.

O'Brien had seen old man Haggerty take a beating from his wife when caught ogling the voluptuous woman more than fifty years younger than him. But even with his wife's mean swing of a purse, he still spent most of every service working to angle himself for one more glimpse of Deb's partially exposed body.

Joslyn, on the other hand, was much more reserved in her appearance. But what she held in reserve by dress, she made up for in action. She was a toucher. More than once during her departure from the church, the tight-bodied blonde had made a point of hugging him. The things she whispered in his ears were enough to make a sailor blush and forced him to immediately make an Act of Contrition. If the hugs and whispering weren't enough, Joslyn, on three separate occasions, had grabbed his crotch. Now, when possible, he avoided her like the plague.

The two temptresses sat side by side, directly in Father Donny's line of sight, as he stepped to the podium to deliver his homily. The outside of his left eye, along his upper cheek, was still slightly discolored in a subtle yellow-ish-purple hue from a punch Mike Kelly had landed during last Thursday's session at Pops's gym. It had been a heck of an overhand right delivered by his lifelong friend. He brushed it absentmindedly, the tenderness of the three-day-old bruise temporarily distracting him from Deb's cleavage.

He cleared his throat and adjusted his collar as he looked outward.

"With Thanksgiving around the corner, I wanted to take a moment and talk about cleaning the plate. And I don't mean after your third trip to the dessert table."

A ripple of laughter circulated through the congregation.

"I'm talking about your spiritual plate. It becomes burdensome to carry the heavy load of sin. Imagine piling on the turkey, stuffing, and mashed potatoes, and going back for seconds before eating your first. The weight of your dinner plate would eventually slip from your hands and likely shatter on the floor. I know I've got your stomachs rumbling at all this talk of food. Don't worry, you'll be getting your Eucharist soon enough."

The reference to the small, light-as-air wafer earned another chuckle from the group.

"But in all seriousness, your spiritual health is important to me. Without clearing away buildup on your soul, you run the risk of shattering your faith. I think you can see the number of churchgoers has dropped in recent years. Much is due to the weight of sin. Hard to walk through those three arched doors behind you when you feel unworthy of God's grace."

The group seemed to sense the seriousness in his normally uplifting tone and grew solemn. Even Deb adjusted her shirt, partially shielding her breasts from view.

"There is a simple way to wipe clean your plate. To start fresh in the eyes of God. And that's through the Sacrament of Penance. I haven't seen many of you lining up at the confessional lately. But not to worry, I have faith today will be different. After Mass, why don't you take a bit of your busy Sunday to stop in. Lighten your spiritual load before you tackle the turkey of life."

A little laugh enlivened the group. Joslyn seemed to take the invitation to stop by the confessional as some secret code for a romantic tryst, because she bit the bottom of her lip and winked. Father Donny felt warm and knew his normally pale cheeks had reddened.

"Let us stand," he said, concluding his sermon and resuming the ritualistic aspect of the Mass.

This priest was good, the man in back thought to himself. It seemed as if today's homily was written just for him. The words were powerful in and of themselves, but he knew now the importance of his life's purpose. God spoke to him. The priest was a mere vessel to deliver his message, but he heard it loud and clear. When he first entered the church, he wasn't exactly sure of his direction. He had it now. A cleansing in the biblical sense. And what better place to do it.

Although not a parishioner of this particular church, the man had been raised Catholic, and the routines of most services were universal. Up, down, kneel. He had never been inside this church before today, but he'd been called to it.

The Mass ended, but the man remained. He lowered the cushioned hassock and knelt. The closing hymn echoed along the vaulted ceiling as the priest and his entourage of altar boys solemnly paced down the center aisle toward the back of the church. As they passed each row, the members of the congregation began their clamorous departure. The man did not look up when the priest passed by. His hands were folded in prayer, and he rested the center of his forehead on his scarred knuckles. His eyes were closed, and he slipped into a deep prayer, beginning his own private penance before meeting with the priest. His spiritual plate was full and needed cleaning before he set about adding to it.

The last person in the short line to the confessional had exited. A woman with an incredible chest. The man wondered what sorts of sins a woman like this confessed. He would've loved to have been a fly on the wall in there. She hadn't spent long inside the closed room and was leaving in a huff without completing whatever prescribed number of Hail Mary or Our Father prayers she was given to receive her full absolution.

As the woman passed, he wondered what his penance would be for the things he'd done.

The back door to the church boomed as it closed, leaving the interior in a hushed silence. Nobody around except for the kneeling man and the priest enclosed in his section of the confessional. Forty-five minutes until the next Mass was to begin.

The man rose and walked down the middle aisle toward the closed door of the confessional, his footsteps noisy against the tiled floor. He genuflected in front of the altar.

As he neared the door, the priest opened his section and looked out, startled when he saw him.

"I'm sorry, Father. I didn't mean to frighten you." The man secretly enjoyed this unexpected face-to-face interaction with the holy man. "Do you have time for one more?"

The priest looked down at his watch and smiled. "Sure. I don't mean to rush you, but the next Mass will be starting soon, and I've got a little prep to do."

The man bowed slightly and smiled. "It won't take long at all."

The priest retreated inside and closed the door.

Before entering his section of the dim confessional, the man looked around. Still alone. Satisfied, he disappeared inside. He knelt on the pew facing the small covered window. He could feel the warmth of the knees of the woman who'd preceded him.

The priest slid back the solid divider. A dark screen separated the two men. "Do you know the rite? Or would you like me to guide you?" the priest asked, looking forward, away from the kneeling man.

"I know it well, thank you, Father," the man said. "O my God, I am heartily sorry for having offended Thee, and I detest all my sins, because I dread the loss of Heaven and the pains of hell, but most of all because they offend Thee, my God, Who art all good and deserving of all my love. I firmly resolve with the help of Thy grace to confess my sins, to do penance, and to amend my life. Amen." The man recited the words with no hesitation or fumbling.

"Very well, my son. How long has it been since your last confession?"

"Twenty-seven days."

"What sin is it you seek to confess before God?" the priest asked.

"Murder."

The priest shifted in his seat and cleared his throat. "Go on."

"Can you absolve me from something I haven't done?"

The priest gave a sigh of relief. "So you've thought about killing someone? And you'd like absolution?"

"I'm going to kill this person and I'd like forgiveness before I do," the man said softly.

"I'm not sure I can. If you told me who this person is or what they've done to you to make you want to kill them, then maybe I could help." The priest's voice no longer exuded confidence and he choked on the words.

"This person has done nothing to me personally. But they know what they've done."

"I don't understand," the priest said with a tremor. "Who is this person you speak of?"

"You."

The silenced pistol in the man's hand was already positioned against the wood paneling of the thin wall separating the two rooms. The shot toppled the priest from his chair. The man rose and took aim through the screen, preparing to fire an additional bullet for good measure but quickly realized it wasn't necessary.

Then he knelt once more into the dimpled fabric and completed his prayer.

2

The shopping cart's front left wheel wobbled wildly, pulling it to the left and forcing Michael Kelly to pay extra care to navigating it past other shoppers. He did so with some failing, crashing the side of the cart into the grocery aisle refrigeration section's retaining wall for the second time in less than a minute. He now understood the purpose of the black rubber bumper lining the knee-high retaining wall of the fruits and vegetables, a guardrail designed to protect against any wayward cart drivers cruising the thorough-fare of Stop & Shop's tiled aisles. As if adding insult to injury, his latest crash was accompanied by a deafening squeak of the wheel, drawing the attention of a few nearby shoppers. Kelly smiled, throwing his shoulders up into a shrug.

He leaned down and reached for a bag of Brussels sprouts as the timed mist sprayed down from above, dampening his outstretched arm. *Perfect! When it rains it pours.* He wasn't a big fan of grocery shopping, and this latest venture only added to his dislike. The one bright spot was the company he'd brought along with him.

Kelly fished out a family-sized bag of sprouts and tossed it into the cart. Embry looked up at him, her green eyes wide with fear, as if she had just seen a bear pop out from behind a tree.

"Are you kidding me, Dad?" she asked, staring down at the newest item added to the cart.

Kelly smiled. "Come on, they're good for you. Plus, the way I cook them, they're not that healthy. Trust me, they'll be delicious. I think you're old enough to at least give it a try. I'm going to be cooking them with bacon. You love bacon."

Embry stuck her tongue out in a gagging gesture and slowly shook her head from left to right, eyes still holding a feigned, wide-eyed look of shock at his suggestion that she try something so horrible as fresh Brussels sprouts on Thanksgiving. "Great, now I don't even get to look forward to bacon."

"Don't worry. I bought two packs. One for the sprouts and one for the pancakes the next morning."

"As long as they're not Brussels sprout pancakes."

Kelly's turn to roll his eyes.

"So, tell me more. When is she coming?" And just like that his daughter flipped the conversation back to their previous discussion. She batted her eyes with a coy, mocking gesture as she continued to subtly tease her father, which she had done since they first entered the store.

Actually, the taunting began when his daughter learned about their guest at this year's Thanksgiving dinner. Embry had met Kristen Barnes before, but not since the two of them decided to try their hand at a relationship. And much to Kelly's misery, Embry was taking far too much pleasure in tormenting him for it.

"Look, like I told you before, Kris will be stopping by. No big deal. She's just a friend. Kris isn't coming to dinner. She'll only be over for dessert." Kelly tried to downplay his excitement, but he could see by Embry's eye-rolling that she wasn't buying into it.

"Maybe she's skipping dinner to avoid your Brussels sprouts?"

Kelly laughed. Embry would make a hell of an interrogator someday, although he said a silent prayer every night that she would never choose to follow in his footsteps.

"I'm sure she's very upset at the prospect of missing out on my secret recipe. But she's got a family tradition of her own. Kris has never missed a Thanksgiving dinner with her parents unless work interfered, and I don't want to be the reason she misses tomorrow's."

"Why?" Embry asked with genuine interest.

"It's an important time for her. I don't know if I told you, but she was in foster care for a long time."

"Her mom didn't want her?"

It was a foreign concept to a child like Embry, who'd never experienced anything like that. Kelly thought of the recent revelation regarding his own biological mother and his secret adoption, something he had not yet shared with his daughter. He wasn't sure when the time would be appropriate to do so, especially since he was still processing the news himself.

"Not every mother can keep their child."

"That's sad," Embry said solemnly.

Kelly was always impressed with his daughter's ability to empathize. "It is, and I'm sure it was for Kris, but some good came of it. She was eventually adopted by a loving family who couldn't have children of their own."

"But I still don't understand why she can't come to our house for dinner."

Kelly was delighted to hear his daughter so intent on having Barnes over. If for no other reason than to have a partner to commiserate with her suffering in having to eat the sprouts.

"Thanksgiving holds particular significance for Kris and her family. It was the day her adoption was finalized. For her, it was the first family meal she had in a very long time. So, for her, it's not just Thanksgiving, it's a time when she reconnects to that point when she was first brought home. When she gained a home after living so long in the foster care system without one." Kelly somewhat regretted the serious tone in the conversation because he saw the glimmer dissipate from Embry's eyes as she looked up at him.

"I get it, Dad. But still, when is she coming?"

"Like I said, dessert. So maybe sometime between 5:00 and 6:00."

"And how long is she going to stay? Hopefully she'll join us for game night. If she's going to be your girlfriend then she should stay for games."

"I told you, we're just friends," Kelly said a little more emphatically than intended. His denial made the truth more obvious.

Ignoring his attempts at concealing the nature of their relationship, Embry continued, "I think you should dress up. Better idea, I should dress you. How about that? Let me get you ready for your big date."

"Embry, I told you, she's just a friend. I invited her over for dessert. She's my partner. You don't make a big deal when Mainelli stops by. Or the times that we've met some of my other partners out at a restaurant for dinner."

"This is different, Dad, and you know it," she said. "They aren't girls."

"True, but they're still cops. She's a cop. A good cop at that."

"I know, Dad. You told me the stories. I get it. But I also know you, and I can see plainly that there is a little more to this visit than you're letting on. You're trying to be cool about it. And guess what? It's not working."

Kelly pushed the squeaky cart forward, fighting to keep it straight as they moved down the aisle.

"Does it bother you?" he asked.

"What?" Embry smirked.

She was going to make him say the words. "If it was a date? If she was more than a coworker? Would it bother you?"

Kelly had wanted to ask this question of his daughter since he first broached the idea of having Barnes over for Thanksgiving.

It had been well over a year since the relationship between Embry's mother and Kelly had dissolved completely. And although she had moved on, he, for all intents and purposes, had not. He hadn't dated, and he had never brought a woman home with him, never introduced a new potential prospect to his daughter. This would be a first for him. He was entering uncharted territory and he was worried—actually terrified—how his soon-to-be nine-year-old would take the news.

She seemed fine with her mother's boyfriend, so it was reasonable to assume Embry would accept it when Kelly found someone else and be open-minded to it. But now that it was upon him, he was worried maybe it was too soon. Maybe she wasn't ready.

The two had always been close as far as fathers and daughters went. With the circumstances of their relationship, and Kelly being a single parent, he was closer to her now than ever before. He feared introducing a new woman into his daughter's life would have negative consequences, damaging the bond formed.

"I'm happy for you, Dad. You've seemed so lonely since you and Mom split. And I like the idea of you dating now."

Kelly leaned down and kissed her forehead. She smiled and tucked a loose curl of auburn hair behind her ear.

"Hey, and if she's as cool as you say she is, then I'm sure to like her."

And just like that, the burden was lifted from Kelly's shoulders. The worry of the past couple months, the trepidation that his decision was a selfish one, evaporated. His daughter had given him her blessing, and with that, he suddenly felt more comfortable with the idea of moving forward with his relationship. Kelly also had a newfound respect for his young daughter and the wisdom she possessed at such an early age. Sometimes life and its circumstances taught children lessons that would be better learned later.

But Kelly couldn't change the past. He couldn't mend the damage done in those dark times after his partner's death and the fallout it had on his family. What he could do, what he had been doing since the dissolution of his marriage, was to put his energy into his daughter and the relationship they had, balancing work against life as a single dad. Something that took some adjustment, especially after being assigned to Boston PD's illustrious Homicide unit and the endless sea of cases crossing his desk. Suffice it to say, looking at his daughter now, they'd both adjusted well enough to the circumstances. Their bond and relationship were stronger now than ever before.

"Tell you what, Dad, I'll try a Brussels sprout if you let me sit next to Kristen when she comes for dessert."

Kelly felt his cheeks reddening. "Of course. You win. A Brussels sprout for a ticket to sit next to the guest of honor seems like a fair trade."

She giggled. It was an excited, infectious giggle, and he was beginning to hear it often. Embry seemed to have thoroughly bounced back from the initial fallout of her parents' divorce.

Kelly shook off the cold from the vegetable refrigeration unit as they pushed the noisy cart toward the Stop & Shop's meat and dairy section.

"Well, it sounds like this Thanksgiving is going to shape up to be just perfect," Kelly said.

"Except for the Brussels sprouts," Embry muttered under her breath.

Just then Kelly felt his cell phone vibrate in his pocket and stopped the cart. He pulled it out to see a familiar number and answered on the second ring.

"Hey, Donny, what's going on in the world of God?"

The response came in the form of ragged breaths. Donny sounded as if he was running, and at first Kelly thought maybe his childhood-friend-turned-Catholic-priest was out for a jog. Keeping himself fit was something that he did on top of taking care of the parishioners he served. Perhaps Donny had butt-dialed him, and he was just catching the rubbings of his phone against his arm or pocket.

"Donny, are you there?" Kelly asked, louder now.

"Hey, Mike, I really need to talk to you. Something awful has happened."

Kelly stopped, giving his full attention to his friend, a man who prided himself on remaining calm. The priest had heard and seen horrible things in his time serving the Dorchester community and always managed to keep a level head. To hear the panic in his voice concerned Kelly immensely.

"Donny, what is it?"

Another ragged breath and a sigh. "It's Father Tomlin. He's dead. Somebody's killed him, Mike...here at Saint Peter's!"

Kelly paused for a second, considering his friend's words. "Somebody killed a priest inside your church? When?"

"Shot him. I just found him dead in the confessional. Gunshot to his head. They shot him through the confessional, Mike. Who does that? Who murders a priest, let alone murders him inside a confessional inside of God's house? Who does such a thing?"

The ragged breathing changed into a whimper as his friend cried softly through the receiver.

"I'll be there as quick as I can. I just got to drop off Embry and then I'm heading your way. You already called the police, right?"

"I called you first."

"Donny, hang up and dial 911. The cops need to be there right now. They need to hold the scene. They need to secure it. Don't let anybody in, and anybody that's in there, do your best to keep them there until the cavalry arrive. Do you hear me? Call 911 now. Report it. They'll send marked units. I will be there shortly, I promise."

Kelly's tone was serious as he tried to snap his friend out of the dazed and confused mindset he was stuck in so that he could do the right thing.

"I'm hanging up now, Donny. Do you hear me? I'm hanging up the phone now. You're going to dial 911. I am going to be there as soon as I can."

Kelly ended the call, slipped his phone back into his pocket, and looked at his daughter, who had only heard half of the conversation. Her eyes were now as wide as when he had grabbed the Brussels sprouts, but now they were layered with a serious undertone. She knew something bad had happened. He always tried his best as a parent and cop to shield his daughter from the horrors of his job, but sometimes it wasn't possible.

Kelly rarely, if ever, talked about his case work, and never brought his work home with him, at least not where she could see. He alone carried the emotional burdens of the things he experienced. He tucked them deep, sheltering his daughter from such horrors and working hard not to impact her childhood.

But this situation was unavoidable. Had Kelly known it was a call from work, he would have stepped further away from his daughter and spoken in hushed tones, something she'd become accustomed to. Embry knew that when her father answered a call and walked away, it was most likely work and she was not privy to the details. He'd caught her eavesdropping only once and had nipped that in the bud. But this time, she had caught the full force of the conversation.

"Honey, we've got to go now. Donny needs me. Something bad's happened."

"Is he okay?" Embry asked.

"He's fine," Kelly half-lied, knowing that his friend was physically fine but would have emotional scars that lasted a lifetime. "Donny's tough. He's from the old neighborhood. He'll be okay. I just got to get you home so I can take care of him and help him out. Do you understand?"

Embry nodded.

He reversed the squeaky cart, abandoning the last few items on his shopping list. Kelly shoved the cart forward to the self-checkout aisle, making quick work of the few items that he had, bagging them, and then heading out the door with Embry in tow.

A dead priest the Sunday before Thanksgiving was no way to start the holiday festivities.

Marked cruisers posted at each end of Bowdoin Street had effectively shut it down in a one-block radius of Saint Peter's Church. The squad cars, their distinctive powder-blue-and-white color pattern unique to the Boston PD, successfully cut off any vehicular traffic. Although the patrol cars' positioning stopped civilian vehicles from entering the area, the officers assigned to securing the perimeter were still in the process of extending the distinctive yellow crime scene tape so onlookers and civilian foot traffic couldn't enter the space.

Kelly stopped his unmarked Caprice near the grassy park area at the disjointed three-way intersection where Bowdoin met with Adams and Church Street. He stepped out and surveyed the scene, taking in the initial perimeter being set. It was better to start big and collapse the scene inward than try to expand it, which made for all sorts of challenges regarding evidence collection and scene integrity. From Kelly's initial take, the on-scene patrol supervisor seemed to have done a decent job of giving a wide berth to the investigative area around the church.

It was cool, not cold, and Kelly only had a department-issued navy-blue windbreaker over his hooded lightweight gray sweatshirt. Even though his jacket had the BPD logo on the front and lettering on the back denoting his unit, Homicide, Kelly tugged at his beaded chain necklace, releasing the worn leather of his badge carrier. His detective shield was now prominently displayed outside his jacket at the center of his chest.

He dipped low, slipping under the tape, his badge swinging freely. Kelly recognized the patrolman who was busy unraveling the plastic tape nearby.

"Been a while, Kelly. How's the murder beat treating you?" Officer George Arundale asked.

"Not bad. It's a front-row seat to the show," Kelly offered, a standard response he'd begun giving with more frequency. The truth was, his recent position had exposed him to the underbelly of the criminal world, some of which had its roots in the department itself. A revelation Kelly wished he never uncovered and something that left a bitter taste in his mouth.

Kelly knew Arundale from when he worked the Eleven back in the day. Although the two had been on opposite shifts, they'd gotten along well enough, even if only through locker room jocularity.

"I'm thinking of taking the detective's exam next time it comes up," Arundale said, eyebrows raised. "What d'ya think?"

"Go for it. Best of luck." Kelly gave him a goodbye wave and moved quickly toward the front steps of the church, the same church where not too long ago he had flattened the nose of Connor Walsh's enforcer, Tommy Sullivan.

An eternity seemed to have passed since that clash, yet in reality it had only been a couple of months. In that time Kelly had settled into the responsibilities of his job as a homicide detective, temporarily putting on hold his battle with Boston's most notorious crime lord. His caseload had diverted him from his efforts at putting the boss in custody. His inability to focus his investigative energy on taking down the kingpin had nothing to do with finding out that Walsh was his biological father.

Father Donovan O'Brien was speaking to two patrolmen at the top of the steps. He looked distraught, and the cool breeze whipping around the building was blowing his hair wildly. Kelly could see that Donny was nearing a state of shock, an understandable reaction after having just witnessed the death of his colleague.

As Kelly made quick work of the stone steps, Donny looked past the officer questioning him, his eyes brightening slightly upon seeing his friend approach.

Kelly put his hand on the patrolman's shoulder and said, "I've got it from here for now. Would you guys mind giving me a second with him?"

The two patrolmen looked at each other and shrugged, knowing that Kelly's homicide detective status meant his decisions on scenes like this trumped theirs. They'd have to get whatever information they were seeking for their initial report later.

The two jogged down the stairs and back to the sidewalk, where they began talking with the shift supervisor, likely explaining why they were no longer questioning the priest.

Kelly recognized the on-scene supervisor and gave a friendly wave to Sergeant Connolly. The seasoned sergeant gave a nod, his silent approval.

Kelly turned back to his friend. "Okay, Donny, run me through it right now. Tell me what you found. Take your time—no detail is too small."

"It was crazy, Mike. I mean, I had just finished Mass. I had gone into the back to arrange things and straighten up for Father Tomlin, who'd be delivering the next service."

"Why was he in the confessional?"

"We offer it after each Mass. It was Tomlin's turn to hear confession. We rotate."

"And how many people were waiting to be seen by him?"

O'Brien shrugged. "I have no idea. To be honest, I wasn't paying any attention. After I see the parishioners off, there's lots of prep to be done in advance of the next service."

"What about the people in church today? Do you remember anything that stood out among any of the attendees?"

"I mean, it's a pretty big parish, Mike. You might remember, when you used to attend on a regular basis."

Kelly took the subtle blow in stride. He had long since stopped going to Mass, even though his friend reminded him of his absence on a regular basis, particularly on Thursday nights when they boxed at Pops' gym. Kelly always came up with a reason why he couldn't attend. The reality was that after years of seeing the things he'd witnessed as a street cop, then as a narcotics detective, and now in Homicide, he felt a sense of disconnect that he couldn't quite place. Baxter Green's death had been the nail in his soul's coffin, severing the last thread in his belief in a higher power. Although he continued to raise his daughter in the principles of the Catholic faith, he himself had become a wayward follower at best.

"I get it, Donny. You can slap me on the wrist for not attending some other time. But did you see anyone during or after Mass who may have stood out from the rest, somebody you haven't seen before?"

Donny flexed his brow, thinking hard. Kelly let his friend silently process the question.

"Honestly, Mike, I can't think of anybody who stood out. I mean, it was the usual crowd. Familiar faces and unfamiliar ones. We get visitors, family members in from out of town. Heck, Mike, it's just before Thanksgiving, people are in town for the holidays. There were plenty of new faces, and none that stood out as being a criminal or a murderer. I mean, what would I be looking for anyway?"

Kelly knew he was right. Murderers didn't always wear dark hooded masks and sunglasses and look like the Unabomber or Charles Manson. He'd met many a killer, confronted them face-to-face after seeing what they were capable of, and there was no way to tell just by looking. If you passed them in an aisle at your local Stop & Shop, the average citizen would never look twice. Some of the most dangerous killers in the world were able to pull off normal lives, hiding the darkness of their hearts from outsiders. Ted Bundy charmed people, making himself invisible in plain sight, even after the legal system had exposed him for the monster he was. Kelly knew it would be impossible for Donny to identify the killer unless he had actually seen someone with a gun.

"Okay. I knew it was a long shot but had to ask. Tell me about your routine. Walk me through what you did this morning after Mass ended."

Kelly wanted to establish a clear and concise timeline. From there, he could build his investigation around the avenues of approach and escape for the person, or persons, who committed the crime. He planned to check the neighboring buildings and surrounding area for any video surveillance that might pick up foot or vehicular traffic. A tight timeline greatly reduced the hours of tedium when reviewing surveillance footage.

Kelly had to explore all the angles if he was to approach the case in a way that would yield the highest solvability. The first step in moving in that direction would be to establish the timeline.

"Well," Donnie began, "after the parishioners left, I cleared the altar area and staged it for the opening of the next Mass. I had to refill the communion hosts and wine decanters. The bottle was nearly empty, so I went to the back of the church where the reserves are kept."

"How long were you in the back?"

"Not long. I came back to replace the empty bottle."

"Did you notice anybody in the church at that time?" Kelly asked. Now that his friend was mentally walking through the moments leading up to the discovery of Father Tomlin's body, it was easier to access memory recall by breaking things down into smaller, more specific chunks of time.

"Nothing in particular. Wait—I saw Debbie Shoemaker. She was lingering about." Donny paused and looked wide-eyed at Kelly. "You don't think Deb could've done this, do you?"

"Honestly, I try not to jump that far ahead. I just put one foot in front of the other and see where things take me." Kelly realized from his friend's shocked expression that the answer he'd just given didn't do anything to alleviate his worry. "But you and I have known Debbie for a long time. I seriously doubt she's a cold-hearted killer, but it definitely gives me another person to talk to after I leave here."

Donny looked temporarily relieved.

"Continue," Kelly said.

"After replacing the wine, I went into the sacristy and changed out of my vestments. I wasn't going to be presiding over the next service. Father Tomlin would have been taking the second half of today's Mass schedule."

"Is that normal? Do priests usually rotate?"

"No, not always. Depends. But today we split the workload. Father Tomlin's trying to establish himself within the community, and the more the parishioners see his face in front of the crowd, the more comfortable they'll be with him."

"Okay, so you were in the sacristy," Kelly confirmed. "And then what?"

"There was still about thirty minutes until the next service was scheduled to begin, so I went to my office in the back to catch up on Sports Center. The Pats are playing at three."

Kelly saw his friend mentally punish himself for giving in to the guilty pleasure of his fandom. After a tragic event, people tended to play the "what if?" game. And Kelly knew his friend would find a way to blame himself for leaving the main space of the church. The priest's Irish-Catholic guilt would be working its magic for a long time to come.

"Okay, you had another Mass coming in thirty minutes or so? When do you typically wrap up confession before the next Mass?"

"Again, it really depends on the number of people waiting to receive their penance. But we try to stop hearing confession about fifteen minutes before the next wave of congregants enter. I guess it's roughly a thirty-minute window where confessions can be heard. Anyone who didn't get a chance would be asked to come back at another time." O'Brien shrugged. "To be honest, there usually aren't too many lingering to confess their sins after a service ends. Most are rushing for the door."

A thirty-minute window at best. Kelly made a mental note. He'd document it later in his notebook but wanted to give Donny his full attention now. "Who else was in the church? Any of the parish staff?"

"In the main area of the church it was just Father Tomlin and me. The altar boys had already changed and were long gone. Those kids can't get out of those clothes quick enough and get back out on the street. You remember how it was, right, Mike?"

Again, Donny was reminding him of a different time, and Kelly's service as an altar boy within the Archdiocese of Boston. And yes, he could remember how quickly he could disrobe from his religious wear before cutting out to the street to play with friends.

"Was anybody here when you found the priest?"

"No," Donny answered. "Nobody was here."

"Nobody? Debbie wasn't still present?"

Donny shook his head. "Whoever did this had to have been the last person Father Tomlin had seen."

"Do you keep a running list of who comes in? Is there a sign-in book for confession?"

"No, we'd never do that. That'd be like asking someone to put a placard out saying that they've sinned and 'look at me.' We don't keep track of those who come. It's supposed to be anonymous. That's why we still use the closed confessional box, Mike." Then Donny paused, and when he spoke next, his voice cracked slightly. "Do you want me to show you his body?"

"No, that's not the way it works. I can't have you re-enter the church until we're done processing it. And I'm not walking into a scene until I've got as complete a picture as I can establish. With that being said, how many people have been in the church since you called me?"

"Just those two cops you saw me talking to. They entered the church to make sure nobody was hiding in there. They searched the area, confirmed that Father Tomlin was dead, and then came back out. So besides me, just those two officers down there."

Kelly took out his notepad for the first time since they'd begun talking and jotted down the notes he'd mentally accumulated. "And about what time was that, Donny, if you had to guess?"

"Oh, I don't know, Mike. Probably fifteen minutes or so before you arrived."

Looking at his watch, Kelly noted the time. "And before they arrived, when you called me, you had just found Father Tomlin?"

"Yes." Donny nodded.

"Okay, good, that gives me a nice window of time to work with. If you had to guess, how long of a gap between the last time you saw Father Tomlin and when you made that call to me? How much time had passed?"

"I don't know, Mike, maybe fifteen or twenty minutes, if I had to guess."

Again, Kelly noted the time with a squiggly line to denote the approximate nature of it. But looking at it, he realized the murder would've happened at the very tail end of the confessional time period that Donny had explained earlier. The killer appeared to have waited until they were the last person inside the church. Unless more than one party was involved.

"Okay. That's good, Donny. That was really good. I think you've given me some stuff to work on."

"Thanks, Mike." Donny looked relieved.

Kelly knew his friend wanted to feel as though he was contributing, helping in some way, especially in such dire circumstances.

"One more thing," Kelly said. "Was anything missing from the church? Money or any items of value?"

"I don't know. I don't think so—I could check."

Kelly jotted this down and looked up. "We can figure that out later. Just asking. Not a big deal right now. I know this is all a bit overwhelming."

"So, what's next, Mike?" Donny asked, looking around as the crowd for the next Mass began to fill in along the yellow police tape, panic in their eyes.

Kelly turned and looked around. "Well, it's going to be pretty crazy for a bit. The media will be all over the place. We're going to have to contain it as best we can. But as for me, I'm going to wait for my team to get here, and then we're going to walk through the scene by the numbers. We're very methodical in how we approach something like this. We don't do anything quickly. So Mass is going to be canceled for the day. We will be holding your church hostage for about a day until we get the scene processed, depending on what we find when we get inside. Do you have somebody you need to call, one of the higher-ups, to explain what's going on? Have you done that already?"

"I already made a call to Father Winslow, who said he'd notify the archdiocese of the situation. He seemed extremely upset."

"Father Winslow, you said?" Kelly confirmed the name and then jotted it in his notepad. "Do you keep files, like personnel files, here in the church?"

Donny cocked an eyebrow. "You mean like HR forms for priests?"

"Yeah," Kelly said, "something that says where so-and-so lives, their background, maybe a bank account. I know you have some stipend that you live on, right? Something that I could use to get a background into Father Tomlin's life so I can start looking at all the angles."

"Oh sure. Yeah. We have a record system. It's back in the rectory area. I can get it for you."

"Not yet," Kelly said, "I just wanted to know if you had access to that. When we clear the scene and you're free to go back in the church, make sure you find that and get it to me, okay? That's going to help me out a lot."

"Sure thing, Mike," Donny said quietly.

"Hey, Kelly, what are you doing, assigning yourself your own cases now?" a voice called out from behind him.

Kelly turned. Standing next to Sergeant Connolly were Anthony Acevedo and Charlie McGarrity, two detectives from his Homicide unit. They also happened to be the next crew up for rotation, the next in line. Kelly had hoped to beat them to the punch and then jockey for position to take the case, since it was in his own neighborhood and directly involved one of his lifelong friends. He had a personal connection to the case and wouldn't feel comfortable leaving it in the hands of these two.

"Good to see you guys," Kelly said, sarcasm permeating his tone. "I thought you'd never get here." He looked at his watch, adding insult to injury. The fact that he hadn't been dispatched to the homicide yet beat the assigned detective squad there would sting.

"Very funny, Kelly. Just because a body drops in Dorchester doesn't mean you get first dibs. There's a pecking order here. Being a new guy to Homicide, maybe you should start learning how things work and the way cases are assigned."

Kelly threw his hands up in mock apology. "Hey, guys, no hard feelings. I was just talking to a friend of mine. There just happens to be a dead body inside," he said a little quieter, trying to keep his banter out of earshot of the onlookers.

The two detectives approached Kelly. They weren't smiling and didn't seem to find any humor in his attempts at levity.

"Seriously, Kelly, take a hike," Acevedo said as he got closer. "This isn't your case, and you being here means you get to write the first supplemental report. Maybe you should open with—'Dear Chief, I can't seem to mind my own damn business and ended up on somebody else's crime scene.' Sound good? Do you like writing supplemental reports on other homicide detectives' cases?"

"Not particularly," Kelly said, still not backing down from the younger detective.

Acevedo had been with Homicide longer than Kelly but had less experience on the street. He'd only been on the job for a little over six years and had fast-tracked his way into the unit. Acevedo's father was a captain and ranking member of the union. To say he had pull would be an understatement. His father had undoubtedly greased the wheels for his son's career ascension, giving Acevedo the prestigious position of homicide detective over those more deserving. As far as respect went, Kelly had little for the man.

Kelly wasn't just irked by the fact that nepotism had given Acevedo a leg up. This was Boston, and there was plenty of that to go around. His dislike for the detective came more from his work ethic. Kelly didn't trust his ability to handle the heavy load.

Kelly knew Acevedo and McGarrity were up for this case. When he received the call from Donny, he had rushed to the scene, not only to help his friend but also hoping he could beat the pair and take over the case. Because the likelihood of it getting solved under their watch was far less than if Kelly kept the ball in his court. Their closure rating was somewhere around forty percent, twenty percent lower than the average in Homicide, yet somehow Acevedo was able to maintain his position within the unit.

"What gives, Kelly, seriously? This isn't how business is done in Homicide. We don't just pick our cases. You get me? So go home! Take the rest of the day. And then tomorrow when you come in, how about you type up that supplement and put it on my desk? Sound fair, reasonable?"

"Everything—except the whole me-going-home thing and writing-you-a-supplement thing. I'm not writing a supplemental report."

"Why not?" Acevedo asked, getting a little too close for Kelly's comfort.

Under different circumstances, Kelly might've punched the man. But not here, not in the public eye, and definitely not on the scene of a homicide. He tabled his frustration and looked him square in the eye. "Because this is my case."

Acevedo looked to McGarrity and then back at Kelly, trying to process the situation. And while he was doing so, Kelly pulled out his phone and dialed the number he was preparing to call had he not been so rudely interrupted by the pair.

It rang once, and the gruff voice on the other end didn't seem pleased to hear from Kelly. "Mike, why are you calling me on a Sunday morning?"

Kelly assumed Sutherland already had gotten word through the universal message system, which notified when a body dropped just in case someone was out having a good time.

"Hey, Sarge, sorry to bother you, but I'm on the scene of a homicide, and I just wanted your take on things."

He heard the man sigh loudly. "What are you doing, Mike?"

Kelly distanced himself from Acevedo so he could privately converse with the sergeant of his squad. "Look, Sarge, you've got to back me on this one. You owe me."

Kelly didn't like using that as leverage, but Sutherland knew it was true. He hadn't backed Kelly previously when he needed him to, and Kelly was playing the trump card now.

"You can't give it to these two clowns. Sarge, this is going to be a big one.

We've got a dead priest inside this church right now with a gunshot wound to his head. And whoever did it ghosted. I'm not sure what we're looking at—a robbery gone bad, something personal, a hit. Who knows? Regardless, it's going to be a media circus within the next fifteen minutes. And do you really want the face of this case to be Anthony Acevedo?"

Kelly waited. The other end of the line was silent. He knew his boss was probably rubbing his thick, stubby fingers against his hair and rolling his eyes. But deep down the pause was because he knew the truth. To let those two handle a major case would be a detriment to the case itself and potentially result in a black eye for the PD. And in an image-conscious world, the department couldn't afford another one of those.

Sutherland exhaled loudly, as if he'd been holding his breath for the past several seconds. "Fine, Mike, I'll make the call and talk to their sergeant. The case is yours. Send them packing."

Kelly clicked the phone off and walked back to the two men.

"And?" Acevedo folded his arms. He was shorter than Kelly, wire-thin and not in a good way, similar to the twigs of a willow branch. He was neither physically imposing nor mentally domineering. And watching him try to intimidate Kelly, his superior on both counts, was almost comical.

Kelly, not one for cockiness, ignored the gesture. "I'll be seeing you guys. Have a good Sunday."

"That's what we thought," Acevedo said with a smug look, nodding toward McGarrity.

"Happy trails," McGarrity added, his sarcastic overtone apparent for all within earshot.

A split-second later, Acevedo's phone began to vibrate and chirp, and he looked down at the incoming call. Kelly knew it would be their direct supervisor, Sergeant Chad Williams. When Acevedo put the phone to his ear, Kelly watched the color fade from the man's tan face.

Kelly heard Acevedo's side of the brief conversation as he muttered, "Okay," in a barely audible voice. "You know, I think this is... "

The phone call must've ended abruptly because Acevedo never finished his complaint. He pulled the phone from his ear but didn't pocket it as he turned to look at Kelly with indignation.

"Have fun, you smug son of a bitch." Acevedo accented each word, almost spitting them at Kelly's face before turning and storming down the steps.

McGarrity followed, the two making their way back toward their car.

Donny said to Kelly, "What was that all about?"

"I pissed in somebody's cornflakes."

"Do you ever have a day where you don't do that?" Donny offered, the softball joke the first indication that he was going to be okay.

"Not lately."

Kelly's eyes were still tracking the pair of disgruntled detectives when he saw a familiar face working her way through the crowd. Kristen Barnes brushed past Acevedo.

4

Standing outside the church, Kelly and his cohorts made their plan of attack; dividing and conquering the work was required to process a scene as potentially large as this one.

"Why don't we divide into three?" Kelly said. "Kris and I will take the center aisle, work our way down. We'll do the preliminary walk-through without photographs. Take mental notes of potential areas of interest. Then we'll come back through and do a full evidentiary layout with photos. I'd like to get a feel for what we're up against."

"I'm good with it," Barnes said.

Kelly continued, "This goes without saying, but mind your movements in there."

"Thanks, Dad," Mainelli said with a sardonic overtone.

Kelly dismissed the comment. "Maybe we'll be able to identify a tighter area for our evidence collection. It's a big church. Hopefully we can pick apart our doer's path, figure out his probable entry and egress point, get an idea of where we need to start searching for any potential trace evidence."

"Sounds like you've gotten the hang of this thing," Ray Charles said with a rare smile, only big enough to let Kelly know his approval.

Kelly took the compliment in stride and looked over at Mainelli. "Jimmy, why don't you take the right side? Ray, if you don't mind, work your way down the left?"

"As you command, my fearless leader," Mainelli jested, following his comment with a slight head bow.

Kristen Barnes had remained relatively quiet since arriving on scene. Something was obviously bothering her about standing at the threshold of a church where a dead priest was lying. Kelly wished he could read her mind, and not just because of the current circumstances. There was a deep complexity to her, and he wasn't sure of her feelings about a lot of things...in particular, their relationship.

Working Homicide had its challenges. In Kelly's opinion, the hardest part of beginning a murder investigation was knowing that every step taken into a scene had the potential of contaminating it, of ruining evidence that might otherwise break the case open. Especially one like this, which would undoubtedly be under the scrutiny of both his supervisors and the media.

It wasn't every day that a priest wound up dead in Boston, though the Church was not without its enemies. The fallout of negative press the Catholic Church of Boston received during *The Globe's* 2002 Spotlight investigation into the sexual abuse and coverup of multiple young victims, resulting in the arrest and conviction of five priests, continued to this day. Kelly wondered if this was possibly related. All possibilities for motive had to be considered.

Kelly temporarily suspended the thought. He never entered a crime scene with a preconceived notion of the why. He tried to take on each bit of information as fresh and new, in the hope that as more evidence piled up, the picture would become clear. To enter a crime scene with an idea of what might've happened tainted the direction and flow in which the scene was processed. It might pigeonhole him into making decisions or seeking out evidence in areas he wouldn't normally have done.

Kelly's eyes were wide open to all the possibilities that lay ahead once those doors were opened.

He looked down at his watch. "Mark the time. 11:13 a.m. We're beginning our preliminary search and walk-through now." He scribbled the time in his notebook and then tucked it away, leaving his hands free. He didn't want any distraction to interrupt his focus on the scene.

Each member of the team donned Tyvek booties over their shoes and slipped on a pair of latex gloves, then the group entered through the church's center door.

Even though it was sunny outside, cold air worked its way past Kelly's windbreaker, sending a shiver up his spine. At least that was what he told himself. In reality, a dead priest in a church shattered the norm and left him feeling a bit unhinged.

Taking the lead, Kelly pulled the door open and was immediately greeted by the intense scent of the frankincense oil used during Mass, which seemed to linger and permeate every square inch of the church's interior. The incense, burned as a purification ritual dating back to biblical times, tickled the back of Kelly's throat.

Stepping further across the threshold, he saw the light penetrating through the ornate stained glass high above the main entrance, decorated in a vibrant array of colors and arranged to look like a six-petaled flower. As the door closed behind them, the colorful beams streaming through the glass warmed the church's interior. High gabled arches lined the ceiling in three columns leading down to the altar. The intricate details of the hand-carved wood bore testament to the incredible effort made in the artistic construction of this impressive church.

Kelly knew the church well, having spent most of his youth in it, either forced by his father, or later, once he had passed, under the watchful eye of his mother. He was reminded of the ritualistic up-down-kneel his Roman Catholic upbringing offered, a fate no boy born of Irish descent in the Dorchester neighborhood could avoid. He had a love-hate relationship with the church, but being here now, and under these circumstances, was difficult to process. The murder of a priest was a tough pill to swallow.

Kelly no longer needed to command his group of seasoned investigators. No one would touch anything and would only call out if they noted a potential piece of evidence, which would be photographed once they formally processed the scene. This walk-through was designed to give the grander scope, a wide-lens perspective of what they were up against before they dove deep into the minutiae that came with any crime scene.

Every fourth step, Kelly paused. He scanned the pew to his right and then his left, eyes moving down to the floor in a slow, methodical visual processing of each row. Not that he was expecting to see a loaded pistol resting on one of the wooden benches, but there was always the chance of something left behind, an article of clothing or the like.

He continued his measured approach to the altar, reversing the path Donny would've walked at the completion of the Mass. Mainelli did the same to his right and Ray Charles to his left, each man keeping an even pace with him and Barnes.

She leaned over, her skin a combination of Irish Spring soap and something sweet like honey, and whispered, "This is crazy, right, Mike? Somebody shooting a priest? Worse yet, somebody shooting a priest inside a Catholic church. That's got to be a first, right?"

Kelly stopped and looked at his partner, his date for his family's upcoming Thanksgiving dinner. The lines were definitely beginning to blur. He found it harder and harder to separate his feelings for her from their work relationship. "I've never heard of anything like this. You seem a little more unnerved than usual. You okay?" he asked, recalling her reaction while standing outside the church door. Now, out of earshot of the other two, he was glad to be able to check in on his partner's wellbeing. "What's eating at you?"

Kris initially shook her head. "It's nothing. It's... I just..."

"What?" Kelly whispered, keeping his voice from echoing in the openness of the sanctuary.

"Just brought back some memories, things I had tucked away long ago."

Kelly furrowed a brow. "From before? During your foster care time? I mean, before you were adopted?" He wanted to approach the subject delicately to avoid offending her or bringing up something too intense to be dealt with adequately in the current circumstances.

"Yeah, I guess so. It's funny what you can force yourself to forget." Barnes visibly shook herself. "Anyway, I'm sorry. I was a little off when we first came in. I'm good now. I promise. My head's in the game. Let's figure out what's going on here. Focus on finding the killer."

"Or killers," Kelly added. An assumption that one person was responsible immediately closed the investigative mind to other possibilities. It created a barrier, clouding judgment and, at times, overriding logical reasoning. If multiple people were involved, they'd have to take into account the possibility of lookouts or getaway drivers. And more importantly, the modus operandi going into the decision to commit the crime. Right now, everything was possible until proven otherwise. *Eyes wide open*, Kelly thought.

"You're right," she said, "or killers. I guess we won't know until we really get down into this thing, huh?"

"We never do."

They continued plodding down the aisle until they reached the altar.

Kelly felt strange getting a backdoor view into the church. His Irish-Catholic guilt kicked in, making him feel like somewhat of a heathen for not attending Mass in several years, especially after serving as an altar boy in his youth. This sacred place within the church carried an invisible barrier to all those parishioners who approached to receive communion, and Kelly felt it press against him now. It didn't block him from continuing forward, though; he walked up the three short steps to the altar with Barnes beside him. She went left and he right as they circled the altar. They saw nothing leading to the back door, which Kelly knew led to the private area where the priest and his altar boys prepared for the day's sermon.

Kelly's childhood memories returned full blast as he remembered sitting next to the priest. He remembered the sermons. He remembered his job there, the removal of the communion, the bringing of the wine, the servitude. As much as he hated dressing up and performing the task, he loved the routine of it, the same comfort he found at Pops' gym. The ritual and routine, the warmup. The structure was steadying. And maybe that was what so unnerved Kelly about murder. It broke every norm. It divided and shattered the idea of conformity. Murder was the biggest act of nonconformity a person could do to another. The taking of another human life was uniquely outside the bounds of society's norms. That was what drew Kelly to this line of work in the first place.

Satisfied they hadn't missed anything of value or seen anything worth noting on the initial pass, he turned to Kris. "Time to see the body."

"Ray, Jimmy, anything on your end?"

"Looks clean so far," Charles said.

"Let's bring it tight. Over by the confessional."

The confessional was another part of the church's impressive design. Albeit smaller in scope, it was nonetheless as intricately detailed as its surroundings and set along the marble wall left of center when facing the altar. It extended upward approximately ten feet into three arches, the center one rising a foot above the others, each adorned with a cross. The lacquered mahogany was a blend of dark and light brown, a testament to its antiquity and the years of upkeep required for maintaining its pristine condition.

Two doors with black steel handles led to the area where priest and parishioner could meet in anonymity, a closet designed to cleanse the soul for those who sought absolution. The door on the right was closed. The left was slightly ajar, the shadowed image of the priest's curled body barely visible within the dark confines.

The group was uncharacteristically silent. A murder cop's dark humor usually reared its ugly head during moments like this, but this time, the levity that served to ease the horror was uncharacteristically absent.

The four investigators stepped closer but kept their distance, stopping just outside the confessional. Kelly saw a footprint, the burnt umber of dried blood. It moved out from the partially open door and trailed off in the direction of the center aisle, fading away near the toe of Kelly's right shoe.

"Looks like one of the guys dragged a little evidence with them on their way out," Charles said.

"They always do," Mainelli added. "At least the medics or FD didn't come through. Those guys can destroy a scene."

Kelly laughed. It was true. Cops commonly referred to their medical counterparts as the Evidence Eradication Team. All done with good intentions, but sometimes the most detrimental things were caused by them. Kelly knew well enough, from having been on patrol as a first responder on scene, as everyone in the group had been at one point in their police career, that the collection and preservation of evidence always had to be weighed with the preservation of human life. And if there was any chance the priest had still been alive, they had to render aid. To do so meant they'd have to enter the invisible barrier of the crime scene and make contact. This life-saving effort would result in an exchange. The obvious one was the priest's blood being transferred to one or more of the responding officers' shoes. The patrolmen would have to note that in their initial report.

Charles would have to photograph the boot, do a tread comparison. As tedious as the work was, and with little evidentiary value for the case itself, it ensured that if a suspect developed later, a defense attorney couldn't cast doubt on a potential case's veracity.

A bloody shoe print at a crime scene was a great way for the defense attorney to cast doubt, therefore it was imperative they take the extra step in identifying who it belonged to. No punishment would befall the officers. They were just doing their job.

In those initial moments when first responding to any crime, life trumped evidence every time.

The confessional door was ajar, either opened by the responding officers or by the killer himself, which was doubtful. A quick conversation with the responding officers would clear that up.

Peering through the gap in the door, Kelly found it plainly obvious that the priest could not have survived the gunshot wound to his left temple. The exit wound had been devastating, leaving its scattered remains on the interior wall. Kelly stepped to the left and looked at the outside wall of the confessional, where a section of the dark wood bulged. "Looks like the round didn't penetrate the outer wall. That's good for us."

"I've already made a mental note of it," Charles said.

Both sides of the lacquered box—where the priest dispensed penance and the congregant confessed their sins—contained potentially vital evidence that could lead to the killer, based on what was left behind. Locard's exchange, a principle of forensic science, stated every criminal brought something of themselves into a crime and took something from the scene with them when they left. It was up to Kelly and his team, and particularly the in-depth forensic analysis of Senior Crime Scene Technician Ray Charles, to find that link. No matter how minute the exchange.

The pieces of trace evidence could break a case wide open, whether it was DNA, a fingerprint, a fiber from clothing unique to the person, or the thousands of other potential variables at work during the physical exchange. They'd be searching for anything to give them a leg up in finding the killer or killers. A round recovered on scene would be a good place to start. Kelly's mood brightened a bit at the prospect of recovering the spent bullet from the confessional's outer wall; hopefully, it would be intact enough to make a comparison.

"Looks like we can tighten our search to the area around here, but I still think we should leave the external barrier that patrol set on the surrounding streets," Ray said, asserting himself as the evidence expert. "It looked pretty good. We're going to have to sweep the area. Maybe we'll get lucky and find a surveillance camera system that picked up something useful. Inside the church, I think our focal point for evidence collection should be here." He indicated the confessional.

Raymond Charles was the most senior of the group when it came to evidence recovery, and the most seasoned when it came to the handling of crime scenes. He'd served as a mentor to Kelly since he first arrived at Homicide, cutting his teeth on the Faith Wilson case. Charles had proven to be somebody Kelly could rely on when dealing with the uniquely different scenes he'd encountered in his short time in the unit.

"I'm completely in agreement," Kelly said. "Let's back out. We'll do our official walk-through with photographs, and then we'll focus on the internal scene for processing. Does that sound good to everybody?"

The group nodded in agreement. Mainelli added a grunt.

They retreated outside, exiting through the same door they had entered twenty minutes ago.

"All right. Unless you want to be in the first shots, you might want to step back." Charles fished out his Nikon from his oversized duffle.

Kelly, Mainelli, and Barnes walked down the split concrete stairwell, out of view of the first few shots. Cops did their best to make sure they were out of sight when any crime scene photography was underway. Nothing worse than getting snagged in a photo and then being called into court to explain something you were doing. Another prime opportunity for the defense to attack a case, a tactic used quite often, especially with patrolmen captured by the camera.

Kelly allowed Charles to do his photography and lead the team back into the scene. They followed the same entry point, retracing their steps.

Charles was taking overalls, capturing the big-picture visual overview of the church, then working his way down the aisle to the place where the victim lay. Kelly and his team stayed a few steps behind the technician, moving at his pace.

Kelly, notepad in hand, took a moment to do a rough sketch of the church's interior, a basic outline of the entryway leading to the confessional.

Measurements would be taken later, but he would use this sketch to orient himself to the scene after he left.

The progression down the center aisle was slightly quicker this time because they knew from their preliminary walk-through that there was no noticeable evidence in the pews and aisle areas leading up to Father Tomlin's body.

Kelly marked the first piece of evidence, laying a triangular yellow placard with the number one in black boldface print at the faded bloody boot print just outside the confessional.

Charles focused his lens and began taking photos from different angles of the partially open confessional area containing the priest's crumpled body.

"Let's open it up," Charles said, still holding the camera to his face.

Mainelli stepped around the bloody shoe print and reached up to the top of the door with gloved hands, minimizing his risk of contaminating any potential trace along the handle.

The hinge creaked noisily at the movement, seeming louder due to the silence.

Father Tomlin's knees were folded awkwardly, as if he had been seated— which he most likely had been when the bullet struck his head. The impact sent him to the floor. The room's small confines didn't give the dead man much in the way of wiggle room. He was partially tucked underneath the wooden bench attached to the back wall, his body folded into an awkward Z pattern—his legs tucked underneath his buttocks and his body bent forward. The dead priest's head rested alongside the left wall, just beneath a smattering of blood and brain matter.

"Mike, I need to get a measurement on that entry wound on his left temple. Can you put up a point of reference for me?" Charles asked.

Kelly did as he was asked. Retrieving a disposable ruler, he lay it alongside the wound, taking care not to make contact. He kept several measuring strips with him in his homicide go bag in the event one got soiled.

Charles took several photographs, adjusting the settings on the camera to accommodate for the limited light within the confessional room. "All right, I've got my photos."

"We've got a small hole in the wall just above that chunk of brain matter," Kelly said.

"I see it, Mike," Charles said.

Kelly knew the crime scene tech was also documenting his visual findings on the voice recorder he kept tucked in his shirt pocket.

"Let's mark that as well," he added. "Can you get up another measurement?"

Kelly marked and measured as Charles took the photographs.

"All right, we can work on retrieving the round later. I'll probably take the whole wall with us," Charles muttered. "I need to get some close-ups."

Kelly backed out of the confessional box as Charles cautiously stepped over the priest's body. He used his camera's low light setting to capture the inside of the dimpled hole.

"Son of a bitch," Charles said, partially to himself but loud enough for Kelly to hear.

"What do you got, Ray?"

"It's not there."

"What's not there?"

"The round. It's not in the hole. I mean, unless I've suddenly gone blind."

"Maybe it's all that chicory your wife keeps putting in your coffee?" Kelly continued their long-running joke regarding his wife's decision to cut expenses by taking away his one true love: Dunkin' Donuts coffee.

"Give me a little extra light."

Kelly pulled a flashlight from his pocket and angled it over Ray's right shoulder. Both now could easily see that the hole where the round should have been was empty.

"Strange," Kelly said.

"Maybe it popped back out," Charles said doubtfully.

"Ever seen something like that before?"

"Never in my life, but there's always a first for something."

They scanned the floorboard area without moving the body, but Kelly saw no sign of the round. "We'll do a more thorough search once we remove the priest's body, but I'm not holding out hope. Not a good sign," he said.

"Definitely not."

Charles took a few more photographs while standing over the priest, then said, "I'm good. Ready to roll?"

"Ready. Hey, Jimmy, can you grab his feet? We're going to do a roll," Kelly called out to Mainelli, who made an agreeable grunt. He was now used to his friend's nonverbal responses to work.

"All right, on three. One, two, three."

Tomlin's body now rested on his left side. He was cold, but rigor hadn't begun to set, making the roll easier than most.

Charles took several photos from underneath the priest's right side and then of the exit wound outside his right temple area, which was much larger than the entrance wound.

"We need a quick photo of that, with scale," Charles said.

Kelly, already one step ahead of him, had the scale ready to go.

After a few clicks of the camera, Charles said, "All set with that. Let's back out."

Kelly worked himself out of the tight space, leaving the priest's body resting in its new position.

"What the hell is that?" Barnes asked.

"What's what?" Kelly glanced around, excited at the prospect she had spotted the missing round.

"That mark on his hand." Barnes was now peering over Mainelli's shoulder as Kelly and Charles squatted lower, hovering over the body.

"Oh my God," Kelly said, seeing the carved X on the web of the priest's right hand between his thumb, knuckle, and index finger. That same mark had been left on his partner, Danny Rourke—the perpetual red card on his murder board. An overlooked piece of evidence when his body was found over eight years ago.

"This just went from bad to worse," Barnes said.

The group's shocked silence affirmed her words.

"Let's run through it again," Kelly said.

Mainelli rubbed his eyes and then buried his face in his large hands, completely masking his facial expression. But Kelly knew the tortured look he wore.

Even with the conference room's moderated temperature, Mainelli was sweating profusely. The fitness-resistant investigator was beginning to show signs of wear from the long day, which started at the church and was now closing in on its tenth consecutive hour of tedium, with the last four taking place inside the BPD Homicide unit's conference room, affectionately referred to as The Depot. The room's name started as a joke that stuck, though nobody could pinpoint its origin. It was a reference to the end of the line, a homage to the city's public transportation rail system.

At first glance, The Depot was anything but extraordinary, just an average-size conference room with a long outstretched table, several chairs, computer screens on both walls, and several keyboards enabling the detectives to access different files and pull them up for everyone to view. What made the room special were the cases solved within its walls.

Kelly was old school when it came time to hash out a case, as were most of the people in the room with him. He used the room's technology sparingly, preferring to spread the case out on the table and manipulate the tangible documents rather than use the monitor displays. And right now, he was looking down at the series of photographs Charles had taken at the scene, in particular those of Tomlin's body in the confessional's cramped space.

They were reviewing the crime scene again, and Mainelli couldn't have looked more annoyed at the prospect. "Seriously, Mike?" he complained. "How many times do you want to look at it today? Why don't we take a break, call it a day, come back with this thing early in the morning, fresh? Who knows? Maybe we sleep on it, something pops into our minds."

"We're all tired. But I don't think we've hit a stopping point yet," Kelly offered. Trying to coax Mainelli into focusing on the case was getting harder with each passing second.

"All I'm saying is a break might be nice, Mike."

Kelly gave him a stern look. Although Mainelli had been with Homicide for more years than Kelly, in the last few months Kelly had shown a tenacious drive mechanism that put some of his more senior partners to shame.

Barnes sat at the table, unfazed at reinvestigating the scene from beginning to end in their fruitless attempt at finding the evidentiary needle in the haystack, the clue that could be lying just within arm's reach.

Currently, they'd hit a stalemate. As if to punctuate the real reason for Mainelli's request for an evening recess, his stomach rumbled loudly.

"Jimmy, feel free to cut loose at any time. I'm going to look at it again. I understand if you've got some things to take care of; go do it. No one's holding you back. Kris and I can hold down the fort."

Mainelli looked at his watch and sighed, then followed with an exasperated roll of his eyes. Kelly knew he had won the battle by calling him out as the only member who would be leaving, an attack on his ego. Pride prevented his departure. Kelly played the card and it worked. Mainelli would be staying for another session of round table discussion, an additional examination of the crime scene and the clues spread out before them.

"All right, good. We're all in agreement, then," Kelly said. "Let's start at the beginning and look at what we've got so far. Maybe we can find something to add to the board."

Heads turned to the dry erase board affixed to the wall nearest Kelly. The board wasn't held in much reverence by his colleagues, but for Kelly it was a tool he felt very comfortable with. He had used it during his time as a crisis negotiator and found the board's visual fluidity an excellent way to highlight case facts and keep them in sight of the group. As the brainstorming continued, details would be added as needed, its simplicity a great way to keep a finger on the pulse of an investigation. Kelly always made sure he photographed the board prior to departing The Depot. The men and women of Homicide had a penchant for doodling, and he learned the hard way to capture and wipe the board prior to leaving for the night.

The smudged writing on the board displayed key notes they'd obtained since the onset of the investigation. The list did not adequately convey the effort it took to reach its current state, a bleak outlook thus far for the case's progression.

Vic: *Benjamin Tomlin, age 46 (priest)*
Timeline: *10:00-10:30 a.m.*
MOD: *Gunshot left temple*
Caliber unk
No round No casing
Wit: *Donovan O'Brien*
Interview: *Y*
Deborah Shoemaker
Interview: *N*
Surveillance Cameras
Interior: *N*
Exterior: *3 (patrol checking)*
Forensics: *Pending*
Autopsy: *Pending*
UID: *Mark on hand*
Suspect: *None*

"We're looking at a lot of dead ends on this board," Kelly said. "The bloody footprints were confirmed to be from Officer Chandler's boot, so that's another dead end." The comparison had been quickly completed by Charles and his young crime scene tech protégé Dawes, photographed, and was now in the pile of pictures spread out on the tabletop.

Kelly stared at the board, lost in thought. "So we've got no witnesses, no close-in cameras that may have picked anything up immediately around the church or on the inside. Patrol is checking a few externals from surrounding businesses, but I'm not holding my breath."

"I've got a call into Jenkins at the Eleven," Mainelli offered. "He'll give us a heads-up if anything comes from it. His guys are working on pulling the tapes."

"O'Brien appears to have been first contact with the decedent. Nothing else we've discovered points to the contrary. With that, I think we have a pretty solid timeline established, and it's an extremely tight window. Right now we have no description for a suspect. Shoemaker will be coming in tomorrow morning for an interview. More disturbing, though..." Kelly paused, focusing his attention on the lower half of the board. "We've got a single gunshot wound to the left side of Father Tomlin's temple, exit wound right-side temple, and pass-through with heavy cranial damage. The round struck the wall of the confessional on the opposite side. Charles has confirmed after carefully evaluating the impact area and confessional chamber after the body removal that no round was found on scene. That's a big problem for me. For a whole lot of reasons."

Kelly turned to face Barnes and Mainelli, who were seated side by side across the table. "I don't like to make conjectures this early into an investigation, but for our suspect to remove the round from the wall shows me we have somebody with practical experience—possibly dealing with a professional."

Mainelli rubbed his eyes for the second time in not as many seconds. "Like I've said before, anybody with internet and YouTube access can find ways to beat a crime scene. Or at least make it harder. Every banger we come across lately seems to know better than to leave their shell casings on scene, at least if they're not too high or drunk to do so. We're only catching the stupid ones now."

"Maybe you're right and this wasn't a professional, but I'm with Mike," Barnes weighed in. "Somebody took the time to make sure the round wasn't on scene and no casing was left behind. You take those two pieces of evidence out of the equation and we're grabbing at thin air."

Mainelli was the portrait of frustration. They'd been stuck in this loop since Charles had confirmed the missing evidence.

"I get it, but we have to consider that possibility. And then there's the other problem." Kelly tapped the capped end of the dry erase marker in his hand against the board. This was the elephant in the room, the unspoken piece nobody really wanted to talk about. Were they looking at a serial killer? The mark cut into the priest's hand was identical to the one carved into murdered BPD Patrolman Danny Rourke's hand. The photograph from the case file of Kelly's former patrol partner was nearby and open. The view of the strange X marked on his partner's right hand in the web joining his thumb and index finger stared back at him.

Kelly typed on the keyboard, and the monitor on the wall came to life with a side-by-side comparison of both photographs. Without going into the forensic aspect of what tool could have left the mark, on first inspection they looked eerily identical.

"You think whoever did your partner is the same guy? He reappears after —what, eight, almost nine years to kill a priest? Please, tell me the connection. I've got to understand this." A hint of sarcasm was sprinkled not too lightly into Mainelli's words.

It was Kelly's turn to rub his eyes in exhaustion. "If I knew the connection, we'd already be heading out of this room to find the perp. I can't make sense of it. That's why I've got it up on the screen and on the board. And you should know better than most that there's no such thing as coincidence in what we do."

Barnes had remained silent for the majority of this round of conversation but decided now would be the time to insert herself. "I agree with Mike. It's just too damn coincidental, too close, too connected to not be the same. And what about Phillip Smalls, the rapist we found dead during the Wilson case? He had the same mark on his left hand."

A third picture popped up on the screen in line with the rest. All three hands bore the distinctive X on the outside web.

"Tell me what it means, then," Mainelli said.

"I don't have a clue. All I know is we have three unsolved murders with one glaring connection. We need some fresh perspective on this."

"And that's why we've brought in some help," a voice grumbled from The Depot's door as it opened. Sergeant Sutherland surveyed the room, taking in the screen, the papers strewn across the table, and the notes on the whiteboard.

Behind him stood a clean-cut, athletically built man Kelly didn't recognize.

"Team, I'd like to introduce FBI Special Agent Sterling Gray."

Kelly heard Mainelli curse quietly under his breath. Seeing the agent was like the nail in the coffin for his partner. With the FBI getting involved this late in the day, he now knew he wouldn't be going home anytime soon. Kelly watched as this prospect sank into Mainelli, completely sucking the wind out of his partner's sails until he had deflated like a punctured helium balloon.

"Hi, guys," Sterling said in a casual manner. His accent sounded as though he might be from the Southwest, or maybe even Texas. Hard to tell, but one thing was for certain: he definitely didn't grow up local.

Kelly had come to know many of the local FBI agents within the Boston network of task forces, but he was unfamiliar with Gray. His first guess was this was an out-of-towner.

"I'm not trying to take over your scene, your case," Sterling said. "This is your baby. I understand that, and the FBI does too."

"Then why are you here?" Kelly asked, exhaustion adding an unintended edge of frustration to his voice. "If you're not here to take over, then why is the FBI getting involved with the case?"

It was Sutherland who answered. "Media is already swirling into a real shit storm, Mike. They're breathing down the mayor's neck. And it's starting to roll downhill. Everybody wants an answer. This murder has the community up in arms. It's not every day that a priest is executed, and within the confines of a church to boot. It's got people unnerved, unhinged. So we're doing everything we can to show the people of Boston we're taking this seriously. We're bringing in all the heavy hitters and every resource at our disposal, one of which happens to be the Federal Bureau of Investigation. Do we have a problem, Mike?"

Sergeant Dale Sutherland rarely spoke so forcefully, but it wasn't the first time Kelly had seen him bend to the power and strength of the command staff. Most recently, the sergeant had turned a blind eye to the politics that polluted Kelly's investigation into a rogue undercover. It left him with a sour taste in his mouth with regards to Sutherland, but more importantly, some of the senior brass at the department. None of his personal misgivings changed the fact that a priest was murdered in his neighborhood. He was going to make sure he did everything in his power to bring about justice for that terrible wrong.

And at this point, as he stared at the board and the markings on the three victims with their similarities but no connection, he was desperate for some assistance, whether he openly admitted it or not. Kelly was secretly interested in seeing what the FBI had to offer.

"Like I said," Agent Gray offered, softening the aggressive introduction by Kelly's direct supervisor, "I'm not here to step on any toes. I know how Boston PD handles their cases. Your Homicide unit is top-notch and I'm just happy to have an opportunity to lend a hand. The resources of the FBI are at your disposal. Hopefully, it will help bring about a quick end to this case and give your community the closure it deserves."

Community, Kelly thought. *What does this guy know about the neighborhood? He didn't grow up there. He doesn't know what it's like. He doesn't have the connection to the people and places. He's not a hometown boy. He's not a townie.* His motivations had to be purely political. Maybe he was a rising star in the FBI, and this was his way to get the face time he needed to climb the next rung. Or maybe he was considered an expert in this type of investigation. Whatever the reason, Kelly wasn't confident Gray would bring about much of a change in the course of things, but at this point, something was better than nothing.

"Okay, Agent Gray, welcome to the team," he said.

"It's Sterling. Feel free to drop the 'agent' stuff. No need for it."

Kelly couldn't have agreed more and hearing the bureau man say it immediately improved his opinion of him. Rank was a hindrance to an investigation and held cops back from speaking plainly. It muddied the waters.

Gray looked at the three images on the monitor. "I might be able to help with those."

Kelly's interest was piqued.

"Before you get into all that, a press conference is about to begin," Sutherland said.

"Son of a bitch," Mainelli hissed, throwing his head back and staring at the ceiling.

Sutherland cleared his throat loudly. "Jimmy, are you volunteering to speak? I know how much you like talking to the press."

Mainelli reset himself, leaning forward on an open case file atop the conference table.

"It's being held in the community room. When the brass delivers their message, they want the face of Boston Homicide standing alongside the FBI. So best get yourselves cleaned up." Sutherland added a wry smile. "You're going to be on camera."

Kelly rolled his eyes. The thought of standing in front of a crew of reporters never jived with him, but it made even less sense at this point in an investigation. He didn't do the job for the accolades or publicity. He did it for the sole purpose of delivering justice to those who needed it most, fighting for the people who couldn't fight for themselves.

Since being assigned to Homicide, he understood his role. It was to speak for the dead, and the best way he could effectively do that was to find their killer.

"I see the look on your faces. This isn't an ask or polite request. It's an order, and it comes from the top down. I'm just the messenger. Get yourselves prettied up." Sutherland eyed Mainelli. "Especially you. You look like a wet sack of dog crap."

"Your kindness knows no bounds," Mainelli retorted.

"Oh yeah, almost forgot: be downstairs in five minutes. The press briefing will begin shortly thereafter."

"They want us to talk, Sarge?" Mainelli asked.

"Absolutely not. You're the last person the Boston public needs to hear from. You'll remove all sense of safety if you open that big mouth of yours."

"Gee, Sarge, I never knew you loved me so much," Mainelli fired back.

"Look, you guys know I'm at the end of my career. I don't need to ruffle any feathers. I want a smooth transition out of this PD. You understand me?"

"You've been saying that ever since you banged your knee," Mainelli said, keeping the banter going.

Every detective in Homicide knew the gruff sergeant had been working on getting his disability claim to reach a percentage that would enable him to take an early retirement. It was an ongoing battle, one the union had been fighting for several years. The longer the city jerked him around, the more disgruntled the once gregarious sergeant became.

"Time's a ticking. Suit up and be downstairs," Sutherland said, walking out the door and into the main space containing the cubicles of the thirty-eight detectives assigned to Homicide.

Gray remained in the doorway. "For what it's worth, I'm glad to be part of the team and I'll do whatever I can to help. Hopefully, there's no hard feelings."

Barnes and Mainelli got up, almost in unison. They shook Gray's hand, exchanging brief introductions and pleasantries before heading out of the room.

"Well, welcome to the show," Kelly said, eyeing the screen image of the X on the priest's hand.

6

The first floor of the Boston Police Department had a room set aside for press conferences. News of the dead priest had spread like wildfire, and the room was packed with reporters, all vying to get their questions heard and hoping to break a new detail in the story.

Kelly had been through enough high-interest cases in his time as a city police officer to know somebody somewhere in the department had probably already leaked some of the case facts. This was usually done for the teller's personal benefit, whether financial or positional. On the street, the saying was "snitches get stitches," but the joke around the department was a play on those words: "snitches get promotions." In a city as politically charged as Boston, somebody was always jockeying to get the upper hand, to see their name in print, to control the outcome of a case, or to make themselves look more favorable.

These were the aspects of law enforcement Kelly hated most of all. He liked the simplicity of the not-so-simple crimes. He preferred to deal with things on the street level. Under no circumstances could he see himself working to be promoted beyond his current rank and position. Detective was as far up the ladder as he'd hoped to climb. Beyond his personal motivation to remain an investigator, Kelly had zero interest in standing at a podium fielding questions and speaking in front of the cameras while hundreds of onlookers jotted notes.

No, that was not the life for Michael Kelly. His work was predominantly done behind the scenes, and he liked it that way. Being called now to stand by while the brass took the podium drove him mad. These few wasted minutes, pressing flesh and making comments and standing pretty for the cameras, was time taken away from the investigation, time that would be better served in search of the killer. Few people truly understood the dynamics of a homicide investigation and how rapidly the tide could shift. Substantial leads could dissipate as quickly as morning rain striking the pavement on a hot summer's day.

Sergeant Dale Sutherland led his entourage toward the podium, where Superintendent Juan Carlos Acevedo was standing ready. Acevedo was the poster child for the department and a potential candidate to be the next chief. His polyester uniform was sharply pressed, his jet-black hair meticulously combed underneath his eight-point hat. He was the epitome of professionalism in looks and appearance.

Kelly didn't mind the man. He saw him for what he was, a politician in a policeman's uniform. Over the years, Kelly had dealt with the superintendent on too few occasions to form an opinion of him. Although the fact that he was Detective Tony Acevedo's father did cast him in a slightly dimmer light, since, in Kelly's opinion, the biproduct of his loins was substandard as both a person and a cop.

Sutherland walked up and greeted Superintendent Acevedo with a firm handshake.

"Sergeant Sutherland, good to see you and your team here. Although from what I hear, your team wasn't originally assigned this case. Isn't there a certain order to how things operate down in Homicide? Or have they changed that much since I worked there?"

Sutherland threw up his hands in a gruff, disgruntled manner. "Hey, Superintendent. You don't like the way I do business, feel free to expedite my disability claim and I'll be happy to be out of your hair."

"Don't get yourself all worked up, Dale," Acevedo said through gritted teeth.

The superintendent then gave a disingenuous smile before losing interest in the banter and turning his gaze to Kelly. The fake smile vanished instantly. *Great. I can add Acevedo Senior to my fan club too*, Kelly thought as he met the superintendent's stare. Kelly cracked a slight smile and considered adding a wink just to piss him off further but decided not to push his luck.

The superintendent turned his attention back to the sea of reporters and prepared himself for the upcoming briefing, looking down at the notecards resting on the slanted wood of the podium.

Mainelli whispered in his ear, "Jeez, Mikey, he looks pissed."

"Strange. I thought he looked quite happy to see me. Maybe it's you?"

Barnes, positioned between them, jabbed each of them in a subtle gesture reminding them to shut up and prepare for the cameras.

Agent Sterling Gray stood nearby, close but not too close to the four-man detective unit assigned to handle this homicide. Gray was an integral part of this briefing, and Kelly knew it. The FBI needed to be seen with them, but at this point, after only the brief introduction minutes ago, there wasn't any kinship. Kelly noted Gray did his best to present himself as if he were a member of the team: chin held high, body straight, posture rigid as if standing at attention. To Kelly, Gray looked like a prep-school boy preparing to meet with the headmaster.

All were wearing a shirt and tie, except for Barnes, who'd changed into a blouse. Sterling Gray was a notch above with his navy-blue sports coat. Kelly had thrown on his blazer, the same one he'd worn earlier while working the scene. His Boston PD emblem was visible, but his badge remained tucked in. No need to display his shield in the room full of reporters. Mainelli looked as though his shirt and tie had been pulled out from a crumpled heap in his locker, because it had been. Looking back at his disheveled coworker, Kelly noticed a yellowish stain, most likely mustard, prominently centered on the silk paisley design.

"You might want to stand behind me a little bit," Kelly said to Mainelli, poking his finger on the stain.

The heavyset Italian detective began his innate resistance to suggestion, until he looked down to see the blotch. Mainelli dipped in behind Barnes, using her to block his unkempt appearance.

Lieutenant Jack Rosario, the department's brand-new public affairs officer, or PAO, stepped in front of the superintendent and adjusted the microphone, causing an awkward squelching sound. He, too, was clean-cut, well-groomed, and in full dress attire. Under normal circumstances, Rosario would be giving the daily briefing, but as this was a much higher-profile case than normal, the superintendent would take the lead. Politics in policing.

"The briefing will begin shortly," he announced. "Please take your seats and set your cell phones to silent if you haven't done so already. For those who don't know me, I'm Lieutenant Rosario and have recently been appointed as Boston PD's PAO. I will remain your point of contact within the department, but today's briefing will be handled by Superintendent Juan Carlos Acevedo. We will begin shortly with the superintendent's remarks. Please hold all questions until the end. We will not get to all of your questions, but hopefully by the time this briefing is over, we'll have given you everything that we have at this time.

"I want to remind you that this is an active investigation and the things we say now may dynamically change in the hours and days to come. Please bear in mind the information we will provide tonight will be an overview of what we have thus far, and there will be no information as to the particulars of the case. This is done to keep from compromising the ongoing investigation being conducted by these fine detectives behind me here. Without further ado, may I introduce Superintendent Juan Carlos Acevedo."

The lieutenant stepped down from the platform and onto the maroon carpeting. He backed away and stood next to an American flag posted near the rear wall.

Kelly and his team, coupled with Sterling Gray, were staggered to the superintendent's left. Kelly was doing his best to keep his head slightly down and out of the line of cameras. There was no telling whose image would make the front page of the local papers, and he wanted to minimize the likelihood of his face being plastered beside an unflattering headline. Kelly wouldn't be one of those cops with a box full of clippings when he retired. He hoped when the day came to turn in his badge, his memory of the awful things he had witnessed during his career would go with it. Doubtful, he knew.

He tried to tuck himself away, wedging between Sutherland's girth and Barnes's slender frame. Kelly felt his hand brush against hers. The contact jolted him, instantly transporting him away. He wanted nothing more than to reach out and hold her hand. Although they spent copious amounts of time together on the job, it was not the kind of quality time either hoped for. Being in her presence on a near constant basis left him longing for the private time they rarely got, whether due to her schedule or his, his time with Embry, or just the daunting caseload they continually worked.

So Kelly took these unexpected moments of contact, brief and benign, and made them his escape to normalcy.

Since the budding of their relationship, it had been quite difficult to create a normal most people would have accepted. He took this opportunity —the brief glancing touch of his pinky finger against her hand—as a moment of connectedness to her on a personal level, even though it was under professional circumstances. He wondered if she felt the same. He hoped so. Maybe if time permitted, tonight he would ask her.

The superintendent's clear, perfectly enunciated voice interrupted Kelly's thought process, taking him back to the here and now and away from his momentary slip from his investigator role.

"Good evening. As the lieutenant said, I'm Superintendent Acevedo, head of the Bureau of Investigative Affairs, and I'll be handling tonight's briefing. As many of you know, this morning we had a tragic incident occur in our Dorchester neighborhood. Father Benjamin Tomlin, who worked at Saint Peter's Catholic Church on Bowdoin Street, was shot and killed shortly after Mass.

"As of now, we are actively investigating the case. Any leads and information generated at this point will be held from release so as not to interfere with those who are pursuing justice. I can tell you this—this tragic circumstance is of the utmost importance to the Boston Police Department. We will bring the full investigative strength of the Criminal Investigation Division to bear on this.

"We've solicited the support of the Federal Bureau of Investigation, and they have readily supplied us with Agent Sterling Gray, who will be acting in a supporting role to our detective unit, and in particular our homicide investigators. I can tell you we welcome the resources the FBI brings to the Boston Police. Although we are quite adept at handling cases of all shapes and sizes, this one obviously carries with it a significant concern. I know that the people of this city, and in particular the neighborhood of Dorchester, are heartbroken at the news of losing one of their parish's own. I will tell you right now, we have some of the department's best and brightest working on this case, and they will not rest until they find the person or persons responsible for this murder."

Disregarding the lieutenant's initial order about holding questions to the end, several reporters, upon hearing the word "murder," shot up their hands.

Superintendent Acevedo scanned the crowd. "We're going to answer very few questions regarding this case. This is an active investigation, and the reason for the press conference is simple: we are asking anybody watching this broadcast who has information relevant to the case, please do not hesitate to contact the Boston Police Department. You can do it anonymously or in person. We have detectives and officers standing by to talk to you.

"At the bottom of the screen, for those of you who are watching this at home, we have provided a number for our tip line where you can remain completely anonymous when giving any information you think would benefit this investigation. With that being said, I can see several reporters in the audience have questions. Let me start by taking..."

"Colleen Maxwell from the *Herald*." Colleen was a tall redhead with a feisty temper and a tenacious investigative journalistic reputation.

Hearing her voice above the others, Kelly raised his head and eyed her. She had dragged him through the mud after the Baxter Green shooting death. She destroyed him in the paper in the initial wake of that case, adding insult to the injury of the circumstances leading to the young boy's death. Most of what she had initially reported had been incorrect, filled with half-truths taken out of context from whoever her point of contact was within the police department. Seeing that Superintendent Acevedo picked her first, he now wondered if he had been that source, a tit for tat, some favor, something owed. Politics in policing at work.

It left a bitter taste in Kelly's mouth. The shooting death of Baxter Green had been traumatic enough for him. Having his name bashed for all to read had worsened his ability to process it. Even though she later printed a retraction, a corrective piece in which she highlighted his efforts to bring about a resolution and the sound tactics used to do so, it had come a year later. A year of anguish for Kelly, a lifetime of frustration. She had waited until the internal investigation had closed and all wrongs had been cleared before making any effort to try to clear his name in the paper.

But as with everything, a year was a long time. In that same year, Kelly had lost his wife to divorce and his job had become burdensome. When she printed her second version of the incident, it was barely a blip in the world of newspaper journalism and had little effect. Seeing her getting the first question worried him. What would she have to say about this case before she had all the facts?

Kelly had learned long ago not to spend much time looking at the paper. It rarely, if ever, helped to follow any articles revolving around active criminal investigations. More likely it would only infuriate him when facts and details laid out in arrest affidavits and police reports were either incorrectly cited in the abridgement, miscommunicated, or flat-out disregarded. Best to turn a blind eye to it altogether.

"From what I understand, your department has ruled out any chance that this was a self-inflicted gunshot wound?"

Kelly held back from rolling his eyes. With his luck, that would be when the camera was pointed in his direction. Somebody had leaked to her about the gunshot wound, which went against everything they were working toward. Zero details, just the death of a priest, that's what Sutherland had advised would be said: a quick briefing to let the public know they were on the case and all efforts were being made to bring about a resolution. A briefing designed to put people's minds at ease and buy them time. Details released, like "single gunshot wound to the head," would skew any caller information that came in. It would taint any witness accounts.

"Thank you for the question, Colleen. Yes, we are ruling this a homicide. We have no evidence at this point in the investigation to indicate it was a suicide. And unless something changes, we will continue to investigate it as such."

She followed up and Acevedo let her speak again, much to the chagrin of the other reporters competing for the opportunity to have their questions heard.

"A single gunshot wound to the head? Any details on what type of gun was used? Any surveillance cameras, any suspect possibilities, things that we in the general public can be on the lookout for?"

How much information had she been fed?

"I'm not at liberty to discuss anything further with regard to the details of the case. It's an active homicide investigation, and we will update you as soon as we have anything further."

Another reporter, a heavyset man seated near the front row, spoke without being called upon. "Do you have anything on a motive? I mean, who would kill a priest? In a church, at that? I mean, do we have any history with this priest? Any open investigations about impropriety involving Tomlin? I know Boston has got a long history as far as clergymen go."

Acevedo sighed audibly, his breath striking the microphone's foam padding and making a hissing sound as he narrowed his eyes at the man. "Like I said, we are not getting into a motive or potential motive, the method in which the crime was committed, or any other factors that may hamper or hinder the investigation, as it is a current and ongoing one. What I will reaffirm to everyone here in this room and who may be watching at home on TV right now is this: the Boston Police Department's finest are on the case. They are working hand-in-hand with the FBI. And we will bring about a resolution."

Acevedo shot a glance toward Sterling Gray, giving him a half-smile and nod before turning back to the cameras.

"Everything at our disposal will be put forth to bringing to justice the people or person responsible for this heinous crime. Thank you very much for your time. There'll be another briefing tomorrow morning at 8:00 a.m. Lieutenant Rosario will be handling that one. Hopefully, less than twelve hours from now, we'll have more information to give you.

"As of right now, I say to those of you watching, if you have any information that can help, please don't hesitate to contact our department. Thank you for your understanding. Good night."

A roar came from the crowd as other reporters leaned forward, trying to have their voices heard before the termination of the briefing. Hands were raised and questions were hurled as the superintendent and lieutenant moved off stage and out the side door, marked *Authorized Personnel Only*.

Colleen Maxwell gave Kelly a smile. Her green eyes flickered. He couldn't tell if she was taunting him or trying to be genuine. Either way, he didn't like it and offered nothing in return.

He turned and walked away, following his team, this time with Sterling Gray at the lead. There was a lot of work to be done, especially if the department planned to give another press conference twelve hours from now. It looked like sleep would not be coming tonight.

"Well, that went famously," Barnes whispered as they moved into the hallway.

"Yeah, right?" Kelly said. "I mean, every Tom, Dick, and Harry is going to be calling in what they now think they know. Our workload has just tripled, so whoever leaked the fact about it being a single gunshot wound screwed us. We have our work cut out for us now. We've got to get ahead of it."

"At least they didn't mention the round and casing were missing from the scene."

Kelly raised his eyebrows. "Exactly. Whoever tipped off Maxwell, either they didn't have that information or knew it would've been too obvious a tip-off from whoever was feeding the beast. The pressure's definitely on now. Do you feel it?"

"I guess nobody's going home early tonight, huh, Mike?" Mainelli grumbled.

"Might as well fire up a fresh pot of coffee."

The four detectives plus their newest addition, Special Agent Gray, waited for the elevator to take them up to the second floor and back into The Depot.

7

Kelly poured a cup of coffee from the pot, the deep stains penetrating the percolator's steel walls from years of use adding a flavoring all its own. The aromatic scents infused the surrounding air. Kelly had read somewhere that the smell of coffee was therapeutic and activated the brain in similar ways to the caffeine contained within. Science aside, he loved the smell and held the mug close to his face before taking his first sip of the morning.

The kitchen was cold. His mother kept the heat set low, claiming she "ran hot." Kelly knew her sensitivity had more to do with cost than comfort. It was as though his mother had a built-in thermostat in her head. When he was a child, she seemed to always know if Kelly made even the most subtle adjustment to it.

Ma Kelly was as tough as they came, and Kelly had been raised under her roof and accepted her way. But now, at 5:30 in the morning, he was grateful for the warm mug in his hand that was hard at work chipping away at the cold surrounding him. The steam licked at his face as he took his first sip, the hot liquid working its way down his throat and warming him from the inside. The caffeine tore the cobwebs from his mind, the fog of exhaustion lifting with each gulp.

Kelly closed his eyes around 2:00 a.m. and managed less than three hours of restless sleep before he was back up.

He'd showered before hitting the sack, which didn't help him sleep any better, but he was tired enough that it didn't much matter. He always liked to wash himself, especially after a day like yesterday. Having spent time in his childhood church under such tragic circumstances didn't give his mind any peace as he tried to settle in for some sleep. The focus of the murder investigation would be his fuel as he revved up for the coming day's events. He had already accepted that sleep would come in spurts, and usually not long ones.

He was grateful for this quiet moment, alone with his thoughts. Kelly had peeked in on Embry, who was sound asleep, before coming downstairs. It was his morning to take her to school, rounding out his weekend with her. The call-in and subsequent murder investigation threw a kink in his plans, and he would need his mother to fill in as chauffeur again. Now that her broken hip was healed enough, she could drive short distances without too much discomfort and was better able to assist in matters like this, but she still had a long road of recovery. She had even begun working more hours at the package store, though she really didn't need to be there as much as she was. Kelly's Liquors, their family-owned business started by his late father, was in the watchful hands of Reyansh Gupta, the manager she'd hired. He'd proven to be as honest and hardworking as any they'd ever had in the past, if not more so. The store was in good hands, but Kelly knew his mother needed to keep busy.

Ma Kelly never refused any of his requests to assist in raising Embry. She'd taken great joy when Michael had returned to his childhood house after the divorce, and especially on the weekends and nights his daughter slept over. Even so, he felt a modicum of guilt for his constant need for help.

Kelly grabbed a slip of paper from the magnetized pad stuck to the outdated beige fridge, removing a clean sheet from underneath the running shopping list.

He took a second to write a quick note to his daughter: "I love you. I'll miss you. But we'll see each other on Turkey Day. - Gobble Gobble." Much to his frustration, Embry had received notes like this more times than he cared to admit. He wanted to wake her and tell her in person but couldn't bring himself to disrupt her sleep just to fulfill his selfish need to tell her that he loved her. That's why he made sure to tell her at every opportunity, especially when he was on a case. Working with the dead called to mind the importance of those he loved most. A side benefit to the darkness of his profession.

Simple acts of kindness had lasting effects, especially for those left behind. His job had given him an amazing perspective on that particular aspect of life, and he tried to keep that in mind.

Kelly finished the note with a cartoon caricature of a turkey that looked more like a fat duck with big, dreamy eyes. He learned how to draw the eyes while watching his daughter doodle. She taught him how to make what she called "emoji love eyes," and he found himself scribbling them on scraps of paper around the office. It came in handy on days like today. He was hoping she'd be pleased when she found the note, easing some of the guilt he had for leaving before she was awake.

He heard a creak on the floorboard behind him and turned to see his mother's bright eyes and soft curled hair, white as fresh snow. She was standing there in her nightgown and slippers, giving him a warm smile.

"We're up early, Mike," she said, kissing him on the cheek before moving past him to retrieve her own cup from the mug tree that dangled a variety of choices. She picked one with a hand-painted sunflower, a gift Embry had recently given her. Setting it down, she poured herself a cup from the percolator. "Smells good. It actually woke me up. You do something different this time?"

"No. Same old pot. Same old coffee, Ma. Nothing different."

"Hmm. Well, it smells different. Either way, I'd rather wake up to the scent of coffee than our neighbor's damn car alarm. Can't you do something about it, Mike? For the last week and a half, that red Jetta's car alarm goes off at godawful times of the night. I have half a mind to go out there and smash it with a rock."

"Ma, please don't do that," Kelly said, knowing her Irish temper could get the best of her and turn an idle comment into action. He regretted staying for the second cup of coffee that kept him from avoiding this conversation. He'd meant to address the problem when it was first brought to his attention. "Like I said, Ma, I'll look into it."

"When? You're not home all that much."

Kelly let the verbal jab slide off his chin. Too early for a back-and-forth. As far as the car alarm went, he assumed the person probably worked late or left early. Probably something as simple as an accidental push of the panic button instead of the door unlock, simple mistakes, but at 3:00 in the morning, those sounds were exacerbated.

Back in the days of Kelly's youth, his mother probably would have walked around until she found the neighbor and had a polite but direct conversation about common courtesy, but in today's world, that was a dangerous thing. Neighbors were not so neighborly, and overreactions could be disastrous. Most people now took to social media, putting neighborly disputes on blast for the world to see. Kelly had advised his mother to leave the problem to him, but right now, it was the last thing on his mind. He had a long list of things on his agenda to complete before the day was up.

His mother looked down at the note he had scribbled and then back at him. "I guess I'll be taking Embry to school today, huh?"

Kelly shrugged. "I was going to leave a note for you too, Ma. I'm sorry. I caught a bad one."

"Mike," she interrupted. "You do not have to explain. I saw the news. I actually saw you on it. Looked like you were trying to hide from the cameras. I don't know why. You're so handsome."

Kelly blushed slightly at his mother's compliment.

"But I know what you're doing and what you're working on. It's important. The people are very nervous. It's a scary time for the neighborhood. You've got plenty on your plate. I understand that you have to go, and Embry will too." She looked down at the note again. "She sure does love getting them. I just wish you didn't have to write them so often."

"Me, too," Kelly said quietly, more to himself than his mother.

They'd had this conversation before, and she was well aware of the guilt he felt over Embry.

"And you don't have to worry about picking her up, Ma. Samantha is going to get her from school," Kelly said. "We'll get her back on Thanksgiving Day. We'll split the day with Sam and get her just in time for dinner. Good news is we'll have her for the rest of the week after that, so you'll only have to drive her this morning."

His mother gave a dismissive wave. "You know I don't mind doing this for you and her whenever you need."

"I know," Kelly said. "Just wish you didn't have to."

He drained the last bit of his coffee, then kissed his mother on her forehead before grabbing his to-go mug and moving toward the door.

"You be safe out there, Michael Kelly."

"Always am."

Kelly's early morning commute didn't take long. Construction had begun in some spots, but he was able to bypass most of it and make quick work of the drive from Dorchester to downtown.

Kelly entered police headquarters through the side access, fob-only entrance and took the stairs to the second floor. The doors to the Homicide unit were always locked, regardless of the time of day or night, a security measure designed to maintain case integrity. The list of authorized personnel was limited. There was a phone on the outside wall where non-cleared members of the department could call in. Nowadays, most usually sent a text message to coordinate their entry.

When Kelly reached the door, he could see a light on through the window.

Typically, he was the first one in. Somebody was either burning the midnight oil or had come in early to work a case.

As he made his way to the main office area, he saw Barnes at their unit's cubicle cluster, which housed her, Kelly, and Mainelli. He wasn't surprised to see Barnes; she matched his work ethic and was the one person he could always count on to stay late or come in early, and on days like today, sometimes beat him at both.

"Morning, Kris," Kelly said as he approached.

"Well, look who's dragging themselves in a little late this morning."

"What time did you get here?"

She smiled. "Only a few minutes ago. But that's because I went for a jog first."

"You went for a run and still beat me here. I've got to start upping my game. You're making me look bad." Kelly chuckled.

"I'm not the only one who's here early."

Kelly looked around and, seeing no one else, furrowed his brow. "What gives?"

Then he heard a toilet flush, and moments later, Sterling Gray exited the restroom. He tossed a paper towel in the trash can and gave a friendly wave. Kelly nodded at the man and looked over at Barnes.

"Don't look at me. He was waiting outside the door when I got here, said he couldn't sleep, wanted to get an early start."

"I did," Gray said as he walked up. "I came in on this investigation behind the power curve and wanted to get caught up on things. I want to look at it from my perspective and see what I can bring to the table so I can make myself useful. If you don't mind, I'm going to head into the conference room."

"You mean The Depot. If you're going to be part of the team, you've got to start using the lingo," Kelly said.

"Yeah, right, The Depot."

They had explained to him the nomenclature used for Homicide's main conference room.

"Give me a few seconds to get settled in," Kelly said. "I can come in and see if we can put our collective brain power to work, if you'd like?"

"Sounds good to me," Gray said, grabbing his laptop and heading into The Depot. The motion-activated lights kicked on as the agent took up a spot at the table and began looking through some of the files.

"We've got a big day today," Kelly said to Barnes. "Debbie Shoemaker's going to be coming in this morning." He looked at his watch. "Maybe she can give us something useful. I'm going to ask that Sutherland pick some other stand-ins today for the press conference. It's the other reason I called and got Shoemaker's interview pushed up to 8:00. We've got the autopsy afterward. Then we'll see where it all gets us. I'm not too hopeful about Shoemaker, but I definitely want you in on that interview with me."

"Of course. What are partners for? She's from your neighborhood, right?"

"She is," Kelly said.

"Am I supposed to read any further into that?"

"Nothing between us. Never has been, but she's definitely flirtatious."

Barnes's smile broadened. "Flirtatious, as in former love interest?"

"One-sided completely," Kelly said. "And not just me. She had it in for everybody. In particular, Father O'Brien. She chased him around all through high school."

"Funny. And she still attends his services."

Kelly smiled. "I think that's *the reason* she attends his services."

"Maybe we should consider taking out a stalking order against her." The two laughed.

Kelly sat down at his desk and started to organize his handwritten notes, along with his field sketch from the scene at the church. He then began the tedious task of reading through the supplemental reports completed by the patrolmen assigned to check surveillance and canvass the area around the church.

As of right now, they were batting zeros. Of the three potential surveillance cameras in the area, one was totally defunct, there solely for deterrence purposes. The report documented that no wire was physically attached inside the store that owned it. The other two cameras of interest were reviewed. One was blurred so horribly that the reviewing officer couldn't make out pedestrian traffic within a few feet of the camera, and it was well over forty feet from the church and angled poorly. The last camera, his only hope, came from a barber shop across the street, though it was pointed away from the church's door. All of the tape had been pulled and placed into a digital evidentiary file for later review, but nothing seemed worth their investigative time at this point.

The canvass conducted by officers going door to door in the neighboring residential section revealed nobody heard or saw anything. A total of forty-eight people had been interviewed so far, and not one person had any information. This caused concern for Kelly. A dead priest with a gunshot wound to the head, shot at close quarters in a church where the open space was designed to reverberate sound, yet nothing was heard. Either people didn't hear it, or it was designed not to be heard. A bullet missing from the scene, along with no shell casing, pointed to the latter. Lots of holes, none of which were good.

Kelly figured it was time to pick Gray's brain without anyone else around and get a feel for what the Bureau had to offer.

8

Kelly entered The Depot and pulled up a seat beside Gray. He had a laptop open and was scrolling through something when he looked over at Kelly.

"What are you working on?" Kelly asked, expecting the federal agent to close the screen and pleasantly surprised when he didn't.

"Remember yesterday, when I said I might be able to give you a little guidance in the case and maybe explain what those marks on the hand might mean, the significance of them?"

"Of course, been waiting for you to open that can of worms."

"Yeah. Sorry about the delay. I was playing catch-up on what you guys had been working on. It's a pretty extensive crime scene and very meticulously handled. Kudos to you, your team, and in particular your crime scene technicians."

"Thanks. They're top-notch," Kelly offered in return.

"I had to wait to get clearance before I could share this information with you. You've got to understand how things work where I come from."

Kelly nodded. He understood the bureaucratic red tape. There was plenty of that to go around at his agency. Not a big leap to assume it was commonplace everywhere else.

"What I'm about to show you stays within the confines of this team and this team alone. That means you, Barnes, Mainelli, and Sutherland. Outside of that group, I would have to go back and speak with my superiors to get authorization to disseminate it any further."

Interesting. It usually worked the other way, with the upper echelon controlling access to the people on the ground level who needed it most. It was refreshing to hear the opposite was true. Kelly wondered if this came at Gray's direction.

Kelly's interest was thoroughly piqued. Up until now, Sterling Gray had offered little in the way of assistance during his short time in Boston.

Gray appeared to have taken a step back, allowing Kelly's team to process yesterday's crime scene uninterrupted. He was more of a fly on the wall, listening to the back-and-forth banter and the heavy resistance offered by Mainelli.

Smart move to enter into any new organization and observe, just as Kelly had done when he came to Homicide as their newest investigator. He'd found it best to watch and get the feel of things rather than assert himself before he'd learned the protocols.

Gray had obviously reached his comfort level and received the approval required for sharing whatever he had to offer.

"I'm all ears. What do you got?" Kelly asked, trying to look beyond Gray's shoulder at the monitor.

Gray turned it toward him. The digital image of a hand—in particular, the meaty web of the left hand—was similar to the side-by-side comparisons of Danny Rourke, Phillip Smalls, and the most recent victim, Benjamin Tomlin. In fact, when Kelly first looked at Gray's screen, he thought for a moment the photographs were from their case files. The close-up showed the flesh near the web of the hand and the X cut into it.

"That's not one of ours, is it?" Kelly asked.

"No, and that's the real reason I'm here."

Kelly was quiet for a moment as he processed Gray's words. "So, you have been working cases where you've seen this before? Where you've come across this X pattern in other victims? Are we looking at a serial here?"

Gray let out a shallow exhale. "It's not an X."

"What do you mean it's not an X? I'm looking at it. It's an X." Kelly was suddenly tense.

"It's a cross."

Gray hit a button and the image on the screen shifted, rotating ninety degrees to the right.

Kelly was immediately kicking himself for not seeing it earlier. How long had he stared at the wound on his partner's hand? How many times had he sought its meaning? Once the image had been rotated, it became readily apparent that one of the lines was a fraction longer than the others, and when turned to its current position, it clearly showed a cross.

X, cross, a mark is a mark, right? Kelly sought, to no avail, to absolve himself for his shortsightedness. "What's the significance of the cross?"

"We're clear on the fact that everything I say stays here, correct?" Gray asked.

"Of course." In Kelly's past experiences with his department's upper echelon and the recent cover-up he had tried to expose, his circle of trust was extremely small, and currently limited to the members of his immediate team. "You can trust me."

"I got that feeling about you," Gray said.

"I'm guessing its meaning is something significant?"

"We've been hunting this person for a long time."

"You know who he is? You've got a line on our killer and you waited until now to let us in on it?" Kelly asked, leaning toward frustration.

"Well, yes and no," Gray said flatly. "BAU has done an extensive workup on our guy. He's been busy, not just here in Boston but around the northeast and across the country."

"So we are dealing with a serial killer?"

"Yes and no."

"You keep saying that. I'm hoping you plan on getting around to filling me in."

"Well, to answer your first question...Yes, we do know who he is. But not in the way you're thinking."

"Do you always speak in riddles?"

Gray gave a wire-thin smile. "The more definitive answer is we know the type of person he is. BAU has done an extensive workup based on the findings we've accumulated over the years."

Kelly knew the reputation of the FBI's prestigious Behavioral Analysis Unit, made famous in recent years by the TV show *Criminal Minds*, Hollywood's representation of the unit. Their true capabilities were far different from the television portrayal and much less dramatic, but, just like on TV, real-life profilers did analyze extensive amounts of data accumulated from crime scenes and case facts, and apply expertise in developing a behavioral makeup of the suspect. By doing this they were able to effectively render a profile to aid law enforcement's investigative efforts.

BAU developed a set of identifiers that, when applied to suspect searches, improved the likelihood of identifying a person of interest where normal investigative efforts had failed. The FBI didn't have an endless supply of agents to work every violent crime, but in bigger cases they were brought in to assist. It was a useful tool in identifying unknown perps, at least to give a starting point of establishing patterns.

And their unit, as small as it was and based out of Quantico, was tasked with only the highest priority cases, ones that drew the most attention. Apparently a dead priest had hit the jackpot and raised a red flag. Kelly wondered why Rourke's death hadn't caught the FBI's attention, but then he remembered what Charles had said when he found the mark on Phillip Small's hand. In the Rourke case the X was initially passed off as a non-related wound, and not categorized in any way that might have alerted the FBI to the presence of the killer in Boston city limits.

"What's the meaning behind the cross?" Kelly asked.

Gray gave a half smile. He had the chiseled jawline and close-cropped hair of ex-military, and the look of somebody who had served.

"It carries religious significance. Because of that, we named him The Penitent One."

Kelly took a sip of his coffee and rubbed his weary eyes. "You've given him a nickname?"

"Every killer gets one until their real identity is revealed. His official label is Unsub 05-80920. The identifier is the year and zip code of the first known body. I don't know who came up with the nickname, but whoever did—it stuck."

"I guess it's ironic that the case that brought us together took place in the penitential confines of the confessional."

"That's definitely a unique twist and a bit of a departure from the way he carries out his business," Gray said.

"So I'm guessing you've got a list of unique identifiers for this Penitent One? At least an idea of the type of person we're looking for?" Kelly asked.

"I do." Gray tapped a couple keystrokes on his laptop, and a document populated the screen.

"Here's your killer." Gray turned the screen toward Kelly and pushed back slightly in his chair.

Kelly's eyes widened at the depth and detail of the list the BAU team had compiled for this killer. It was the first break in the case.

Kelly stood and walked over to the whiteboard, uncapping a red marker. Drawing an arrow extending from the suspect line into the open space to its right, Kelly began jotting a bulletized list extracted from the BAU report.

First was the notation *ex-military/police.*

Kelly finished copying the list as the phone rang at his desk.

Barnes answered and hollered down the hall to him, "Debbie Shoemaker's on her way in."

Shoemaker, who had arrived at the police department lobby ahead of schedule, strode to the main desk area. Her heavy perfume managed to penetrate the bullet-resistant encasement where the main desk officer took walk-in complaints, causing him to cough.

"Debbie Shoemaker. I'm here to see Detective Michael Kelly, hon," Shoemaker said between smacks of the gum in her mouth.

"Is he expecting you?" Officer Lewis asked gruffly.

Contrary to the majority of receptionists around the world, most police departments made sure they selected some of their less-friendly faces to be the receivers of the walk-in complaint.

Many of those complaints handled in the lobby required limited police involvement. A gruff gatekeeper was always appreciated by those on the investigative floors for keeping the loony tunes from consuming valuable time with their rants and insane complaints.

Today's gatekeeper, Jeffrey Lewis, choked by the woman's perfume, held up one finger and retreated to his desk to call upstairs to Homicide.

Kelly answered the phone.

"It's Lewis down at the main desk. Got a Debbie Shoemaker here, says she's here to see you." Lewis was equally surly when addressing Kelly. It was his nature.

Kelly looked at his watch. She was half an hour early, which was fine. The quicker he got done with this, the quicker he could bring the team up to speed on the new information Gray had revealed before he headed over to the autopsy.

"I'll be down in a minute," Kelly said. After hanging up the phone, he made his way to the elevator, which required a fob access, as did pretty much everything within the walls of headquarters. Therefore, either the main desk officer would have to escort a lobby visitor upstairs, which would've sent Lewis into a tizzy, or Kelly could go down and receive his own guest. He frequently chose the less confrontational option, not out of intimidation but because he liked the aspect of control it gave him. The small talk enabled him to build rapport before the more intense portion of an interview began.

As the steel doors parted, exposing Kelly to the lobby, he caught the overwhelming smell of jasmine and lavender. It hung heavy in the air, almost making his eyes water.

Debbie Shoemaker, who was lingering by the main desk, turned when the elevator doors opened.

Kelly held his finger on the button, keeping the doors open, and stuck his head into the lobby. "Hey, Deb, I'm over here."

She perked up and began to saunter toward him.

At 7:30 a.m., Debbie Shoemaker was dressed as if she were heading out for a long night of bar hopping. She wore three-inch heels that clicked loudly on the tile floor as she walked, and tight jeans that accentuated every feature her body had to offer. She had an exaggerated swagger to her walk, and she was wearing a fuzzy coat unzipped just enough to reveal a skin-tight black top underneath.

And much to Kelly's consternation, he could tell she was *overly excited* to see him.

Her makeup was done, and she had pulled her hair back with an oversize clip. Not that it was needed. Shoemaker's black wavy curls were coated in the visible sheen of whatever can of hairspray she'd emptied on them.

Seeing her all done up was like being transported back to the mid-nineties, as if she were trying to relive the first time they met in the freshman hallway.

Her lips smacked loudly on the piece of chewing gum in her mouth. "Hi, Mikey. It's been a while."

She spoke with an overt coyness he already found exhausting.

Shoemaker entered the small confines of the elevator, and as the doors closed, Kelly had to force himself not to gag at her fragrant trail, which worsened as she spun to face him.

"Hey, Deb, I really appreciate you coming in this morning. I'm sorry to hear that you had a family emergency yesterday. I hope everything's okay."

"It was my aunt. She's got the cancer. Smoked all her life, still smoking now. Can't stop her, but she was pretty sick yesterday. I had to go and see her. My sister—you remember Josie—she said that we're coming up on her last days, so..."

"I'm sorry to hear that," Kelly said, offering a genuine apology. As rough as Debbie Shoemaker's external appearance was, Kelly knew deep down she had a heart of gold. "I won't take up too much of your time. I just want to get a feel for what you saw yesterday. My partner and I are going to run through some questions with you in the interview room, and then we'll get you on your way as quick as possible."

"I'll stay as long as you want, Mikey. You know that."

There it was again, Kelly thought. He wondered how long the flirtations would last or how bad they would get. He'd have to suffer through them—his penance today.

Kelly ignored the remark and was grateful when the bell dinged as they reached the second floor.

"It's just down this way, Deb."

He led, she followed. He brought her to the doors and fobbed his way in.

"Ooh, Mikey. Fancy digs," she said, entering the office space.

"We have an interview room already set up."

He took her down the hallway to Interview Room A. The office was relatively empty, and only a few detectives were beginning to trickle in. Nobody had scheduled an interview this early in the morning, although as the day progressed the rooms would begin to fill.

The door was already open. Kelly flicked a switch on the wall outside the interview room.

"Debbie, just so you know, I just activated a camera system in here. We have to record everything in our interviews."

He walked her in. A table in the center had a chair on one side and two on the opposite side where Kelly and Barnes would sit. He showed her the camera system tucked in the corner. It would be looking down at the back of Kelly's and Barnes's heads, but into Shoemaker's face.

A traditional interview was always designed to record as much of the suspect's reactions as possible. It was equally important to do so in a witness interview so that they could check the veracity of the statements made during the course of questioning. There were few differences between criminal and witness interviews other than the tone of the questions.

Rapport would be built, although Kelly and Shoemaker had a long-standing history, and based on the comments she'd already made, she seemed to be open to any and all questions he asked.

"Deb, can I get you a cup of coffee? Glass of water? Soda? Anything?"

"I'll take a coffee, Mike. Thanks." She plopped herself into the plastic seat and made herself comfortable.

"Just give me a second. I've got to grab my partner and that cup of coffee, and I'll be back here in just a moment. I am going to shut the door, though."

Kelly left. His first stop was the break room, where he poured a cup of coffee from the pot that was already brewed. He grabbed two creamers, a handful of sugars, and a stir stick so she could make the coffee as she liked. Then he turned his head toward Barnes. "You ready to do this, Kris?"

"Sure thing." She grabbed a notepad and stood up from her cubicle.

As she walked closer, he was grateful for the break from the heavy perfume. Kristen Barnes always kept her clean scent subtle.

"You're in for a real treat," Kelly whispered.

"Oh, I can't wait!" Barnes said. "This is your old high school girlfriend, right?"

Kelly rolled his eyes because he had already briefed her that he had known Debbie back in the day. "Not a girlfriend, Kris, although you're going to get to witness some heavy flirtations from her this morning."

"This morning just keeps getting better and better."

"Shall we?"

The two entered Interview Room A, and Kelly was once again assaulted by Debbie Shoemaker's overwhelming aroma.

She was their first and, at present, only witness to the killer the FBI called The Penitent One.

9

They'd spent the better part of the last forty minutes in the gas chamber of perfume with Debbie Shoemaker recounting how her life led to where she was now. She'd worked herself up from the bottom and now owned her own beauty salon, which might explain the liberal application of makeup, hairspray, and perfume. Kelly had spent a great deal of effort guiding his former high school classmate back to the purpose of their conversation. The interview was not to reminisce on times past or a social catch-up, but designed for a specific recounting of any particulars from yesterday, when she had attended church at Saint Peter's and potentially witnessed the would-be killer, whether she knew it or not.

For the seventh time in the last few minutes, Kelly had to cut off Shoemaker's long-winded dissertation and guide her back on track.

"Listen, Debbie, it's been great catching up, seriously. I'm glad for you. Good to hear things are going well in your life, but I think you're forgetting why we're talking here today. Take me back to yesterday morning, the point where you were at church. Walk me through the time from when you entered the church, where you sat, and anything you may have noticed when you left."

"Well, like I said, I attend church every Sunday. I thoroughly enjoy Father

Donny's sermons. They seem to speak to me." She winked at Kelly, and he knew the underlying meaning of her words, so obviously stated.

The wink was added for his benefit. Barnes noticed and nudged him under the table. Kelly tried to ignore the contact.

"I like to sit up front so I can be close to really hear what he has to say," Shoemaker said, pausing for effect. "I don't remember seeing anybody that stuck out. How am I supposed to know what a killer looks like?"

Kelly knew this was true. This was the same conversation that he'd had with O'Brien. There was no way to pinpoint or identify a killer by looks alone.

Historically, in the early stages of criminology, eighteenth-century French physician Franz Josef Gall believed human behavior could be directly linked to physiological traits; in particular, he believed the shape of the skull served as a predictive trait. Certain measurements of the cranial cavity, known as phrenology, stated the size and shape would dictate a person's propensity for violence and criminal activity. It had been proven over the years to be an inaccurate scientific approach and debunked, although movies and television still exacerbated the theory that a person could spot a bad guy by looks alone. Kelly knew this was not true, but it was important he ask anyway, to see if anything caught her eye.

He believed people had an innate ability to perceive threats in a subconscious manner, like an animal who knew it was prey and scurried away. That feeling, the tingle at the back of the neck, was where thousands of years of evolution and survival instinct kicked in.

The subconscious brain perceived threats at different levels, but whether the person brought it to the forefront, recognized, and reacted to it was another story. These mental walk-throughs, slow and paced, were designed to call to the forefront of a witness's mind things their conscious had dismissed.

As far as Debbie Shoemaker's recall of anything usable, they were batting zero.

"Like I said, Mikey, I don't remember anybody that stood out from the crowd except, of course, Father Donny. Now if you'd been there in the crowd, I would have noticed." She gave a coy smile and batted her eyelashes.

It was like being stuck in a bad movie with a B actress overplaying her flirtations. Worsened by the fact that Barnes, sitting to his left, was thoroughly enjoying every single second of it. She hadn't interjected once, leaving Kelly to fend for himself against the outlandish comments.

The banter, the back-and-forth between Shoemaker and Kelly, and Kelly's uncomfortable responses seemed to amuse Barnes to no end. He knew that when this interview was over, she would not hesitate to bring it up endlessly.

"All right. So nothing during the service that stood out, or when you went in, or people around you. How about afterward? Am I correct in assuming that you stayed to go to confession?"

She took a sip of her coffee and chortled a scratchy, raspy version of a school-girl giggle. "I don't stay to confess my sins, Mike. I hit the confessional every once in a while in the hopes that I'll get a little private time with Father Donny. Much to my disappointment"—her brow furrowed—"he wasn't there. It was Father Tomlin."

"And how did you know? Isn't there a screen vent between the two rooms that obscures you from seeing each other?"

"I knew as soon as I heard Tomlin's voice. As soon as I realized this priest was expecting me to confess my deep, dark sins, I apologized, made the sign of the cross, and left."

"And that was it, you left? Was there anybody else in the church when you departed?"

Shoemaker started to shake her head no, and then stopped herself. "Yeah, come to think of it. I don't know why I didn't remember this before. There was a guy..."

For the first time since meeting with Shoemaker, Kelly was fully interested in what was going to come out of her mouth next. She made a smacking sound as she continued to chew the gum, even though she had already started drinking her coffee, now lukewarm if not cold. A disgusting combination that Kelly tried to ignore. Her incessant gum chewing became more erratic and noticeably louder. The nervousness was obviously setting in.

"Okay. Take it slow. You saw somebody else in the church. Do you remember if they were standing or seated?"

"I believe he was seated a few rows back from the front of the church. I can't exactly remember where. I do remember that as I passed by, something caught my eye. I really wasn't paying any attention. Not my business. I'm no busybody."

Kelly held back from laughing out loud, knowing that in her job as a hairdresser and owner of a beauty salon, she was a master of gossip. "Okay. Well, what can you remember about the person? It was a male, you said *guy*."

"I do remember that. He was definitely a TDH."

Kelly shot a glance over at Barnes, who shrugged. "TDH?" Kelly asked.

"Tall, Dark, and Handsome."

Kelly fought the urge to roll his eyes. He had never heard the acronym before, but again, he was out of the loop when it came to that sort of thing. He was sure some type of emoji would go along with it if it were sent via text message. Another aspect of modern life that seemed to have slipped by him. "Okay, so tall, dark, and handsome. But you said he was seated, that you remember."

"He was," Shoemaker answered. "But I could tell he was a tall man." She paused. "He didn't pay me any mind. He was kneeling in prayer."

Kelly listened intently, allowing Shoemaker to revisit the images in her mind. Better for her to do it than for him to assist. If this case led to arrest and prosecution, Kelly didn't want a defense attorney to say he led the witness to describe the person. He sat patiently, letting her work it out on her own, as painful as the process was.

"He looked fit, but it was hard to tell. He just had that look of a guy who likes to work out. Ya know—a strong jaw, kind of like an action hero, and dark hair, but short and clean-cut, like one of those military guys. Not too different from you."

And then she stopped altogether and finished the last sip of coffee.

"Anything else? Anything at all that you can remember?"

Debbie rubbed her temples and closed her eyes, as if trying to visualize the man. "Glasses—I think he had glasses. I'm not sure. I want to say he had glasses."

Kelly nodded, making a mental note.

"That's all I can remember. I left right after that. I got the text from my sister about my aunt, and I rushed out. I guess I pretty much forgot it all until now. Strange. I really couldn't remember him at first. I didn't think I would be able to help at all, but I did. Right, Mike? What I told you helps?"

She seemed eager to please him, excited at the prospect of potentially helping the case, maybe to put herself in Father Donny's good graces.

"You did great, Deb. Thank you so much for coming in." Kelly noted the interview's end time in his notepad and looked up at the hair stylist who'd give Tammy Faye Bakker a run for her money in the liberal application of makeup. "I've got your number and you've got mine. Should anything else come to mind, please don't hesitate to reach out."

She reached across the table unexpectedly and placed her hand on Kelly's, rubbing it gently and looking him in the eyes. "You can call me anytime, Michael Kelly. Any time."

Kelly blushed red. He felt Barnes's knee jab his and knew he would never hear the end of this conversation.

Kelly returned from escorting Shoemaker to the lobby to see Mainelli sitting at his desk. He looked at his watch. It was nearing 9:00. "Wow, Jimmy. Making good time today. You look like dog crap."

Mainelli raised a glass mug in mock cheers. "Thanks so much, Mike. Always appreciate your kindness." He took a swig of coffee. "The wife put me on the couch last night. It's our rule. If I come home after midnight, there's no bed for me. I'm not going to lie to ya, sleep didn't come easy. Didn't even wake up when the kids got up."

Imagining Jimmy Mainelli not waking up in his house was shocking and a testament to the man's obvious fatigue. Kelly had witnessed firsthand the war zone that was his children's daily norm.

It didn't bode well for Mainelli's work output for the remainder of the day. Kelly had worked alongside the man long enough to know that once he was beleaguered by either hunger or fatigue, his investigative skillset dropped dramatically. On those days, Kelly typically assigned him alternative duties rather than the tip-of-the-spear work. Looking at his watch, he knew they had a little time to get across the city to meet with the medical examiner and go through Father Tomlin's autopsy. Better to take Barnes. Mainelli could stand by and assist should any of the forensic evidence start to trickle in from Charles and Dawes's office. Kelly could focus on the primary responsibilities, especially since this was officially his case and everyone else on the team would be in a supporting role.

"Well, Jimmy, since you look so chipper this morning, how about you hang back? I'm going to grab Barnes and head over to see what we've got with Tomlin's body. Who knows? Maybe something will pop on the autopsy today."

"You're not going to get an argument from me," Mainelli said, offering no resistance.

"I'd like to tag along, if you don't mind." Gray poked his head out of the conference room, where he'd spent most of the morning.

"I don't see a problem with that. You been to many autopsies with the Bureau?"

Gray shrugged nonchalantly. "I've been to my fair share."

"Okay, then, let's head out. I don't want to keep the ME waiting."

Kelly spoke with the receptionist, notifying her that Boston PD Homicide was there for Tomlin's autopsy. The trio waited only a few minutes in the cool antiseptic lobby before the door opened.

Luck be damned. Standing in the threshold was Ithaca Best. Kelly felt his heart sink at the awkwardness of seeing the forensic pathologist; they'd recently gone on a date, during which Kelly had to ditch her for a shooting. He had ended any potential of a romantic relationship without giving it much of a chance. Now, he stood next to Barnes, feeling completely out of place.

Gray was oblivious to the tension as they strode up. Kelly made quick introductions, although Best knew Barnes already, having worked with her on prior cases. For Kelly, this was the first time he had attended an autopsy with Best since their failed attempt at a dating relationship. Although he had told her that it wasn't the right time, that he wasn't ready for a relationship, and she said she understood, upon seeing her face-to-face, he felt wholly wrong about his handling of it.

"Ithaca, this is Sterling Gray. He's with the FBI, attached to Homicide on the Tomlin case," Kelly said.

She extended her hand. "Ithaca Best. Welcome to the dead zone." A quirky sense of humor was needed when you worked among the dead.

"The pleasure's all mine," Gray said.

Kelly noted that their handshake lingered a bit. Maybe she'd moved on from him as quickly as he had from her.

"Well, let's get to it, shall we?" Best led them into the sterile hallway and down to the autopsy room where Father Tomlin was the guest of honor.

His body was set on the cold metal tray, prepped and ready for the autopsy to begin. Two technicians were standing by to assist, for which Kelly was grateful. When the medical examiner was overloaded with bodies, he'd had to do some of the moving and manipulation during the course of an autopsy. He preferred to remain distant, maintaining his role as an observer and taking copious notes.

A detective wasn't required to be on scene for an autopsy. They were recorded by audio and video, and extensive photographs were taken. Kelly always applied a layer of redundancy to his cases, and being physically present on a crime scene or autopsy was different from watching it on video.

Best tapped the voice recorder on the stainless-steel tray nearby, indicating to the group the recording was about to begin. As was ritual, Best made her opening remarks.

"Today is Monday, November twenty-fifth, two thousand nineteen. I, Doctor Ithaca Best, pathologist for the Massachusetts Office of the Medical Examiner, will be performing today's autopsy of Benjamin Tomlin, age forty-six. Pathology Technicians Thomas Robichaud and Adrian Markus will be assisting. Detectives Michael Kelly and Kristen Barnes of Boston Police Department's Homicide Division are in attendance and will be observing the procedure. Also in attendance is Special Agent Sterling Gray of the Federal Bureau of Investigation. Time on the clock reads 10:27 a.m."

Processing a body followed a similar pattern to working a crime scene. Best began by taking photographs, starting with overalls and then working her way down from the head toward the feet on the right side of the body. She moved in a clockwork fashion around Tomlin's gray body, working her way back up on the left.

Kelly and his team stood off to the side and watched, waiting patiently and hoping something in this initial part of the investigation would give them some evidentiary find that would propel things forward.

"We've got a single gunshot entry wound left temple, exit wound right side slightly above the temple region. Major damage to the brain. We'll know the extent once we remove the skull cap. No stippling except on the outside of the entry wound. We see debris embedded, appears to be bits of splintered wood, in and around the entrance wound."

The gunshot was fired through the confessional screen. The round that traveled into the priest's skull would have carried with it bits and fragments of the handcrafted wood lathing screen divider.

Ithaca continued her summation of the head wound. At her direction, the technicians rolled the body. The exit wound was measured, and the diameter of both entry and exit wounds was noted.

Kelly took notes. "Any idea on potential caliber?" he asked, knowing from past experience that a specific caliber couldn't be generated, but a rough guesstimate could be made based on an entry and exit wound.

"Given the approximate distance from where the weapon was fired, I'd say we're looking at a weapon no greater than .40 caliber. Looking at the exit wound, I would guess—and this is just a guess, mind you—we might be looking at a hollow point, something that would do some expanding on exit, based on the size and damage of the wound. When I remove the skull cap and take a closer look at the brain, I should be able to give you a better estimate. But I think we're safe to say that greater than a .22 and less than a .40 caliber."

That really doesn't narrow things much, Kelly thought. A wide variety of weapons and calibers were capable of producing such a wound.

Best continued her overalls. "I see the hands are bagged. I'll check for any type of defensive wounds or manipulation."

Kelly interrupted, "There's a wound to his left hand, Ithaca. It's going to be at the webbing between the thumb and index finger. Could you take special care in noting that and documenting any potential findings for an instrument that would have left such a mark?"

"Will do." She manipulated the bagged hand slightly, looking at it more carefully. "Some type of an X, a stamp of some sort," she said. "Possibly a Phillips head screwdriver."

"Not an X, a cross," Gray said.

"Huh," she said, not dismissing his comment but absorbing it. "Tell you what. When this is all done, I should have at least a potential workup of what could cause the wound. Who knows? Maybe I'll get lucky and be able to scrape something usable out of it. Anyway, that's going to take a bit of time and we're going to have to wait for the lab for analysis, but I'll put it on expedite."

"Thanks," Kelly said.

"Moving on."

No truer statement, Kelly thought. He couldn't help but think of the list Gray had provided, and the killer who was somewhere on the loose within the city of Boston.

10

"What do we think?" Kelly asked.

The group sat inside The Depot and stared at the board. The new information extending out from the suspect line detailed the description provided by the Behavioral Analysis Unit's analysts, their bureau's profilers. Added to it was the information gathered from Debbie Shoemaker's potential eyewitness account of the killer.

It was fascinating to see the parallels, the connections the analysis unit in Quantico had made to the descriptors, albeit limited in scope, to those Shoemaker had provided. They married up on several points, one being the suspect's physical size.

Height: *5'11" – 6'2"*
Build: *Muscular*
Hand: *Right*
Age: *Mid to late 40s*
Glasses: *(?)*
Education: *College +*

But what haunted Kelly most was the top line: ex-military/police likely.
What Shoemaker had given them did little in the way of providing a

detailed-enough description to use with a sketch artist. At this point they had almost nothing in the way of any specific details they could disseminate to the public.

TDH. Shoemaker described a tall, dark, and handsome man with rigid facial features and glasses, although she was less confident in her recollection of the eyewear. It was a more complete picture than when the investigation began, but still not enough to pursue any one particular person. Not by a longshot.

"Why the left hand?" Barnes asked. "Why not the right?"

"Well..." Gray had become the group's go-to on the killer's psyche. "There are several indications in the Bible that the left is the side for evil. The analysis team pulled together several passages that seem to fit the rationale in why a killer would be using the left hand to leave his mark." Gray rattled off three different passages, then provided the group with the religious significance of the markings on the victims' left hands, citing several more biblical references to support the assertion, referencing verses from Matthew Chapter 25. "He will put the sheep on His right, and the goats on the left. Then He will also say to those on His left, 'Depart from Me, accursed ones, into the eternal fire which has been prepared for the devil.'" Gray's summation was that judgment was passed for those who stood on Christ's left, and salvation was reserved for those on his right. BAU asserted the killings were done as a passing of final judgment, and thus the moniker "The Penitent One" was born.

The victims didn't fit a specific pattern, which was why the FBI had difficulty tracking him. The three Boston victims had no apparent connection. A cop, a rapist, and a priest. It sounded like the start of a really bad joke.

"Why the religious markings? Why the cross?" Mainelli said aloud, apparently not making the connection.

Gray took the floor and, turning to the group, said, "It's been theorized that our doer, our unsub, The Penitent One or TPO, was most likely raised Catholic. From all indications, and from the actions he's taken coupled with the significance of leaving behind a religious marker, his teachings had to have been intense, to say the least."

Kelly thought about his own upbringing in the Roman Catholic Church in South Boston's Dorchester neighborhood. He knew families who were extremely devout and followed the doctrine and teachings of the church to a T. Accepting the FBI's assessment was a challenge for him. Why commit one of the most cardinal sins—murder? It just seemed off.

"If he was raised in the religion, it seems backward that he would use it as a means to convey some type of message," Kelly said.

"Well, maybe it has a negative connotation in his mind," Gray offered. "This is what the profilers believe. The TPO's religious upbringing was in the strictest of fashions, and more likely than not, religion was presented in a punitive form, making it difficult for us to relate. They further theorized that as he grew older, a deep-rooted resentment resurfaced in the form of an insatiable rage.

"A love-hate relationship. The TPO is conflicted. He was raised to believe in the teachings of God, especially under the Roman Catholic discipline, but he was physically punished by the same hand who had taught him. The markings seem to be both a statement of his devotion and his hatred for those who instilled it."

"Great," Barnes muttered. "We've got a religious fanatic who kills people at will. A ghost managing to elude capture from both local authorities and the federal government for at least, what...fifteen years?"

"Fifteen years is a long time," Mainelli blurted out. "We're going against a killer who has managed to maintain his anonymity for more than a decade. Not a single photograph or piece of DNA linking him to any case. You basically have nothing on him."

He was blunt to a fault. Kelly noted Mainelli was more alert today, a change from his recent norm. His sleep situation must have improved overnight, a sign that the man would be a more useful member of the group today.

"It's true, he's been a ghost," Gray said. "Trust me—since this case was handed off to me a few years back, I've spent countless hours going over the old files, looking at connections, trying to find the pieces that fit...only to come up empty-handed every time. And you're right. As of right now, we have no photographic evidence. He's been impeccably meticulous, leaving no evidence behind. The only thing connecting the cases right now is the mark on the left hand. The one saving grace is we've managed to keep that aspect from the public. Right now, it's our only link."

Kelly understood the significance of that. Holding back that evidence in the countless murders that had happened in the time since TPO had first come on the radar must've been a monumental task for the FBI. They had to make sure their slim hope of identifying him didn't dissipate into the ether. Had they released the information about a cross-like mark on the victims' left hands, the killer would surely catch wind of it. They would run the risk of him changing his calling card and therefore being nearly impossible to connect to future cases.

Historically, some killers continued their pattern even after it was identified by the media. The compulsion, an internal drive mechanism forcing them to leave their calling card or token, was innate and extremely hard to change.

"It'd be nice if one of those surveillance cameras would have picked something up," Mainelli said. His voice was loud, almost a shout.

"Well, I wasn't holding out hope," Kelly said. "Nothing came up on the department intel camera set up at Church Street."

The BPD Intelligence and Analysis Unit had worked hard in recent years to bring the criminal intelligence division into the digital age by setting up a network of surveillance cameras at many of the city's major intersecting street corners. The cameras were monitored in real time as a way to spotlight crime as it happened and had been used with much success in proactive enforcement and police resource allocation.

The recording devices, working on overdrive all times of the day and night, enabled investigators to backtrack in time and retrieve usable footage from quality cameras. Even though the network was comprehensive, it was costly and therefore not set up everywhere in the city. The intersection at Church and Adams, located three hundred feet from the church's front doors, was covered, but unfortunately the camera was focused mostly on the intersection.

"I've got a bigger concern," Gray offered ominously. "I'm guessing the TPO didn't leave randomly. I think he knew about the camera there and purposely took the alternative route to avoid it." Gray tapped the top line on the dry erase board: ex-military/police. "He's eluded capture for fifteen years, which is increasingly more difficult with the exponential developments in technology. Our unsub has managed to be just a blip on the digital radar.

Never picked up on a surveillance cam, no photos...nothing. The only plausible guess is that he knows how to avoid detection at a scary level."

"Who are we dealing with here?" Mainelli fired back. "The boogeyman? This isn't some type of super soldier movie. This isn't a Jason Bourne novel."

Kelly wanted to agree but couldn't help feeling they were dealing with an entirely different type of killer. While some murders went unsolved in the city, the majority of times it was due to lack of cooperation from a key witness or poor handling of case evidence. Rarely did somebody outwit the system, although Connor Walsh came to mind. He and his crew had ducked several cases. Kelly thought about the gun that had disappeared from evidence, a key piece of evidence that would've undoubtedly put the mob boss behind bars for a very long time. But The Penitent One was proving to operate at a whole different level.

"I'm not sure where we go from here," Kelly said. For the first time in many months, he felt completely baffled by a case. His leads were fairly non-existent. The evidence they'd recovered from the scene was ambiguous at best. There were no DNA hits, no fingerprints left behind. The weapon used was a wide gamut of possible calibers, no shell casing or round recovered for comparison, no witnesses capable of clearly identifying the suspect, and no viable surveillance footage. An endless series of nos. Kelly felt defeated, just like he had when he tried to pick up where investigators left off in his partner's death. No matter how badly he wanted to find the person responsible, he came up empty-handed. It had become his pastime investigation, something he worked on in his spare moments between other assignments. Over the last eight years it had become his white whale, slowly eating away at him. The red card permanently affixed to the murder board at his desk served as a constant reminder of his failure.

Eight years later, and even with the information provided by the FBI, he was no closer to finding the killer. Fifteen years of the killer eluding capture from the FBI's quiet hunt made Kelly feel wholly disheartened at the prospects for this case's resolution.

Kelly's phone vibrated. He looked down to see Donny's name, then stepped out of the room to answer.

"Hey, Donny."

"Mike. I got that stuff you asked me for, but I'd like you to come here and take a look."

Kelly had been so absorbed in the case he'd forgotten what he asked his friend to get.

"I'm sorry, come again?"

"The information on Father Tomlin. You asked me to get his personnel file, remember?" Donny said.

"It's been a crazy couple of days. Yes, you said you have something?"

"I do. Can you come here and take a look?"

"Sure thing. Just give me a few. I'm just wrapping something up here and then I'll head over."

"See you then. I'll be in my office."

Kelly hung up and popped his head back into the room. "Hey, guys, I'm going to cut out and pop over to see O'Brien. He's got Father Tomlin's personnel file."

Kelly didn't wait for any offers to join him, just walked to his desk, grabbed his windbreaker, and headed out the door, leaving the rest of his team to mull over the files in the endless brainstorming session.

Kelly pulled into the lot behind the church and made his way in through the side access door before heading up the stairs to where Father Donovan O'Brien's pastoral office was located. Kelly knew it well from visiting many times in the past. He also knew that when Donny was there, he always left the side door open.

Kelly knocked on the open door's weathered wood frame.

"Hey, Mike," O'Brien said, offering a smile.

He looked genuinely pleased to see Kelly, a far cry from his appearance the other day shortly after he discovered Benjamin Tomlin's body. It was good to see that his friend was able to get back to a working norm so quickly, but it didn't surprise Kelly. Donny had a natural way of putting things in perspective, of clearing his mind from the things he'd heard and witnessed as a priest while ministering to some of the most shattered families in one of the city's toughest neighborhoods.

O'Brien had built a layer of Teflon on the outside of his heart similar to Kelly's, protecting himself from exposure to the tragedies of his congregation.

Kelly pulled up a seat across from his friend. A dark oak desk, stacked with a poorly organized pile of papers, separated the two. The room was small, not much bigger than a walk-in closet. There was barely enough room for a desk, a lamp, and a couple of chairs. Definitely not a space for a large group meeting, but good enough for a couple of people to discuss religious affairs. The bookshelves were loaded with a variety of old texts. A large Bible sat on a small podium next to a globe in the corner. The air was musty.

"Donny, you said you had Tomlin's paperwork. Why the need for secrecy?"

"Here." O'Brien slid a manila file across the desk and tapped it. "Take a look yourself."

Kelly opened the file and saw that it was sparsely filled, not more than three pages. "This is all you found?"

"Yeah, not that I expected a ton more, but it looks like he's got no other religious experience prior to coming here a few months ago. I can't find any of the other parishes that he's worked at in our in-house filing system. So I made a call to the archdiocese to see if there was a master file somewhere with more detail and they said no."

"What did the archdiocese say?"

"They told me not to worry about it. That it's being taken care of and that they'd be in contact with the authorities themselves. To be honest, they seemed a little put off by me asking."

"Who did you speak to over there?" Kelly asked. "Has this ever happened before? Are they normally this secretive about such inquiries?"

"I couldn't say. I've never really dug into another priest's personnel file before. But something about it felt off. Maybe I'm still just shook up. Does it sound strange to you?"

Kelly gave a shrug. "Not sure. Depends. I'll check to see if they ever sent something over to us. It could've gotten lost in the shuffle. I'll check with Sutherland, make sure that somebody at the archdiocese hasn't already forwarded the file over. You know how things get, maybe he just forgot to give it to me."

"It wasn't just the phone call. I remember having a conversation with

Father Tomlin, back when he first arrived. He said he had done some work at Saint Mary's in Alexandria, Virginia, prior to coming here to Saint Peter's. I found it strange there was no record of it in his file here. I was going to call over there, but after getting shut down by the archdiocese, I didn't want to ruffle any feathers by overstepping my bounds and figured I would just leave it to you."

"No worries, I'll check it out."

"Do you think there's something to it, Mike? Do you think there's something going on here I should be worried about?"

"I don't know. Could be nothing. I'll keep you posted. I'll take a look at it and place a call over to that church, see what they can tell me."

"Okay." Donny seemed relieved at hearing this. His mind had obviously run a little wild, and understandably so under the circumstances. Finding a fellow priest murdered would unravel the best of minds. Entertaining a conspiracy theory or two would only be natural.

But that wasn't Kelly's way. Kelly was a fact man. He believed in the tangible, and only when all else failed did he give any credence to wild conjecture. He hoped this wasn't going to be the case now. Although, with Gray's enlightening information, it made the leap to conspiracy theory much easier.

"How are you holding up, Donny? You personally?"

"I'm good. Been a rough week, but I'm doing better. Tough to put the image of Tomlin out of my mind. Thanksgiving seems less festive. I'm going to hopefully take some time to myself and decompress."

"If you need anything, you know I'm just a phone call away." Kelly got up, taking Father Tomlin's thin personnel file with him. "You don't mind if I take this, right?"

"No, that's your copy." Donny switched gears. "Got any big plans for Thanksgiving, Mike?"

"Going to have Barnes over for a little dessert this year."

"Huh," Donnie said, breaking into a grin. "Imagine that."

"Don't give me any grief. I'm catching enough of it from Embry as it is."

"I'm happy for you. It's about time you got your personal life back."

"Thanks."

Kelly headed to his car, still warm from the drive over. He sat for a moment before turning the ignition and grabbing his cell phone. He did a quick Google search, finding only one Saint Mary's in Alexandria, Virginia, and decided to make a quick call.

After a few rings, the call connected. "Hello, Saint Mary's Parish. This is Alice. How may I help you?"

"Hi, Alice, this is Detective Michael Kelly. I'm calling from Boston Police Department's Homicide Unit. I'm investigating the murder of a priest here in Boston, and in doing some research—"

"Oh dear," she interrupted.

"Sorry to be so frank," Kelly said, realizing how shocking his opening remark would have been to an unsuspecting ear. "I've just been working hard on this the past couple of days and forget myself."

"Anything we can do, Detective, please." Her voice reset to its initial pleasant tone.

"Well, digging around in his personnel file didn't have much to offer, and we're trying to get as much background information as we can."

"Sure, understandable." The woman spoke softly, sweetly.

"The decedent told one of the parish's priests that he worked at Saint Mary's before coming here to Boston, but we couldn't find anything supporting that in his personnel record. Is there any way you could take a look for me?"

"Sure, yes. No problem. What is the priest's name?"

"Benjamin Tomlin."

"Okay, Tomlin. T-O-M-L-I-N?"

"Correct." Kelly could hear her typing on the computer keyboard.

"Strange," Alice mumbled.

"Were you able to find anything?"

"No. Not at all. We don't have any record of a Father Benjamin Tomlin. Not anywhere in our system."

"Is it possible it was misfiled?"

"We've recently computerized our records. We used to have an old file system, but I was the one who updated it, put every name into our database," she said, pride emanating from the receiver.

"And there's nothing?"

"No. The database is archived back to the very first priest who presided over our church. There's no history of a Father Tomlin. Nobody by the name Benjamin Tomlin anywhere in our system."

"Strange," Kelly said, repeating the woman's words.

"Sorry I couldn't be of more help, Detective," Alice said kindly.

"You've been plenty of help." Just before ending the call, Kelly asked, "And there's no other Saint Mary's in or around Alexandria that you know of?"

"We're the only one."

"Okay then. Maybe I just got my facts crossed. Does happen," Kelly said, attempting to minimize any worry his inquiry might've caused.

"I hope you find whatever you're looking for, and I hope you find whoever did this."

"Me too," Kelly said, and hung up. Although he felt further away from that possibility with every passing second.

11

The next couple of days proved uneventful in moving the case forward. The additions made to the board all fell into the negative column of things not found or puzzle pieces left uncollected. And for the first time since Kelly's arrival to Homicide, he'd slammed into an investigative brick wall. The internal pressure he placed on himself trumped any hounding by his supervisor or the media, who were still in a frenzied, ravenous quest for an update on a suspect identification. Kelly and his team were no closer to offering one than when they had first briefed the community Sunday evening.

Frustration had set in, etched clearly on the faces of the three men and one woman seated at the oval table staring blankly at the whiteboard. Hoping that by some miracle the answer would appear. While the BAU analysis had been beneficial in painting a clear picture of their potential suspect, it brought them no closer to identifying the actual person responsible. It only served to heighten Kelly's awareness that the likelihood of developing a suspect was diminishing rapidly, if not already completely gone. Sutherland was currently in a closed-door meeting with his immediate supervisors and Superintendent Acevedo, who rarely if ever frequented the actual investigative spaces of headquarters, sticking normally to the command staff level.

Acevedo's presence here today told Kelly the heat was being turned up.

He'd given his boss little to offer in the way of case progression, so the meeting was going to be wholly one-sided.

They'd gone over the case facts a million times. Even Kelly was feeling the tedium of it, although nobody in the room matched the disgusted frustration Jimmy Mainelli wore on his face. He'd complained as soon as he walked in this morning, saying they should have been given the day off seeing that it was Thanksgiving and his wife had a large group coming over.

Death didn't care about holidays. Everybody in the room knew that, even Mainelli.

The meeting ended, and Sutherland trailed after Acevedo and his entourage as they left. A hushed silence fell over the detectives working in the common space as the Criminal Investigation's commanding officer made his way across the bureau floor.

The superintendent stopped briefly at one cluster of desks where his son Tony was seated. A brief exchange between father and son, held out of Kelly and his crew's earshot, could only be about one thing. As the younger Acevedo looked past his father and made eye contact with Kelly, the curl of his thin lips made it obvious that Kelly was the brunt of the joke.

Less than a minute later, the Homicide unit's volume returned to its usual hum as the door closed behind the superintendent leaving with his minions in tow.

Sutherland made his way over to the team. Kelly noticed the sergeant's limp was more pronounced after meeting with the command staff. Dale Sutherland made a point of showing the lameness in his leg when in the presence of his supervisors, not in the hopes of gaining sympathy but in gaining traction with his disability claim.

Sutherland staggered into the opening and leaned against the door frame. The team stared back at him expectantly, the unspoken question, "And what was that all about?" hanging in the air.

"I gave them what we've got so far, which at this point isn't much more than we've had since the start. The case looks like it's stalling out and losing steam." Sutherland said this to the group but focused his stare on Kelly.

"The guy is a ghost, Sarge," Mainelli chirped up. "I don't know what else you want us to do. We've flipped every snitch we could find, pulled every possible surveillance camera in the area. Forensics hasn't put anything useful in our hands. And, no offense to the FBI, but they've given us a fancy list that amounts to nothing more than telling us we're up against somebody who's eluded them for over fifteen years. I don't know what you expect."

"I expect results," Sutherland fired back. "That's what my unit does. We solve the unsolvable cases."

Kelly knew the man was right and was angry at himself for not having more to offer. He wanted nothing more than to counterbalance Mainelli's despondent attitude, but after plowing through all of the case files, comparing every fact and the limited usable evidence, it all circled back to a big fat goose egg.

"Doing the best we can, boss," Kelly muttered.

Sutherland paused at Kelly's comment, and maybe because of the holiday, his gruff exterior softened a bit. "Listen, we've been racking our brains for the past few days on this thing, putting forth extraordinary effort. I know each and every one of you—even you, Mainelli—have given your all. Sometimes an investigation just comes up short."

Kelly slumped in his chair.

"Why don't you guys take the rest of the day, clear your heads, get some good old family time? You've been living in the office, and from the smell of this room, maybe some of you are long overdue for a shower." Sutherland laughed at his own joke. Levity replaced the initial moments since his tongue lashing, delivered by Acevedo.

Nobody moved.

"What're you all still sitting around here for? This is an official order from me to you. Close your case files, lock down The Depot, and head home to your families for the day. We'll pick this thing back up tomorrow. Maybe we look at it with fresh eyes and find something we overlooked. I don't want you to take anything home with you. Leave it all here. Go enjoy your Turkey Day."

Mainelli was already out of his seat.

Kelly hesitated for a moment, hanging back with Barnes, who was the second to last to get out of her seat and move toward the door.

"See you tonight," he whispered out of the rest of the crew's earshot.

"Wouldn't miss it for the world," she said softly.

The excitement Kelly first had on Sunday, when he began his preparations for this Thanksgiving meal and the arrival of his guest of honor, filtered back. It momentarily washed away his defeat at not having moved the case forward. His mind quickly focused on the things he needed to do to prepare for tonight's meal, and he felt suddenly grateful for the distraction.

The crunch next to his ear was loud. Kelly turned to see a bit of broken bacon disappear inside Embry's mouth, the remnants of the salty evidence still crusting the corner of her lips. "If you eat all the bacon before we mix it in with the sprouts, you're going to ruin the flavor."

"The secret is..." He leaned in close and whispered in his daughter's ear, "Nobody likes Brussels sprouts. That's why we bury them in bacon."

She giggled and finished the second half of the piece still in her hand.

Kelly rolled his eyes in defeat. He'd been battling with the bacon thief since he'd fried up the pound of center-cut, maple-flavored goodness.

The cooked pieces drained on a paper towel next to the stove. Kelly used the leftover bacon grease to sauté the Brussels sprouts, softening them and adding in bits of crushed bacon as he went. He salted and peppered the rugged vegetable, drizzling in a touch of Worcestershire sauce and a dab of soy, not following a specific recipe. He'd gotten hooked on cooking shows. It was his secret obsession. Watching the television chefs, Kelly had picked up some tricks of the trade. His favorite thing to do was pour in a little red wine, deglazing the pan and adding a little caramelization as the sugars cooked down. Never letting a good glass of red go to waste, Kelly sampled as he cooked. The downside to his cooking was he could never repeat the process. Each meal, even though he used the same ingredients, always resulted in a different taste. He just hoped this version of sprouts proved to be as good as his last, and enough to win over his daughter's discerning palate.

Embry's resistance to the hearty vegetable was long-standing and stalwart. The deal brokered in the Stop & Shop aisle was worth the trade-off. Brussels sprouts for his seat next to Barnes.

Embry reached across and grabbed another piece of bacon before Kelly could stop her. To his surprise, she bypassed her mouth and crumbled it into the sizzling pan. The smell of the sprouts cooking in the bacon fat carried the note of maple and caused his empty stomach to rumble.

"I'm starving. When are we eating?" Embry asked, as if reading his mind.

"In a few minutes. The sprouts are last, and they're almost done. Everything else is ready and warming in the oven."

She bounced off the stool and skipped into the living room to make the announcement to Kelly's mother and brother, who were watching the football game on TV.

Kelly peeked out, happy to see his brother sipping on an O'Doul's. Ever since coming out of rehab, Brayden had stayed the course set by his inpatient therapy. But on a day like today, he was worried his brother would be tempted by tradition. One in which his younger brother would drink to excess and end up face down before dessert.

Kelly thought it would be okay for him to have a near beer, at least give him the flavor of normal without the negative fallout. He just hoped the taste of it wouldn't send him into a frenzy. When Brayden had bottomed out before, it had taken a heavy toll on the Kelly family. With him living at home again, everybody was making an adjustment.

Brayden had steered clear of the dope, remaining drug free since leaving rehab. He was the healthiest Kelly had seen him in recent years. He finally saw the shadow of his brother's former self in the man sitting in the living room, giving him hope the worst was behind him. Brayden was even picking up a couple hours at the package store.

"Dinner's ready," Embry sang out as Kelly turned off the burner.

The gas feeding the flame flickered and popped before going out. He slid the sprouts into a blue ceramic bowl and then, wearing floral oven mitts, removed the turkey from the oven.

Brayden entered the kitchen. "Smells great! Maybe you should quit being a cop and open a restaurant." He gave Kelly a punch in the ribs, soft but still hard enough to remind Kelly of the playful nature in which they used to box as children. "Let me give you a hand." He grabbed a hot plate and set it on the center of the table before helping remove the potatoes from the oven.

His mother hobbled into the dining room area, forgoing the use of her cane. She was doing this more often as her hip improved. The doctor told her to move without it as often as the pain would permit so that she would begin to strengthen the muscles.

She took her seat at the head of the table, Kelly and Embry sat side by side, and Brayden across from them. For the first time in a long time, as Kelly surveyed the group, he felt like their family was whole again.

Ma Kelly raised her glass. "Family first!"

Kelly, Brayden, and Embry responded in unison with, "Family always."

Dinner ended. The pumpkin pie rested on the warm stove. Kelly handled the dinner while his mother had always taken pride in the sweeter part of the meal. Unlike much larger families, the Kellys didn't overdo the dessert or the food, making just enough with a little left over.

Kelly prepared a plate of turkey, stuffing, mashed potatoes, and a handful of Brussels sprouts. He wrapped the plate in foil and set it on top of the stove, which was still warm from the pie.

The odor of the kitchen transitioned from the savory to the sweet as the pumpkin spice filled the air.

Kelly nervously downed a second glass of wine as he awaited Barnes's arrival. A knock at the door suddenly doubled his anxiety. It would be the first time Embry spent time with Barnes knowing their new relationship status.

"Coming," Embry yelled, sailing down the hallway toward the front door.

Kelly was happy to see his daughter so excited at the prospect of meeting his colleague and, for lack of a better word, girlfriend. Although neither Kelly nor Barnes had ever formally labeled the relationship.

Embry swung the door wide. Barnes entered, chased by a blast of icy cold wind. The temperature had dipped as the sun set, and it appeared the northeast was settling in for a long winter ahead, if November's current temperatures were any indication.

Barnes stood in the doorway for a moment and shook off the cold. Embry, the gracious host, offered to take her coat and threw it on a hook in the mud room. Barnes squatted low as Kelly had seen her do numerous times in their partnership when dealing with a young victim or witness. She had a kind, natural way about her, and she was applying it now with Embry. Kelly couldn't hear what was said, but Embry seemed delighted by it. Barnes gave her a pat on the head, then straightened and followed Kelly's young daughter into the kitchen area.

Kelly wasn't sure about the protocol of their greeting. He walked over and gave her a hug and a kiss on the cheek, cordial but not an overt display of affection. It was lukewarm at best. He wasn't sure how anything more would be received by his daughter. Plus, Kelly was not a fan of PDA by nature.

"Well, look what the cat dragged in," Brayden said, giving her a big hug. It lasted longer than Kelly would have liked, and knowing their past dating relationship—although long ago in their youth—still made for a bit of awkwardness, at least for Kelly. "Come on in and have a seat."

Kelly pulled out a chair and Embry took the seat next to her. Kelly moved around to the other side of the table and took up a spot next to Brayden.

"I'd sit next to you, but I lost a bet."

"What was the bet?" Barnes asked playfully.

"I bet Embry she wouldn't eat my Brussels sprouts; she said she would try them if I let her sit next to you."

"Well, it looks like I am the one who won the bet," Barnes said, smiling down at Kelly's little girl, who looked up at her in delight.

Kelly's mother was the last to sit and had brought the pie with her, wobbling unsteadily as she made her slow progression from the kitchen to the table. Kelly knew better than to try to assist. She was as stubborn as they came.

"I've got a pot of coffee brewing if you'd like, or something stronger," she said with a smile.

Barnes looked over at the glass of red wine in front of Kelly's plate. "I'll take a glass of wine. I can get it, though."

"Let me." Kelly stood and slipped into the kitchen. Upon his return, he heard Embry say, while his mother cut the pie into eighths, "So, do you love my dad?"

Kelly nearly dropped the glass of wine in his hand. He tried to interrupt and made a sound that was somewhere between a cough and a choke.

Barnes took it in stride, laughing out loud.

"How can they be in love?" Brayden said. "They've only been dating for a minute."

"I knew I loved your father the moment I saw him," Ma Kelly said, her brogue adding its lyrical lilt to her voice.

"Here we go again with the love-at-first-sight story." Brayden put his forehead to the table in playful exaggeration.

"I'd personally love to hear it," Barnes said, taking the glass from Kelly, who remained momentarily frozen in shock at how quickly the conversation had deteriorated.

"Well, their father's father ran a small market. Your basic variety of dairy products, milk, eggs, and the like. Back in the day, mind you, they used to deliver door to door."

"The good ole days of the milkman—here we go again," Brayden said under his breath.

"Enough out of your mouth, Brayden Kelly." Ma Kelly gave her youngest a squint of her eyes before continuing. "My mother had ordered a dozen eggs and a couple of bottles of milk. And their father delivered. Although, not so well, I might add." Ma Kelly laughed. "He tripped on our stoop and fell flat on his face, breaking eleven of the twelve eggs. Most of which ended up all over his white aproned uniform. I had come to the door just in time to see the fall. It was quite a sight. When I picked up the egg-covered boy and looked into his eyes, I knew at that moment that he was going to be my husband. Hell or high water, I was going to find a way to marry that klutzy man. And lo and behold, I did. And I have never regretted the time that I spent with him." She raised her glass and took a sip.

As he looked into Kristen Barnes's emerald green eyes, Kelly wondered what his story would be.

12

The dessert session with Barnes had gone better than expected. Kelly finished putting Embry to bed and headed downstairs, where Barnes was hanging out with his mother and Brayden. He went into the kitchen and grabbed the foil-wrapped plate, taking a slice of the pumpkin pie and wrapping it separately, before walking into the living room. Barnes was seated on the couch next to Brayden, and his mother was rocking back in her favorite doily-adorned recliner.

"I hate to break up the party, but it's getting late and I want to get this over to Pops before he leaves for the night," Kelly said, holding the warm plate of covered food.

Barnes said her goodbyes and followed Kelly to the door.

The cold bit at his face as he stepped outside. Barnes was blocking his car in the narrow incline of the driveway. The two stood between the two department-issued unmarkeds, the bumper-to-bumper vehicles mirroring the two drivers as they moved in close.

She moved closer until the plate of food was the only thing separating them. Kelly placed it on his hood and closed the distance.

Barnes gave him a gentle kiss on the lips. "I had a really great time tonight."

"Me too. I think it went well. Embry seems really taken by you," he said.

"Sorry to cut things short."

"Eight o'clock isn't too short, especially when we've got an early day tomorrow." Barnes smiled. "But—I wouldn't mind a longer evening, one of these days."

"Agreed." He retrieved the plate from the cold hood. "Tradition is tradition, and I've got to pay Pops a visit."

Barnes held up a hand and then placed it on his chest, tapping lightly against his well-shaped pectorals. "You don't have to explain yourself to me. I think it's wonderful, the connection you have with him and the way you two take care of each other."

"Family is a strange thing, and it doesn't always come by way of blood," Kelly said.

They kissed again and separated. Kelly watched as Barnes drove off, then made his way down the driveway, wedged between his mother's home and their neighbor's. On the street, he saw the red Jetta that had caused his mother so much grief. Nobody was around. The street vacant. The car served as a reminder of one of the many things Kelly still had to take care of. He needed to set aside some time to have a little chat with the neighbor about their middle-of-the-night disruptions.

After the short commute to Pops's gym, Kelly parked in the back lot. He put his hand on the foil covering, happy to feel it was still warm to the touch.

He entered through the back door, always left open by the old gym owner, day or night, as long as he was inside. It was a way of giving the neighborhood children and young adults a safe haven to escape to any time they needed one. The boxing coach and mentor had proven himself a father figure, protector, and life coach for many of the wayward youth of Dorchester's rough neighborhood, including Michael Kelly.

Thanksgiving was the one Thursday a year, outside of unforeseen circumstances, when Kelly and his three childhood cronies would miss their Thursday night fights. Their boxing matches, rotating weekly between the group of them, held a nostalgic connection to their past, keeping strong the relationships of the present.

Several years back, Kelly had started a tradition of his own on this night, and that was to bring his boxing coach and friend a Thanksgiving meal.

Ever since Pops had lost his son to the criminal justice system, sitting behind bars in maximum security for a murder committed many years ago, he spent Thanksgiving alone. His only real family were those who came through the hallowed halls of this gymnasium.

Kelly made sure on this particular night that Pops was taken care of. He'd invited him numerous times to the house, and Pops had graciously turned down the offer each time, so Kelly took it upon himself to bring the man a plate of food and some dessert. First, Pops was resistant to the gift, but he had come to look forward to this delivery service of sorts.

The lights were off in the gymnasium's main space, Pops saving money where he could in a tough economy.

The smell of sweat and leather clung to the air, even though the gym was closed for recreational use, but Kelly saw the office light on and knew he would find Pops inside. He stepped inside and Pops looked up, clearing away a space at his desk for the expected delivery. Kelly thought of the story his mother had told tonight, his father and the failed egg delivery.

A smile bloomed across Pops's face. He looked up at the clock on the wall, surrounded by clippings and photos of past champions. "I was wondering if you'd be stopping by."

"I know. A little later than normal. I had a visitor tonight, a special guest."

"And who, may I ask, was that?"

"Kristen Barnes." Kelly couldn't help but smile upon saying her name. "I don't know if you remember her. A few months back, she was with me when I dropped off that young Murphy kid after the shooting."

Pops nodded as he accepted the plates of food. "I do. Attractive girl."

"Thanks."

"So, is it serious? Is Michael Kelly ready to settle back down again?"

"I don't know."

Pops laughed. "Sounds like that's something you better figure out. A girl that pretty isn't going to stick around long, especially with a guy who doesn't know whether he's in a relationship or not, or how he feels about her." The life coaching was never on pause.

Pops held the foil to his nose before unwrapping it, taking a deep sniff and closing his eyes. "Smells amazing. Do I detect something different this year?" He cocked an eyebrow.

"Brussels sprouts."

Pops didn't look too excited at the news.

"Don't worry. I think you'll like how I cooked them. Plenty of bacon."

Pops smiled.

"I even got Embry to try them."

"You don't say, and speaking of young Embry, when are you going to be bringing her through the doors? She's about that age where she can start working the bag. Never too young."

Pops was right and Kelly knew it. He'd been meaning to, once he got on a more routine schedule, but Homicide had proven to be anything but routine. His goal was to start bringing Embry to the gym, start her off slow, a day, maybe two days a week, on the nights when he had visitation. Kelly wasn't much older when he got his start.

He figured his daughter would not only learn the art of boxing but also some of the finer pointers life had to offer from the wisdom of the man seated across from Kelly, a man who had proven a guidepost in Kelly's life.

"And please tell me this is your ma's homemade pumpkin pie."

Pops sounded as though he was salivating already and might be eating dessert before dinner.

"It is," Kelly said. "I warmed everything up just before coming over so you wouldn't have to microwave it."

"I like the sound of that." Pops rubbed his hands together in exaggerated anticipation of the meal to come. "You going to stick around for a little bit?"

"I should be getting home. Embry's in bed, but it's unlikely she'll stay there. And I've got an early day tomorrow."

"I heard about the situation down at Saint Peter's. Everybody has. A terrible thing."

Kelly looked down. Until now, he had managed to allow himself to mentally check out on the case. He'd taken his sergeant's orders to heart and disconnected, if only for a few hours, to enjoy some family time. But hearing it mentioned now brought everything crashing back to the forefront. "I'm doing the best I can."

"Michael Kelly, I've known you the better part of your life, and I've never once seen you not give 110% of your energy in anything and everything that you do. There was never a question in my mind that the case was in good hands when I heard it was in yours."

"Thanks, Pops. And I'll be in next Thursday. That's a promise."

"Hopefully we'll see Bobby here too. It's been a while."

Kelly nodded as he walked out. It had been a while. Bobby McDonough, his closest friend turned mob enforcer, had been absent more than he'd been present in the past few months. Kelly knew why and didn't press his friend, knowing that recently things had gotten complicated. Not only in Bobby's life but in the relationship between Kelly and him. His position with his current employer had put their friendship in jeopardy.

"You sure you don't want me to lock up, Pops?" Kelly called back, knowing the answer.

"If I'm here, it's open."

"Happy Thanksgiving, Pops."

"You too, Mikey," Pops said as the door closed behind him and Kelly stepped back out into the night's cold air.

JoJo's Diner, located not too far from Saint Peter's Church, seemed a good place for Kelly to meet with Sterling Gray.

Gray had contacted him via text just before Kelly had gone to bed Thanksgiving night. When he got home, he'd had to read Embry a second round of stories to settle her back in for the evening. The FBI agent asked to meet with him and him alone. The two had bounced brainstorming ideas back and forth in the days following the murder of Father Benjamin Tomlin. Gray proved himself to be an intelligent, thoughtful investigator, and although they weren't any closer to solving the crime, his insight and wisdom were top-notch. Kelly didn't mind taking an opportunity to bend the man's ear.

He'd picked JoJo's to give Gray a taste of the local neighborhood. The diner offered breakfast and lunch only, closing sharply at 2:00 p.m. Typically, the kitchen ran out of its lunch menu about half an hour prior to that, and on most days, the breakfast line outside the small storefront stretched at least a block long, even in the colder months. The minimum wait was an hour, but people endured, the line seeming to grow with each passing weekend.

They'd chosen to meet at 7:00 a.m., ensuring they would make it to the office on time. Kelly beat Gray, but only by a couple of minutes. The agent was proving to be just as tenacious as Kelly and Barnes. Each day since he'd been assigned to their small task force, he'd arrived early and stayed late, showing his dedication and focus.

Gray approached and pleasantries were exchanged. Moments later, a heavyset waitress guided them to a corner booth, where they slid onto the worn brown vinyl seat.

The waitress brought a carafe of coffee and two porcelain mugs. "You boys look like coffee drinkers. I can get you something else if you want, too."

"Coffee's fine by me," Kelly said.

"Same here," Sterling added.

The waitress retreated to tend to the sea of other patrons.

"What gives?" Kelly asked, not wanting to dance around with idle small talk.

"I wanted to meet with you first before I spoke with the group. I got a call from headquarters. They feel that the case is at a stalemate, that we've hit an impassable point. Even with everything the BAU has forwarded, plus the information I've given them on our progress so far, it appears that they cannot extend my time with the team any further."

"What?" Kelly asked, his annoyance conveyed both in his voice and the constrained look in his eyes. "They're calling you back? It hasn't even been a full week."

"It's been five days. And you know better than most, the first day or two of a homicide yields the highest percentile of solution. After that, it drops off dramatically, with the solvability dropping further with each passing day, a negative gradient curve. So, five days is a lifetime in terms of this case." Gray added a spoonful of sugar to his coffee. "I pushed to stay a little longer, just so you know, but they weren't hearing it. There are other cases and other things that I'm needed for."

"I'll bring it up with Sutherland. Maybe he can run it up the flagpole. I'm not letting this go," Kelly said.

"I didn't expect you would. I just wanted you to know that it's been a pleasure. Your team is fantastic, but you, in particular, have shown great ability. Hey, and if you're ever looking maybe to switch sides and come play at the federal level, I'm a phone call away. I can grease the wheels if that's something you're interested in."

Kelly shrugged. "I appreciate it, but Boston is my home, and this is where I'm staying."

"I know. I just figured I'd offer," Gray said. "If something does break in the case, something that points you in a new direction, you'll give me a call. Right?"

"Absolutely. We've valued your expertise on this matter. If we do catch a break, you'll be the first to know."

"We've been hunting him for a long time, Mike. This guy is a ghost and he's a dangerous one. When you're digging around, I want you to be extremely careful and watch your six. He's managed to elude federal and local law enforcement efforts for nearly a decade and a half. It's a testament to his skill and possibly his connections. Not sure which worries me more."

It worried Kelly too.

Ex-military/police was still listed at the top of the board.

Kelly couldn't help thinking that maybe somewhere, somehow, The Penitent One had a law enforcement connection or background. It wasn't too long ago that he'd seen the depth an undercover had gone to in order to cover his tracks when crossing over to the wrong side of the law.

The two ate and engaged in small talk, with the formality and their reason for meeting over.

As they got up to leave, Kelly saw a familiar but unwelcome face in the doorway.

"Great," he said under his breath.

"Problem?" Gray asked.

Connor Walsh stood at the hostess table, but not because he was waiting for a seat. No, that would be taken care of immediately for the crime lord and Dorchester native. He was busy flirting with the hostess, a girl who looked to be no more than twenty, more likely to be his granddaughter than of dating age for the older mob boss.

He caught Kelly approaching out of the corner of his eye and turned, giving his stained, yellow-toothed smile. A Tootsie Pop was tucked in the pocket of his cheek.

"You boys smell that? They must be cooking up some extra bacon in the back."

The overhanded and overused derogatory cop reference went unanswered by Kelly. But the two meatheads standing beside Walsh, his personal security detail, laughed loudly at the joke.

Kelly considered saying nothing to Walsh, but as he got closer to him, he turned and said, "You know, for somebody who prides himself on taking care of his town, looks like your protection isn't what it's cracked up to be."

The smile immediately evaporated from Walsh's face. A low rumble formed in his throat, like the growl of a dog protecting his food bowl. "What did you say to me?"

"I didn't stutter." Kelly stood inches from Walsh's face. He smelled the cherry of the lollipop. "A priest gets killed in your church, and I haven't seen you lift a finger to help."

"I'm sorry. I thought solving crime was your job, sonny boy."

Kelly knew the reason he added the last part but didn't acknowledge it, knowing the others around him probably knew nothing of his biological connection to the mob boss. "It is, and don't worry, your day's coming too."

Kelly pushed through the two men who tried to edge their way in, cutting off his pathway to the door, a subtle gesture at intimidation that failed miserably. Kelly used enough force to knock them aside without making a scene.

"Funny company you're keeping. Can't solve it on your own? You've got to bring in the feds." Walsh spat the words as the door closed behind them.

Gray said nothing and followed Kelly out.

"How'd he know you're a fed?" Kelly asked, looking at Gray.

He shrugged. "Wish I knew."

The statement bothered Kelly, but he couldn't quite place his finger on why.

Kelly and Gray got in their separate vehicles and headed to One Schroeder Plaza so Gray could clear out his space and officially pull back the FBI's support.

13

February *18*

The rattle continued. In the fog of sleep, Kelly thought it was the radiator and fought to ignore it. The nighttime temperatures had consistently dipped below twenty degrees for the past week, and the house's oil-based heating system was working overtime. The boiler pumped steam into the cold pipes, and the metal cried out as it expanded in the form of a banging clatter. This was a constant, but over the past ten days the incessant rattle had intensified to unbearable levels. Even so, Kelly normally slept through it, but for some reason, tonight his brain was unable to disregard the noise.

Kelly rubbed at his eyes, his vision blurring as he tried to look at the clock. It wasn't so much the volume of the noise as much as the rhythm. The pulsing beat, drumming him to a semi-conscious state.

As the digital clock on his nightstand came into view, the glowing red numbers taunted him. 3:53 a.m. His world was coming into focus as the haze of the dream gave way to reality. He realized the rattle wasn't the radiator, but his cell phone's ringtone set to vibrate.

Dazed, he wondered how long it had been ringing. Normally a light sleeper, Kelly was shocked when he looked down to see he had three missed calls. Two from Detective Sergeant Dale Sutherland and one from Kristen Barnes.

Not a good sign, when his unit was ringing him before daybreak. Their squad was up on rotation again, and he could only surmise, from the repeated attempts, that the reason for waking him was not good.

Kelly reached down, swiping open his phone's home screen and preparing to call his supervisor back, when it vibrated in his hand. The fourth incoming call was from Sutherland. Kelly answered it immediately.

He put on his best attempt at alertness, though his voice was still groggy.

"Top of the morning to you, Sarge."

"Never thought I'd have to place this many calls to reach Michael Kelly," Sutherland said.

"I know. I don't know what happened to me. I guess these cold nights put me in hibernation."

"Well, sorry to wake you from your beauty sleep, but we got a fresh one for you. And our team's up at bat."

"Where do you need me?"

"Downtown Crossing. Washington and Milk Street. Across from The Old South Meeting House."

That was the thing about a city like Boston. Modern-day crime didn't care much about historic landmarks. And this part of the country had plenty of both.

"Any details?" Kelly asked.

"Male vic. Multiple stab wounds. Patrol's got the scene locked down with a potential witness. Still trying to reach Mainelli. Spoke with Barnes. Start making your way there. She'll meet you, unless you two want to carpool," Sutherland chided.

Kelly took the comment in stride, partly because he was still shaking the cobwebs free from his brain after being pulled from sleep. But then, more importantly, Kelly was aware his supervisor had picked up on the fact he was dating Barnes. Although neither had openly admitted to it, Sutherland was a cop with a keen eye. With his awareness came the personal jabs, which were becoming more overt and increasing in frequency.

Mainelli had caught wind too. He'd been relentless over the last couple of weeks, especially a few days ago on Valentine's Day. The crusty Italian detective had taken it upon himself to leave a dozen roses on Kelly's desk, along with a giant card. He had signed it with a fat red marker and addressed it to Kelly from Barnes. If the rest of the office hadn't suspected anything was up at that point, they were definitely keyed in now.

When Kelly and Barnes had first considered pursuing a dating relationship, they decided to keep it under wraps. The department had plenty of relationships among their two thousand members. Impossible for it not to happen. But Kelly was concerned by the fact that they both were members of Homicide and part of the same squad in the relatively small specialized unit. They were worried that one of them might get rotated out to another division if somebody raised a red flag, claiming an intimate relationship could be detrimental to the integrity of the unit. Kelly knew the most likely proponent of such a sentiment would stem from the corner of Tony Acevedo and his sidekick, McGarrity.

Acevedo had been gunning for him at every possible turn since Kelly had scooped the Tomlin case out from under him. Since then, he had seen fit to point out any shortcomings in Kelly's ability as an investigator.

The fact that Kelly wasn't a step closer to finding the killer added credence to Acevedo crying foul. Kelly needed a home run on this case to get himself on level footing again.

He threw on some clothes, a heavy overcoat, and a skullcap, then grabbed his badge and gun and headed out the door as quietly as he could. His mother had returned to her uninterrupted sleep since the issue with the red Jetta had been resolved, but no credit could be given to Kelly on that front.

Brayden had taken it upon himself to bring about a solution to the recurring problem, putting some of his old skills to use and disabling the vehicle's car alarm. "Tricks of the trade," he had said when Kelly asked. Kelly pushed no further. One thing was for certain: their mother was extremely pleased. And Brayden was happy to receive her accolades. It had been a long time since he'd done something she was proud of. Kelly let his brother bask in the light of her praise but was angry at himself for not getting to it sooner.

He started the Chevy, which groaned weakly as the cold engine came to life. He put it in drive and took his foot off the brake, letting it roll down the driveway to the street before giving it any gas.

The city was coated in a layer of white, the darkness brightened by the streetlights bouncing their glow off the fresh snow that had fallen in the hours since Kelly had gone to sleep.

It wasn't a heavy snow, just a dusting, maybe an inch or two. Certainly enough to cause a nightmare for the morning commute, but not Kelly's, as only a few cars were on the road at this hour.

Kelly pulled out his cell and called Barnes as the heater worked to thaw the ice box that was his Caprice.

"Morning, sunshine," Barnes answered.

"You already there?"

"Just pulling up now."

"Bad?"

"Nah. Not too many onlookers. I'm sure the snow and cold helped. Plus, it's the middle of the night. Easy scene to contain right now. We'll see what we got when we get inside the boundaries."

"Sullivan said we might have a witness."

"Yeah, he told me the same thing. Said patrol detained somebody."

"All right. I should be there in a few minutes. Any word from Mainelli?" Kelly asked.

"No. Not surprising, though. I'm sure he'll drag his ass in at some point." Her voice conveyed a hint of annoyance. "He always does."

"Not sure who we'll get today, but hopefully it will be Charles or Dawes." The two crime scene techs had become his unit's go-to team when it came to processing a scene. As Kelly had learned in the year since becoming a member of Homicide, some technicians worked better with certain detectives. Charles, as the most senior, had his say in the cases he picked, and lately he'd been stepping up for all of Kelly's. His protege, Dawes—or Freckles, as he was more commonly referred to—had proven to be a quick learner, picking up a lot of the good habits the senior technician had gathered over his thirty plus years of experience working among the dead in the busy city.

As if the senior tech had read his thoughts, Kelly's phone vibrated. Looking down, he saw a text message from Charles. "On my way in, see you soon."

Kelly slowed but didn't stop at a red light, proceeding through back roads into the downtown section. The victim wasn't going anywhere. He was dead. But Kelly felt a sense of urgency. He always did.

The heater of Kelly's Caprice finally began winning the battle against the cold just as he pulled to a stop outside the yellow police tape blocking the intersection of Washington and Milk Street.

He sat for a minute, allowing the heat billowing out of the vent to warm him before he stepped back out into the frigid tundra of Boston in February. He learned long ago as a rookie patrolman to always dress in layers. Easier to take something off than try to put something else on.

As Kelly stepped from the vehicle, a gust of wind carrying a squall of snow pushed against the door, forcing it back against him. It was as if nature itself didn't want him to get out. Nature interfered in the processing of a crime scene in many ways, especially rain. Snow was not an optimal condition for processing a murder scene, but the frozen ground usually aided them in following tracks or any blood trail that might be left. Rain was like God's eraser, washing away critical evidence.

Tarps and canopies were set up over bodies whenever the situation dictated, and this was one of those cases. A large pop tent was set up on the sidewalk near a bank, and officers were posted at various places around the tape, ensuring nobody would cross through.

Kelly was always surprised by how many people would just walk right into or duck under the tape, oblivious to a crime scene, as if they had a right of way through whatever investigation was underway. The inconvenience of detouring was too much for some.

Cell phones exacerbated the situation, making for some of the worst offenders. People walking without looking, staring down at their handheld computer screens. A few years back, as a patrolman, Kelly witnessed a heavyset man plow through the crime scene tape as if he were a runner crossing the finish line after the hundred-meter dash, taking with him the yellow tape strapped across his chest. The large man hadn't even noticed before he was halfway into the scene when another officer standing nearby rushed up to physically stop him.

Kelly remembered the look on the man's face as he glanced up from his cell phone to see where he was. His disconnection from his virtual world to the real one was comical and almost cost him a trip to the slammer for interfering.

The scene he looked at now was well contained. Probably wouldn't be much foot traffic to worry about for the next couple hours. Apparently the media hadn't mobilized yet, since there were no news vans in view. Kelly hated getting to a scene after the media circus had begun. He preferred that their arrival coincided with his departure.

The snow crunched underfoot as he approached Barnes, who was talking to a patrol sergeant. Kelly squinted as the flurries struck his eyelashes, recognizing the uniformed patrol supervisor as Jeremy Parker. A solid cop, he grew up in Dorchester, not far from Kelly. He was a few years older, but the two knew each other. Parker had opted to work the downtown beat, saying he didn't want to arrest his friends and neighbors. Kelly understood, but had taken an entirely different approach, deciding, at least in the early stages of his patrol time, to navigate and protect the citizens he knew best.

Even though Boston was all one city, downtown felt slightly foreign to Kelly, the Dorchester native. It was an amalgamation of businessmen and college students from all over the world and had a much bigger feel than his hometown neighborhood. Although he loved the city in its entirety, whenever he was downtown, he always felt a sense of disconnect.

His badge swung freely as he ducked under the tape and nodded to one of the watch guards standing nearby before making his way along the outskirts of the scene to Barnes and Parker.

His gaze scanned over to where the pop tent had been erected, and he saw the dead man's form standing out against the white of the snow he had collapsed into. He figured it was better to check in with his partner and shift supervisor to get a feel for the scene before he approached.

"Michael Kelly slumming it tonight, hanging with us hoity-toity types," Parker said in jest, knowing Kelly's general disdain for the area.

"Just doing my part to keep the rich folk safe," he said with a laugh. The banter was always the same, regardless of the weather. Detectives and patrolmen always had their one-liner shticks when in the uncomfortable presence of death or working the early stages of a crime scene. It was a way of breaking the ice, creating a norm out of the abnormal.

"What've we got?" Kelly asked.

Barnes spoke, summarizing whatever she had discussed with the sergeant and putting it into Homicide terms. "Our stiff over there was apparently making a withdrawal. At least that's the best guess. The machine still had the printed receipt sticking out of it. He's got three stab wounds. One to the stomach, two to the back. No weapon located on patrol's initial response. And no witnesses."

"Well then, what was all that about with Sutherland saying we had a witness detained?"

"Guess there was a miscommunication," Parker said, inserting himself into the conversation.

"So, no witnesses?"

"Well, not per se," Barnes said. "We've got somebody detained who was with our dead guy earlier in the night. Apparently, he left the bar and wandered off. He was drunk and pissed off."

"So how did he end up at the ATM?" Kelly asked, mostly to himself.

"I guess that's what you detectives are going to have to figure out," Parker said. "Scene wide enough for you?"

"Good enough right now. I'll know more in a few minutes once I do a little quick walk-through and see what we have. I don't want to adjust anything until the crime scene unit gets here. When it comes to manipulation of a crime scene, I like to default to my technicians, and Charles will be here."

"Sounds like you're in good hands. I'll go talk to my guys, tell them to hold the scene. We're here for whatever you need. Shift change is at seven, but we can stay late. You know, my guys wouldn't mind a little bit of overtime, especially when it's just standing by a piece of tape. They live for those kinds of gigs," Parker said. "Maybe not so much on a cold snowy day, but overtime is overtime."

Kelly nodded. He knew many cops lived beyond their means and supplemented their white-collar lifestyle with blue-collar work with excessive amounts of overtime. Kelly didn't do the job for the money. The only overtime he ever accumulated was forced on him by the investigations he worked.

A squeak of brakes cut the stillness. Kelly turned his head and saw Ray Charles pull the crime scene van to a stop near his Caprice. The technician stepped from his vehicle and took a long drag from the cigarette hanging from his mouth. He'd been doing this job for a long time and would never contaminate a scene with a cigarette butt, so he put it out before he entered the world of the dead.

He had a cup of coffee in his hand, homemade. His wife's special brew, as he called it. He washed down the taste of the nicotine with the hot, black liquid. Steam came from his mouth as he exhaled, and he huffed his way over to Kelly and Barnes, who were waiting by the tape to greet him.

"Glad you could make it so quickly, Ray."

"I wouldn't miss it for the world." He rolled his eyes. "What have we got?"

This time it was Kelly's turn to summarize the information. It was like a game of telephone, but instead of the story getting more convoluted with each retelling, it became more refined and concise.

After Kelly finished his summation, Charles said, "Let's take the walk."

The three approached in tandem to where the body lay underneath the canopy. The snow shifted to an icy sleet, clattering noisily against the top of the plastic tarp, like the sound of gravel against a windshield.

"Beautiful weather we're having today," Charles said in jest.

The body lay face down, the man's left arm contorted to the side and his right arm outstretched above his head. His legs were sprawled out, separating in a split.

"Would you look at that?" Charles said.

Kelly and Barnes scanned the snow-covered ground, hoping to see a piece of evidence.

"What do you see, Ray?" Kelly asked.

"It looks like he's making a snow angel." With thirty years of working the dead, the senior crime scene tech's sarcastic, dark humor found a way to rear its ugly head in the first few minutes of the crime scene.

"Have you been working on that one the whole way here?"

"Pretty much," Ray said, taking a swig of his coffee. "I'm glad you liked it."

"Let's get started, shall we?" Barnes asked.

"I just need to grab my gear." Charles switched to a more serious tone.

"Me too," Kelly said.

The three broke off and headed back to their respective vehicles to gather the items they would need to effectively process the scene.

14

Photos and overalls were completed. The body had been rolled, giving Charles more ammo for his dark humor arsenal. The senior tech commented that rolling the heavyset, middle-aged man was like making the iconic Frosty the Snowman.

The information provided by the street boss, Sergeant Parker, had been accurate up to this point. Three distinct stab wounds. One deep puncture in the lower abdomen, right of the center, just above the hip line. The two entry points in the back were higher up. Charles surmised the wound left of the spinal column had been driven in deep. Conjecture, when at the hands of experience, moved a case forward instead of requiring them to wait for the autopsy report. Charles believed this wound, if deep enough, would have penetrated the chest cavity near the heart and was most likely the killing blow. Kelly saw no indication to the contrary.

The white snow surrounding the corpse was now soaked in the dead man's dark blood. With the close-in scene complete, all photographs and evidence collected, the body was now shrouded by a yellow tarp and awaiting the arrival of the ME's office to make the removal.

The gray morning light would be breaking soon, and with it, the commuters would begin heading to work. The media vans had arrived, beginning their breaking news broadcasts under the glow of several bright spotlights. Thankfully, the body was obscured from view.

They hadn't located the murder weapon. As luck would have it, the perp had left a trail of blood that arced in the direction of School Street. The gap between each droplet widened as they progressed away from the body, indicating the suspect picked up the pace.

When they first arrived on scene, Kelly noticed a series of footprints in the snow around the body, freshly coated by the falling snow. Casting a footprint was impossible in snow, but by using proper angles and light coupled with a measurement tool for reference, usable photographs could be obtained. One shoe print had remained relatively undisturbed, protected from the sleet by the canopy. Charles captured the image before it was lost to nature. Definitely not boot treads, meaning the print didn't belong to the responding officers; rather, it was a zigzagged sneaker tread measuring roughly nine inches.

The blood droplets were lined with triangulated orange evidence markers, photographed, and samples were collected. The direction of travel led toward the Faneuil Hall Marketplace.

"We're going to need to get that ATM video footage," Kelly said, staring at a bank's business front. Adjacent to that was a narrow alleyway that would be the perfect spot for somebody to lie in wait in the darkness.

"I'm already on it," Barnes said. "I put a call in to the bank's emergency after-hours number. I left a voicemail, so hopefully we'll get a call back soon. Worst-case scenario, we'll wait until the bank opens and we should be able to access it then."

The receipt sticking out of the ATM had been retrieved.

"Well, we have a pretty damn good timestamp for when this occurred, or at least a close approximate." A transaction for $160 was processed and completed at 2:12 a.m.

No wallet was found on the victim. The detainee, one Charlotte Dupree, who claimed to be the dead man's friend, said his name was Jason Palmer, age forty-eight, of Medford, Massachusetts. When asked why they were in downtown Boston, she said that they were just catching up over a couple of drinks at a bar in Faneuil Hall.

Barnes took the lead on the field interview, quickly breaking the woman down and punching holes in the story. Dupree conceded she and Palmer were having an affair and had met for drinks after a business meeting Palmer had earlier in the day. But during the course of the evening, Palmer had told her that he was ending their relationship and returning to his wife.

He had stormed out of the bar, saying he was going to Uber his way home. When Barnes asked why he would be using the ATM, Dupree explained that Palmer typically paid for anything related to their romantic trysts in cash. Harder for the wife to track. Apparently the two had racked up an impressive bar tab, and Palmer needed the cash to cover the spread for his ride from downtown Boston to the suburbs of Medford. According to the mistress's narrative, Palmer's wife had grown increasingly suspicious in recent months, part of the reason he'd decided to put an end to their relationship.

Dupree vehemently defended the position that Palmer's wife had anything to do with his death. For a mistress, she was surprisingly protective of the now-widowed spouse. Kelly figured the guilt was confronting her under the circumstances.

Dupree's story, told in dramatic fashion, boiled down to the simple fact the two had been drunk and disagreed on the status of their relationship's future. She said Palmer made his angry departure just before last call while she remained and had another drink to wash away her anger. Kelly made a note to confirm this on her bar tab. But in reading the distraught mistress's non-verbal cues, he didn't note anything of suspicion.

She had waited in the back of a marked cruiser for the better part of ninety minutes while Kelly and his team processed the scene. Kelly didn't want her input to slant his investigative eye; he needed to absorb the evidence the picture painted without any taint.

During that time, Dupree's intoxication had slowly transitioned to a brutal hangover. She told Barnes that once the lights went on in the bar, the not-so-subtle reminder for patrons to make their way to the door, Dupree became desperate to talk with Palmer. She called him but he didn't answer. A simple enough check of the phone records would confirm this. Kelly noted it.

In some strange act of desperation that even Dupree couldn't quite fathom, she ran out into the snowy Boston night in search of her lover. Kelly figured the overindulgence in martinis provided the push needed to make such a decision. After wandering the area looking for Palmer, Dupree said she came upon the red and blue strobes of the BPD cruiser.

Kelly had learned from Sergeant Parker that a unit patrolling the post-bar crowd saw the man down and stopped to check on him, assuming he was either a homeless person or a drunk passed out in the snow. Charlotte Dupree had run up and melted down at the sight of Palmer's body.

After concluding her account of the time she'd spent with Palmer, Dupree asked if anything she said would be used in a police report. Barnes fielded the question, saying most of what they talked about could be redacted and she'd only be needed if and when the case proceeded to a jury trial. The reality was, Palmer's wife would be privy to the case, if not while it was ongoing, then at least at its conclusion, receiving the devastating news that on the night her husband of twenty-six years died, he was in the midst of ending a long-time affair. Salt in an open wound.

There was no speculation that Dupree had anything to do with the murder. The first officer on scene described her as distraught and utterly shocked that the man she had just dined with and consumed copious amounts of drinks with was now dead. Gathering exculpatory evidence was also important, and so Charles had taken DNA swabs of her fingernails.

After Dupree was released from the scene, Barnes informed her that they would be in touch if they needed anything further.

"Looks random," Kelly said.

"Possibly. Maybe crime of opportunity, drunk guy at an ATM, somebody walking by. Why knife him, though? Why not just take his money? Why kill him?"

"I don't know. People do stupid things. A lot of the reasons behind the why wouldn't matter much anyway, right? The wallet missing makes me lean toward robbery."

Sutherland called, asking for an update.

"Looks like a street robbery gone bad," Kelly said. "We grabbed some good potential evidence and a usable shoe print. ATM footage gives us a timestamp, and hopefully when we hear back from the bank, we'll have access to the video footage that'll give us something we can use to help ID our doer."

"All right, sounds good. Just keep me posted."

In the background, Kelly heard one of the patrolmen yell, "Found something over here."

"Hold on, Sarge." Kelly lowered the phone and walked over. Across the street, outside the boundaries of the yellow police tape, a patrolman stood beside a trashcan near the T station entrance. The gates were closed to the Blue and Orange Line connector rail.

"What do you got?" Kelly asked as he walked closer.

The patrolman pointed his flashlight into the trashcan. Good cops had good instincts, and apparently this young officer fell into that category, making use of his time as he waited for his shift to end.

Following the beam of light into the can, Kelly saw a brown leather billfold. "Got a wallet," he called out.

Charles walked up to them. "All right, give me a second. I'll photo it in place. We'll mark it with a placard, then retrieve it."

A few minutes later, all was done.

Kelly had half-forgotten his sergeant was still on the line.

"What is it?" Sutherland said, only getting one side of the conversation, most of which had likely been muffled by Kelly's hand.

"Recovered a wallet. It's our victim's. I'm guessing our perp dumped it on the run. Maybe we'll get something usable off this."

"Maybe, maybe not. It's cold as hell tonight. The guy probably had gloves on," Sutherland said in his gruff voice.

"Hey, trust in a little Irish luck once in a while, Sarge."

"It didn't get us anywhere on the Tomlin case, did it?"

A biting blow but one Kelly took in stride. For all intents and purposes, Sutherland was right. No amount of Kelly luck had prevailed in locating The Penitent One.

"Well, maybe I'm due." Kelly clicked off, then turned to the senior crime scene technician. "I think that does it. Ray, it goes without saying, but the wallet and shoe print are going to be top priority."

"Mike, you know I always make your cases my number one."

Kelly was glad the senior technician had taken him under his wing and worked so hard for him when they handled a case together. No sitting around on potential evidence. You'd think after thirty years of working homicides, the jaded nature of the beast would take hold and he would slide. But if anything, Raymond Charles got sharper and more dedicated as the time passed, as if he could see the end of his career coming and wanted to make sure that justice was found for every victim.

"ME is sending somebody to retrieve the body," Kelly said. "Not sure where he's going to fall on their priority list, but I don't think it'll matter too much. Nothing earth-shattering here in terms of complications."

"Hope you're right. It does look promising," Charles replied, walking away.

Barnes and Kelly broke the scene down, leaving Sergeant Parker and his men in charge until the ME removed the body.

As Kelly and Barnes made their way under the tape, they saw Jimmy Mainelli approaching with two large cups of Dunkin' Donuts coffee and an apologetic smile.

Had it not been for the warm cup of coffee, Kelly might've offered a more scathing remark. But after taking the Styrofoam cup and feeling its warmth penetrate his icy hands, he instead said, "Better late than never."

"Well, this looks promising," Barnes said, hanging up the phone. "Check this out."

Kelly and Mainelli got up from their desks and bookended her.

A couple of keystrokes later, an image populated her screen. "The bank got back to me, sent me this link and gave me an access code to pull up the video from the ATM camera."

"My fingers are crossed," Kelly said, leaning in closer and catching her clean-linen scent. It was pleasant until Mainelli's musk overpowered it.

On the screen, a blurred image of a man came into view. Kelly immediately recognized Jason Palmer's pudgy jowls. He had become close with the dead man after spending the last two hours with his frozen corpse.

Seeing him alive was strange, a stark comparison to the lifeless form he'd etched into his mind. Palmer came into focus on the black-and-white footage. He was well-dressed in a blazer and wool trench coat. His tie was loosened, and his Oxford collared shirt was partially untucked. These were the same clothes he was wearing when Kelly saw him.

Kelly watched the drunken businessman swaying inside the ATM enclosure as if being blown by a heavy wind. But he knew that the only wind came from Palmer's undoubtedly high blood alcohol concentration, which must have been off the charts based on the stupor they were witnessing on screen.

Somewhat sad his last moments of life showed him in such an incapacitated state as he ineffectively fiddled with his wallet while trying to retrieve his ATM card.

After an unbearably long effort, he guided the card into the slot and entered his passcode. The camera had no audio, but they could see him reach down to retrieve the money before bringing it up to his face and fanning out the eight twenty-dollar bills.

As he turned to put the wallet in his back pocket, somebody came into view outside the backdrop, nothing more than a shadowy blur. Kelly cursed under his breath, fearful this would be the only image of their potential suspect.

But Palmer shifted, and there, staring back at them, was a man's gaunt face and deep-set eyes. Even with the dark hooded sweatshirt, the light from inside the ATM station clearly illuminated his face.

Palmer was oblivious, staggering onto the sidewalk. The suspect already had the knife in his hand and was waving it around wildly.

Kelly watched and understood why the robbery turned to murder.

Palmer, in his intoxicated state, initiated a drunken haymaker on the skinnier knife-wielding man. A stupid move, and one that cost Palmer everything.

The perp ducked the wild blow and punched the blade into Palmer's midsection. Palmer fell forward and out of view, but Kelly already knew the end.

Snow had already begun to fall, and the scene on screen transitioned from horror to tranquility in a matter of seconds.

The last image was a smudge of darkness, which, based on the pattern of blood droplets, was their perp's departure toward School Street.

"Well, it looks like we've just caught a murderer on tape. Not every day we get to see firsthand the evil our suspects do," Barnes said softly.

Seeing somebody killed in the real world had a far different effect on the psyche than watching an action film or crime drama. Real death was ugly, fast, and horrifying to watch. Seeing the aftermath was bad enough. Watching it happen somehow made it worse. But one thing was for sure, they had a clear visual of their suspect.

"We need to get this screen shot down to intel so they can send it to the rest of patrol, put a BOLO on this guy. Hopefully we can have him grabbed up by the end of the day," Mainelli said.

"I'm hoping we can get him in the next couple hours," Kelly added.

Kelly's phone rang, displaying the four-digit extension for Raymond Charles. He picked it up. "Hey, Ray, won't believe what we just watched."

"Oh yeah, what's that? Mainelli doing police work?" The crusty crime scene tech laughed at his own joke.

"No, nothing that shocking," Kelly retorted. "We just witnessed the murder of Jason Palmer."

"No kidding." Charles sounded genuinely interested. "Guess that ATM footage was good after all. Well then, you're going to love this."

"I can't wait," Kelly said.

"He wasn't wearing gloves."

"No kidding. I guess a little Irish luck is playing out on this one."

"Yeah, I got a full lift, thumbprint outside of the leather. It's a beautiful print. I've already run it through AFIS and got a hit."

"Shut up," Kelly said, shocked.

"You got an image and I got a name. Sounds like a match made in heaven."

Very rarely in police work did a case come together that cleanly and quickly, but when it did, the energy of it was unlike anything else in the investigative world. When a lead shifted into a full-speed manhunt, there was nothing like it. No amount of coffee or nicotine could equal the heart-thumping adrenaline rush of the chase.

"Send it my way."

"Already did. Check your email."

Kelly pulled up an expired driver's license photo and Department of Corrections mugshot for one Wendell Lumpkin. He hit print and a moment later had the two images in hand.

"Got something to add to that video still shot you've got," he said to Barnes excitedly. "Let's go find our guy. We got an old address here on the license. We can start there. I checked in-house already. Nothing within the last couple years."

"Sounds good," Mainelli said, hearing the news.

"Not so fast, sleepyhead." Kelly waved a finger. "Since you decided to sleep through our crime scene while we froze our asses off, I'm letting you type the arrest warrant."

"Come on. Really?" Mainelli offered resistance but knew he didn't have a leg to stand on.

Kelly knew it was fair punishment. The man hated paperwork more than he hated getting up in the morning. It was a soft win for Kelly. Plus, it gave him and Barnes a chance to go and do some digging. He felt the adrenaline coursing through his veins, equal to being inside the ring.

He was close. He could feel it.

15

Wendell Lumpkin's home address turned out to belong to his mother, who was nearing the ripe old age of eighty-three and in poor health. Wendell had burnt his last bridge with his mother after stealing a family heirloom and pawning it, a Rolex her husband had received as a parting gift after thirty years of service to his company. The heirloom fetched Wendell sixty dollars on the trade and had been the tipping point in her tolerance of her son's addiction.

Kelly couldn't help thinking back to Brayden's near-death experience when he heard the story. The turmoil leading up to hitting bottom had pushed the balance of tolerance. His brother's addiction with heroin had nearly severed their relationship.

Facing death breathed life into his brother. Close brushes with death had a tendency to give perspective. The opiate afflicted often were hospitalized three to four times before either kicking the habit or dying.

Upon hearing Wendell Lumpkin's story, Kelly was grateful to have his younger sibling back in the fold of their family. If the past couple months were any indication of the future, Brayden appeared to be winning the battle against his addiction.

Wendell Lumpkin, on the other hand, had not been so lucky. His mother had cast him out after the final straw broke. He turned to the streets, homeless and bouncing from shelter to shelter. Ann Marie Lumpkin said her last contact with her son was nearly a year and a half ago. She had assumed when Kelly and Barnes arrived at her doorstep, they were there to tell her he was dead.

Kelly knew Lumpkin's life, or at least his meager existence, ended the moment he decided to plunge a knife three times into an unarmed man during a robbery. It was a different kind of death. The slow, meandering kind that happened to a person who was apprehended and ripped from society.

Massachusetts had done away with the death penalty in 1984, but cold-blooded murder committed during the commission of another crime carried with it a heavy penalty. Beyond the killing itself, the penalty would be made worse by the fact the attack was captured on video. The defense would be limited, if indeed there was any at all.

Mrs. Lumpkin said Wendell loved the downtown area. It was where she had last seen him when she cared enough to look. He frequented the shelters around Downtown Crossing.

Since Palmer had been murdered not too far from there, Kelly figured it was as good a lead as any.

After leaving Ann Marie's small one-bedroom apartment in the North End, Kelly and Barnes headed downtown. Kelly had mapped the homeless shelters within a one-mile radius of where Jason Palmer's body was found. If nothing popped at their three potentials, they would extend their radial search in one-mile increments.

It was early and Kelly, having worked narcotics, knew the majority of shelters cleared their guests out during the day. Residents needed to sign back in each night.

Two of the shelters had no record of a Wendell Lumpkin in the past couple weeks. The third did, although he had last checked in three days ago. Yet still, it was promising.

Transient populations were difficult to track, but even homeless people had patterns to their behavior. You just needed to take the time to see them. Their unconventional lifestyle did not conform to that of the average citizen, but Kelly had learned the importance of understanding the habitual pattern in the eccentric nature of their existence. He'd spent many days among the homeless population, partly for his job, partly for his own curiosity to better understand them as a culture.

Mental illness permeated the group. Some of the behaviors were erratic, and the thought patterns guiding them were at times unpredictable. Kelly learned even the most socially deviant still maintained a need for basic necessities like food and shelter. The homeless who sought shelter didn't deviate as far from the norm as others who found refuge on the open streets, sleeping in subways tunnels or on the grates.

The good news was that in the winter months, the shelter accepted the wait list for beds earlier in the day, allowing the homeless to get off the street sooner than during the summer.

The attendant at the Hope's Chance Shelter, three blocks from the murder, had told them walk-ins for available beds had to sign in between 5:00 and 7:00 p.m. After that, their doors were shut to new visitors. She said the beds usually filled up early in the winter.

It was nearing 5:00 p.m., so Kelly and Barnes pulled down the street and parked behind a large box truck, keeping the engine running. Too cold to sit for an extended period of time without the heater. No music. The only sound came from the occasional rattle of his unmarked's engine. It had a tendency to rev sporadically while in idle.

A couple weeks had passed since Kelly had gone on a date with Barnes. The last planned outing had been canceled when Embry came down with a cold. Barnes understood, but it still didn't make it any better. Their relationship had to take a backseat to the paperwork and follow-ups of their many cases. The quality of their alone time had been diminished to these moments. They were together, but their minds were focused elsewhere.

His right hand grazed hers, meeting on the center console. Kelly squeezed her hand gently and was about to speak when his phone rang.

"It's Mainelli," Kelly said, picking it up. "What do you got, Jimmy?" He fought to conceal his annoyance at the interruption.

"We're all set. Prosecutor and judge just signed off on the arrest warrant of one Wendell Lumpkin," Mainelli said proudly.

"We're outside the shelter. Fingers crossed he comes through tonight. It's going to be a cold one. I'm hoping he doesn't decide to stay on the street.

They're calling for wind chill to bring it down close to zero." Mother Nature working in their favor tonight.

"You guys need me to come out there and assist?"

Kelly heard the man's question, appreciated the offer, but knew deep down Mainelli was hoping Kelly would allow him to stay in the warm confines of headquarters. Plus, by the time he got to their location and settled into a position, it'd be close to quitting time.

"No, Jimmy, why don't you just stay put? You can assist on processing if we pick this schlub up."

"Fair enough. But don't say I didn't offer. And just give me a call if you need anything else, but you're good to go on the warrant."

Kelly clicked off the phone, their moment of intimacy interrupted. He thought about trying to rekindle it but began to doubt himself. He wasn't sure Barnes had even noticed.

"How do you want this to go?" she asked.

Kelly's heart skipped a beat. *Was she talking about the future of their relationship? Did she think it was faltering?* His mind raced for an answer.

"I mean, this is your case, just want to see how you want to play it if we come across this skell," Barnes said.

Kelly exhaled slowly. *Of course, she was referring to the apprehension of Lumpkin.* He kicked himself for blurring lines and losing focus. It was out of character for Kelly and he didn't like it. If his relationship with Barnes had a negative, it was the unbalance it brought to his thought process.

"Let's go soft, try to talk our way in with him, walk him into the cuffs if we can."

"Fair enough," Barnes said.

It was a misconception by the general public that every apprehension ended in an all-out foot chase, fight, or death match. Most were innocuous and benign, even when it came to the arrest of a murder subject. Kelly preferred the simple ones. They came with a lot less explaining and a lot less paperwork. He didn't allow the job to become personal. Arresting this murderer came with no attachments, no personal connection to the victim. It was just the business end of somebody's bad decision. Today it was Wendell Lumpkin. Tomorrow it would be somebody else. Had Palmer been someone he knew, then Kelly's likelihood of maintaining a soft approach would have been more difficult. Under the circumstances, it was easy to psychologically distance himself from the death of the middle-aged businessman and his drugged-out murderer.

"Well, you take the lead," Barnes said. "I'll follow."

"All right, I have something in mind."

An hour passed, but the silence in the car made it seem much longer. Kelly looked at his watch. It was just past 6:15 p.m. They'd spent the better part of the last hour watching people trickling into the shelter. It was like watching some post-apocalyptic movie as the heavily bundled vagrants staggered along.

Forty-five minutes left until the shelter would close its vacancy list, and with it, their window of opportunity. Kelly didn't want to leave it for another night. Desperate people on the run did desperate things. He wouldn't forgive himself if the killer took another victim before he had a chance to make the arrest, but deep down Kelly didn't see that as Lumpkin's MO. His act of violence was likely due to a drug-induced state, a robbery gone bad. Regardless, Kelly couldn't allow this man to roam free another night.

Just as he was about to speak, he caught sight of somebody sauntering along the sidewalk from the opposite direction. The light from the shelter cast the brightly colored lettering of Hope's Chance in a muted yellow. The street was still bright from the snow. What little snow that had melted during the day was frozen over. Temperatures had not risen above the freezing point, and they were now sitting at a balmy twenty-three degrees.

The man walking toward the shelter wore a heavy coat and hooded sweatshirt, his face tucked down, his hands pressed deep into his pockets. He moved like a tightly wound spring, his steps short and choppy.

"Got something ahead. You see him?"

"I've got him," Barnes said. "Looks to be about the right size from the video. What do you think?"

"He does."

"A little far to tell for sure, but it could be our guy."

The man paused across the street from the shelter and looked around skittishly, then pulled a cigarette from his pocket and lit it. When someone committed a major crime like a murder, they had a halo over them. Investigators called it the spotlight effect. The perps felt that anybody coming close or looking at them knew what they had done, and they reacted accordingly. As he watched the hooded man's body language, Kelly's confidence this was their guy increased tenfold.

They were about a football field away from the man. Kelly cut the engine. In the few seconds after he shut off the motor, the cold began to penetrate the windshield.

"I've got a ruse I hope will work. Just follow my lead on this."

"Like I said, I'll read off your play."

Kelly got out, closing the door quietly. Barnes did the same, and they began their soft-footed approach to the man who was still looking away.

When they got closer, he turned and saw them moving along the snow-covered sidewalk. The crunch of their feet was loud in the early evening quiet.

"Are you okay, buddy?" Kelly hollered, now only thirty feet from the man whose eyes widened.

He held his cigarette near his lips, frozen in place. "You talking to me?" The guy spoke quickly. His head jerked from side to side, looking around to see if someone else was nearby. He was a squirrel on a fence post, frantic and unhinged.

"That's our guy," Kelly whispered under his breath.

"You move, I move," Barnes responded, matching his hushed tone.

"I said, are you all right?" Kelly repeated, loud enough for the man to hear.

"What are you talking about?" Lumpkin asked.

Kelly noted Lumpkin turned his right foot out, away from their approach. He was preparing to run. Body language was the first indicator in a person's thought process. *Watch the body, read the mind.*

"Somebody said a guy matching your description got hit with a bottle, some type of street fight. Did you get jumped? We're Boston PD."

"You're in no sort of trouble," Barnes offered, playing the supporting role.

His foot turned out further as he lowered the cigarette hand. He was definitely preparing to run.

"We got medics around the corner. We've been looking for you. Trying to find you to see if you're okay. The witnesses said it was really bad." Kelly continued to play the concerned detective card.

"What are you guys talking about? Nobody hit me with a bottle."

With each passing second, Kelly and Barnes were able to close their distance. They were now within ten feet of the man.

"So, you weren't just jumped over there by the park?"

Now the man's eyes contorted with a complex twist of his brow. He was thoroughly confused. The drugs he'd purchased with the money he'd stolen from Palmer were in his system, working against his ability to rationalize and process what was happening. He was being approached by two cops, and he knew that he had murdered a man earlier in the morning. Everything in his body and his mind had to be telling him to run, but Kelly's questions froze him in place. Kelly did this by design so he could close the gap.

"Maybe we have the wrong guy. Jeez, I don't know. We're just going off what one of the witnesses said over there. Said it was a pretty nasty fight, guy matching your description." Kelly looked at the man's coat, the same one he'd seen in the ATM video. "Yeah, you match the description, dark coat, hooded sweatshirt underneath."

Five feet and closing.

"There's got to be a million people in this city look like me. It's like freezin' out, ya know!"

"Hey, pal, guess you're right. I just had to check. We had to make sure you're not bleeding out. You mind pulling the hood down so I can see your skull?"

"What?" Lumpkin said.

"Listen, man, to be honest, I don't give two craps about you, but I got to be able to tell my sergeant that I did my best, that I at least investigated this bum fight and talked to somebody. He'll be up my ass if I don't. So, how 'bout you cut me a freakin' break?"

Kelly played the frustrated detective forced to do grunt work. Easy enough. He'd worked with enough cops who fit the bill. Mainelli would have played this role perfectly, without any acting needed. In hindsight, maybe he should have brought the man with him.

"Piss off," Lumpkin said, stepping back and turning away from them. He gave one last glance toward the homeless shelter before starting to run.

Only a few feet away at this point, Kelly and Barnes gave chase.

The drugged-out man was much slower, and in only a matter of seconds Kelly closed the gap. He didn't tackle. Years back, he'd learned a trick of the trade. Never tackle when you can push. If you wanted to win the battle with minimal effort, all you had to do was knock the person off balance.

When Kelly was close enough, he struck out with the palm of his hand, hitting Lumpkin in the base of his neck. The impact sent the murderer's head forward. Ass over tea kettle, the man fell into the snowy hard pack, sprawling out awkwardly before rolling to one side. Kelly and Barnes filled the void.

Kelly dove onto Lumpkin's back and tried to wrangle the man's hands into submission.

Lumpkin twisted his body to the right. Kelly saw the glint of a knife and shoved himself backward, creating some distance.

"Drop the knife or you're dead," Barnes commanded. She already had her pistol out. Barnes kicked Lumpkin in the shin hard, getting his attention while keeping the gun at his head.

Kelly stood, stepping beside Barnes and withdrawing his pistol. He'd disregarded the rule: *Never cuff until you've got control.* An overzealous moment that could've carried with it a deadly consequence.

Barnes had the man's attention. Lumpkin's wide, bloodshot eyes bounced between the two guns aiming down at him. The drugs, the confusion of their ruse, and his current predicament of being flat on his back and facing two department-issued Glocks were causing a whirlwind of uncertainty in the man.

Lumpkin grit his teeth and spat, throwing the knife off to the side. It wasn't over until he was in cuffs and searched. Kelly knew this. He lived by these rules, and they kept him alive.

"On your face," Barnes said.

The man rolled onto his stomach.

"Arms out like an airplane. Do it now," Barnes barked.

Lumpkin complied.

"Slowly," she added.

His ungloved hands crawled across the snowpack, the knife a safe distance away.

Kelly stepped on the blade, making it impossible for the man to get to it in case he had a change of heart, which, under the circumstances, Kelly seriously doubted would happen.

"Put your hands at the small of your back," Barnes said, her voice even but her words commanding.

The man complied. The fight had left him completely.

Kelly nodded to Barnes, a silent confirmation that he was moving in. He then holstered his weapon and unsnapped his handcuffs.

Kelly snapped the cuffs on the man who had just tried to pull a knife on him, who had made the critical error of bringing a knife to a gunfight. Seconds later, Wendell Lumpkin was in custody, and the knife he'd used to murder Jason Palmer was lying in the snow less than seven feet away.

"What the hell is all this about?" Lumpkin said.

"You're under arrest for the murder of Jason Palmer."

"What?" Lumpkin asked, now realizing that his initial reaction of preparing to run when he first saw the detectives had been right.

"You have the right to remain silent. Anything you say or do can be used against you in a court of law. You have the right to have an attorney present prior to or during any questioning. If you cannot afford an attorney, one will be provided to you at no cost. Do you understand the rights that I've read to you?"

Lumpkin nodded.

"Let me hear you say it. Do you understand the rights that I have just advised you of?" Kelly asked, leaning in close. "I want to hear you say it."

"Yeah, I understand, but I ain't talking to you," Lumpkin said.

Kelly pulled the man off the ground and sat him on the icy curbing. He removed his radio from the clip on his belt and called into headquarters, radioing for a caged car to come pick up their perp.

Less than fifteen hours after Jason Palmer was murdered, Kelly and Barnes had their man in bracelets, ready to face prosecution for murder.

Kelly couldn't help comparing the ease of this case with the stalemate of the red card hanging on his murder board. He hadn't even had time to make Palmer's red card, and yet Benjamin Tomlin's and Danny Rourke's killer remained at large. And it still gnawed at him like an itch he couldn't scratch.

16

For the first time in a long time, Kelly arrived at work just before the official start of the day, crossing the threshold into Homicide a minute shy of 8:00 a.m. Jimmy Mainelli had actually beaten him to the office. Kelly couldn't remember the last time that had happened, or if it was a first. He had allowed himself this bit of reprieve from his normal pace and the relentless effort he put forth on a daily basis, the extra couple hours sleep a reward for bringing Wendell Lumpkin to justice so swiftly. The eighteen hours of work that it took to accomplish that feat also contributed to his exhaustion. The extra sleep had been needed for his body's physical recovery from the adrenaline dump.

Kelly had replayed the brief seconds it took to apprehend the transient murderer. Lumpkin's ability to get the blade out before they gained control had haunted him. And it would for a long time to come. Kelly was his own worst critic, hypervigilant when it came to assessing the good and bad of everything he did. It started as a patrolman and only intensified when he obtained his detective shield. After every suspect takedown, whether with SWAT, Narcotics, or Homicide, Kelly conducted his own after-actions review, focusing on any possible mistakes so they wouldn't be repeated the next time around. He applied that same critical eye to the cases he worked. And while to everyone else, Wendell Lumpkin's arrest was as smooth as they come, he knew deep down those final few seconds were anything but. If Barnes hadn't been there to quickly counter the knife with her gun, the end result might have been entirely different. That thought kept him up late into the night.

Once asleep, he'd managed to sleep more soundly than he had in a long time. Catching a homicide suspect had an amazing effect on his psyche. He compared it to winning the Golden Gloves Championship in his boxing career.

As Kelly entered Homicide, he saw Barnes removing her jacket and realized she too must have taken a little bit of extra time this morning. Normally she was his counterpart on the-early-bird-catches-the-worm mantra.

She gave him a smile, simple and genuine, nothing more to it. Mainelli peeked his head up from behind the cubicle wall that divided their squad's four-desk cluster. He wore a wide, shit-eating grin, obviously pleased to have beaten the early riser to work.

Before Mainelli could offer a jab at him, Kelly held up his hand and shook his head sluggishly from side to side. He bypassed his desk and went straight into the break room for a cup of coffee. Kelly, happy to see the pot already full, grabbed a mug from the open shelf and filled it, adding two scoops of sugar and a dash of cream from the fridge before slowly ambling back toward his desk.

He passed by the sergeant's office and was surprised to see Superintendent Acevedo sitting across from Sutherland. Acevedo wasn't accompanied by his normal entourage of lieutenants and ass-kissers. Kelly recognized the only man seated beside him. With his clean-cut, Marine-like haircut graying at the temples, and the dark suit and tie he wore, Paul Halstead, the sergeant assigned to BPD's Internal Affairs Unit, looked more like a bank manager than a city cop.

Kelly's heart skipped a beat. Why was IA meeting with Sutherland? His mind immediately raced to replay last night's arrest. Everything was within the protocols. He didn't step on anybody's toes. Although he knew Acevedo's son, Tony, had been gunning for him. Maybe there was a slip-up? Maybe Lumpkin, who was unwilling to talk after being booked and processed last night, had a change of tune. Or maybe he decided to file a complaint about excessive force. Kelly knew there had been none, but he also knew neither he nor Barnes had a body camera to prove otherwise. It wouldn't be the first unwarranted complaint lodged against Kelly.

Desperate people, especially those arrested for murder, typically did anything in their power to deflect attention from the real matter at hand. In Lumpkin's case, he'd killed a man for what amounted to $160. That said, Kelly also knew the review process within Internal Affairs. If and when a complaint reached their desk, regardless if it was perceived as frivolous, it had to be investigated thoroughly. Supervisors would be notified. The officer who was the target of the investigation would have an opportunity to review the accusation, and in most cases, obtain union representation to deal with the potential fallout.

Not too long ago, Kelly had survived the Internal Affairs review and civil suit revolving around the death of Baxter Green. He employed the union's attorney, Marty Cappelli, who happened to now also be dating Kelly's ex-wife. The thought of having to call him on another matter regarding an IA investigation soured the taste of Kelly's hot coffee.

He approached Mainelli, eyeing the closed-door meeting. "What's going on in there?"

"Beats me. They were in there when I came in." Mainelli shrugged. "So at least twenty minutes now, if not longer."

"Any talk?" Kelly asked, code for the rumor mill.

Mainelli, as lazy as he was, was adept at receiving these whispered rumors. He'd been in Homicide long enough that people trusted and confided in him.

"Nothing. Not a peep." Mainelli absently shuffled the papers on his desk.

Kelly sat down at his desk.

Barnes pushed her chair back, rolling past the divider separating their desks and leaning back to look at Kelly. "You think it has something to do with last night? How we handled Lumpkin?"

Kelly shrugged. "I can't see why. We did everything by the books. It was clean all the way through. I mean, I screwed up with the takedown. Should've seen that coming. Should've waited."

"Don't beat yourself up, Mike. You did good. You caught him. You ran him down. Shit happens. Nobody's perfect. Hell, I'm just glad I was in a position to address it when it went sideways. I hate to think what could have happened otherwise."

"I don't get it. Why is IA in there with Acevedo?"

Mainelli overheard and peeked his head overtop the cubicle. "Maybe his son had something to do with it. He's been pissed off at you ever since you stole the Tomlin case. Wouldn't surprise me if that little prick tried to railroad you on some BS complaint. I'll ask around, see what I can find out."

Kelly nodded slowly, not really one to pry. He usually had the patience to wait these kinds of things out. Closed-door meetings would eventually open. If it involved him, then the turd would land on his desk.

He decided to occupy his mind as he sipped his coffee, thumbing through the paperwork from the Lumpkin case even though it was committed to memory. He eyed it anyway, knowing some supplemental reports were needed, a couple administrative T's to cross before it was closed and forwarded to the prosecutor's office.

He put it aside and stared at his murder board. The red cards for Rourke and Tomlin taunted him amidst the blue solved cases. The fact that he had a blank red card ready to go for Jason Palmer but never even had a chance to fill it out added insult to injury. Kelly never bothered to fill out a red card for the murdered rapist, Phillip Smalls, even though he knew the man was a victim of The Penitent One. A rapist didn't deserve to be on the same board as his former partner and a dead priest.

He opened his drawer and pulled out the thick file on Tomlin, always within arm's reach. Kelly opened it and started scrolling through the pages of reports, photographs, evidence, listings, DNA attempts, fingerprints, and autopsy reports, searching for the clue that would break the case wide.

Mainelli popped back up and looked down at him. "Oh no, not this again, Mike. Let it go. You win some, you lose some. And that right there is a lost cause if I've ever seen one. That guy's in the ether. We're not going to catch him. Hell, the FBI couldn't catch him, and they've been looking for him for almost two decades. Stop beating yourself up." Mainelli cracked his knuckles. "And if I recall, I'm pretty sure Sutherland already told you to push that over to Cold Case and let it rest."

Kelly snapped the file shut and looked at the man whose pudgy fingers were clinging to the top of the divider. "Yeah, I know. It's on my list of things to do."

He put the file back in the drawer and shut it. The case had more to do with the faltering status of his and Barnes's relationship than he cared to admit. She'd been a stalwart supporter of his investigative efforts in every case they'd worked together since she'd come to Homicide after leaving the department's Sexual Assault Unit in mid-summer of last year. But even she had grown tired of talking about the Tomlin murder.

For Kelly, it had become an obsession, one that was driving a wedge between him and everyone in his life. Even when he pretended not to be thinking about it, he was. He'd become disconnected, his mind trapped back three months ago when the case first hit his desk. Kelly had been chasing a ghost ever since. Any open time between the end of a case and the beginning of a new one, he was back on the Tomlin murder. Mainelli was right; he'd been told by Sutherland on more than one occasion that it was time to file it in the unsolved category and shift it over to Cold Case, where it would be lost among the stacks.

But Kelly couldn't allow himself to do it. He couldn't allow himself to give in, to give up. His innate, never-quit, never-say-die attitude that flowed over from his youth wouldn't allow it. The lessons he'd learned in Pops' gym and the streets of Dorchester were only amplified during his time with the PD. Tenacious didn't even begin to describe the fervor with which he attacked a case. Like a pit bull, he never let go. Kelly knew the flipside to the coin could be cataclysmic to his personal life, and yet he still couldn't stop thinking about it.

The murmur of the Homicide floor dropped to a hush. Kelly knew, without looking, that the meeting inside Sutherland's office had come to an end. He peeked around his cubicle and saw Acevedo standing with Halstead beside him. As the three men did a round-robin shake of hands, Kelly carefully watched Sutherland's facial cues. He didn't have his typical disgruntled, angry look. From the looks of things, Sutherland hadn't been admonished by the commander of the Investigative Unit.

Acevedo turned to leave while Halstead lingered behind with Sutherland. The door opened and Kelly dipped back behind his desk. A moment later, a shadow crossed his desk as Superintendent Acevedo moved into view and stood near the opening to Kelly's cubicle. He casually leaned on the divider wall, looking down at Kelly as if they were old friends.

Kelly turned in his chair but did not stand. "What can I do for you, sir?" Kelly was not one typically intimidated by rank, but respectful enough to know his place.

"That was fine work you did yesterday."

"Thank you, sir," Kelly said flatly.

"You're a hell of an investigator, Kelly. Don't let anybody tell you different."

And with that, Acevedo turned on his heel and headed out the door.

Mainelli popped back up. He was in and out of his seat today like a whack-a-mole. "Did I just hear Superintendent Acevedo give you a compliment?"

"Sun shines on a dog's ass every once in a while," Kelly said, repeating a phrase his late father had used on a daily basis.

"Guess so. Color me impressed," Mainelli said, then disappeared back into his hole.

Barnes peeked around the corner again. "Something's happening," she whispered. "Halstead and Sutherland are in there chuckling like schoolgirls."

"I hope they're not laughing at the demise of my career," Kelly offered. His attempt at levity fell somewhat short.

Barnes offered him a conciliatory smile and soft chuckle. "Well, if you go down, I go down."

Kelly hoped that phrase would evolve into something more substantial and be reflective of their relationship at some point. He tried not to overextend and project beyond the current point of his dating relationship with his partner, but at his age, relationships moved faster. He knew what he wanted and approached it with the same mindset he did everything in life. Full tilt, full speed, and all in.

Sutherland approached the squad's cubicles and rapped his knuckles on the metal siding of one of the dividers. "Let me see you guys in The Depot, I've got something I need to talk to you about."

The husky sergeant led the charge into the conference room. Kelly noticed his hobbled gait had dramatically improved, atypical for his boss, who usually played up the bum knee after meeting with anybody from the command staff. Strange that he would not continue his act in the face of the Internal Affairs Supervisor. But Kelly had long since given up trying to figure out Sutherland.

He picked up the case file for Wendell Lumpkin's arrest just as Sutherland turned back before taking a seat in the conference room. "No need for paperwork," he called to Kelly.

Kelly returned the file and followed Barnes and Mainelli into The Depot. Just as Kelly began to close the door behind him, Halstead appeared.

"Got room for one more?" he asked, giving Sutherland a look, some inside joke Kelly wasn't privy to.

Kelly stepped aside, allowing the IA Sergeant to enter.

Sutherland and Halstead sat near the curved head of the oval-shaped conference table. Kelly, Mainelli, and Barnes sat staggered on one side with their backs to the door, a unified front for whatever was coming.

"I have some news. Good, bad, I don't know. Take it however you want. It's good for me," Sutherland said, his gruff nature absent. He was more jovial than he'd been recently. "I've been approved."

"Approved for what?" Mainelli said.

"For my disability rating."

"Nice," Mainelli offered. Kelly and Barnes nodded.

"So, what's that mean, Sarge?" Kelly asked.

"It means this fat bastard is going to take his early retirement and head south to Florida."

"Effective when?" Mainelli asked.

"Pretty much immediately. I got word a couple of weeks ago it was in the final approval process, and I got the official notification this morning. I'm going to be taking my leave of absence. I've got some paid time coming up."

Kelly was conflicted. Although he'd only been in Homicide for just shy of a year, Sutherland had been his supervisor, for better or worse, since he walked in the door. And he had come to understand and read the man, which was critical when dealing with any leadership. Transition always created some level of disruption.

Kelly asked the obvious. "If you're out, then who's in?"

Sutherland reached over and gave Halstead's shoulder a hardy slap. Halstead didn't seem to appreciate the whack, although he took it in stride.

He leveled a serious gaze at them, something he'd become known for during his tenure in Internal Affairs. They called him Iceman because of his unreadable facial expressions and the cold, steely cobalt eyes. A man in his mid-fifties, Halstead barely had a wrinkle, a testament to the fact that he rarely, if ever, betrayed his emotions on his face.

"Most of you know me. For those of you who don't, I'm Paul Halstead. I've been working in IA for the past eight years. I've had my hands or eyes on every controversial case that's come through this department. I may not have been Homicide, but I know my way around an investigation." He paused for effect and scanned the room. "The first order of business is case review. I'm going to be going through all of your active cases. If you have any cases that have hit a stalemate or need to be shifted over to Cold Case, let me know. I'm a numbers man and I want the cases to match what we're actively working on as an investigative unit."

Kelly blew out a long, slow exhale. He knew what case would be up on the chopping block first.

"Well, welcome to the show," Mainelli said. "You're in for a real treat with this crew." He laughed at his own joke.

Sutherland laughed too. It was the first time the man had broken into laughter in a long time, his mood obviously lightened at the news he'd been waiting for years to hear.

Halstead, on the other hand, did not smile. "I look forward to working with each and every one of you, and I also look forward to seeing the kind of case investigations you've put together under Sergeant Sutherland's supervision. I'm not here to change the way things work, I'm just here to make sure they continue to run smoothly."

With that, the group was dismissed. The trio went back to their cubicle stations.

Kelly pulled out Tomlin's file and set it on his desk on top of Lumpkin's arrest paperwork. He wanted to go through it one more time, hoping he could find some piece he missed that was capable of keeping it alive.

17

The bar was abuzz. Conversations increased in volume and intensity with the purchase of each subsequent round. Finnegan's Folly overlooked the harbor and was within easy walking distance of where Jason Palmer's body had been found.

The city now held different sentimental value for Kelly and the other members of his Homicide unit. For the commoner, the civilian, each bar or restaurant or landmark was just that, but not for Kelly. Much of his native Boston was now marred with the invisible scars of the crimes he had worked. The blood and grime that had been long since washed away left only memories, ones Kelly kept stored in his continually growing mental filing cabinet.

People were waiting in line for the tape to be cut and the scene to be cleared so that the bank's ATM could be used again. The death of an unknown person was nothing more than an inconvenience to the average person. Kelly had resigned himself long ago to the fact that everywhere he went, he walked among the dead. The thought of it didn't bother him. It was just the way things were.

Kelly watched the crowd of fellow cops with their mugs of beer or shots of whiskey. Their paycheck came from investigating tragedy, and those investigations paid for these drinks, a symbiotic relationship of sorts. One could not exist without the other. The job never stopped and neither did the drinks, an emotional salve for the trauma observed.

He'd heard more than one cop say, *I wish a day would come when crime was ended and police were no longer needed.* Looking around the bar at his cohorts, Kelly knew that was the furthest thing from the truth. The job was like a rare drug; its euphoric effect became its own driving force. Much like the junkies Kelly dealt with during his time in Narcotics, cops became addicted to the job, attaching their identity to the badge without regard for the world around them.

Maybe Kelly was overthinking it. He'd had more than his share of drinks tonight. Though normally a moderate drinker at best, Kelly lost count a couple rounds ago. That's the way it was at a retirement party. Somebody bought a round, somebody else followed. Beers and shots were shoved into hands and it was difficult, if not impossible, to push back against the rising tide of inebriation. And if Kelly were truly honest with himself, he needed this night. Needed to distance himself from the cases and unshackle the burden they bore on him. Needed to ignore the constant sense of responsibility he felt.

He was jostled from his thoughts as Jimmy Mainelli's burly body shoved up alongside him at the bar. He was double fisting. Both mugs sloshed, overflowing and spilling onto the lacquered surface of the counter. Mainelli barely noticed as his sleeve soaked up the dark beer.

"Saint Michael," Mainelli slurred. "Down here from among high to mingle with the commoners."

If Kelly was feeling the buzz, then Mainelli was two sheets to the wind. His bloodshot eyes and slurred speech bore testament to that, but more so did the jadedness of his words.

Mainelli and Kelly got along fine enough, but there was definitely a difference in approaches when it came to handling the caseloads. It didn't take long for Kelly to figure that out. As a new face in Homicide, he'd been given wiggle room by Mainelli. The senior detective, veteran of the force—in particular Homicide—had let Kelly run free pushing the paces of his cases, assuming, undoubtedly, that he would soon tire. Mainelli warned him the grind was endless, and to survive in a unit where the bodies continued to drop no matter how hard you worked or how many cases you closed, Kelly would need to find a more reserved approach. Mainelli hit his investigative stride years back and, in Kelly's opinion, was operating in neutral, coasting along, and dragging cases out that should be closed.

The friction came when Kelly's pace never changed. If anything, it increased. Nearing a year in the unit and still pushing as hard as he did when he first came in. It had always been that way for Kelly. And always would be.

Kelly was of the firm belief that if someone didn't like the way he worked, they could find someone else to partner with. He never openly pushed people away. He just did things his way.

That was the problem with cops, he thought; everyone was an alpha. Everyone thought they knew best. Everyone was smarter than the next guy. The difference was, Kelly didn't think...he knew. And time and again he proved it. Yet he never spoke it aloud; only in the work did the truth come out. His work ethic was polarizing.

Kelly's investigative efforts were solely for the dead. His job was to speak for them, and he took it seriously.

Kelly didn't engage the heavyset Italian. He knew whatever he said to Mainelli in response would either end in an unnecessary brawl or be forgotten the moment it came out of his mouth. Either way, Kelly saw it as a waste of effort.

"Let me get you a drink," he said, turning the other cheek.

Mainelli tossed back one of the beers. Several loud gulps later, punctuated by an obnoxiously loud burp, he slammed down the empty glass and smiled.

"Well, absolutely," he said. "I've got a free hand."

Kelly flagged the overworked bartender, slid a twenty-dollar bill across the wet counter, and ordered Mainelli another drink. The bartender made quick work of the refill before attending to another of the horde.

Taking his prize, the double-fisting detective disappeared into the crowd. The conversation ended, comment forgotten.

Kelly slammed back the shot of whiskey in front of him and then picked up the Miller Lite bottle in his hand, pushed back from the bar stool, and began looking for Kristin. They hadn't come together. Too obvious. But he'd hoped to spend a little bit of time with her tonight. With the tightly packed crowd, he was hoping no one would notice, and maybe his conversation or proximity to her would go unchecked.

He saw her in the cramped space against the brick wall adorned with framed sienna images of Ireland. Whether they were the bar owner's actual photographs or just purchased for show, Kelly didn't know, nor did he care. He shoved his way through the group, bumping and sliding in and out of the crowd, trying not to dislodge anybody's beer from their grip.

Kelly reached his destination, getting close enough to Barnes to catch her light perfume. Even amongst the sweat and body odor of the others crammed into the tight space, he could pick her scent out of the crowd. He rested his arm on the table and intentionally jostled her, bumping her with his hip. She looked over and smiled, her emerald green eyes by far the brightest thing in the dimly lit bar room. Barnes then turned her attention back to Sutherland.

"I still can't believe you're really leaving us," she said.

"I think you guys are going to be in good hands." Sutherland bobbled slightly. His ability to maintain any falsehood of sobriety was gone completely. Whatever he'd been consuming during the course of the evening had finally caught up to him. Sutherland wobbled and grabbed the back of a chair for stability.

"I'm good," he said as Kelly tried offering assistance. "I'm fine." He straightened himself and then stared bleary-eyed at the two. "You guys are a hell of a team." Then he leaned in and said, not as quietly as intended, "I hope the relationship works out, too."

He reached his meaty paws across the table, using it as a balance point for his protruding midriff as he gripped both by their shoulders and shoved them together slightly. An awkward gesture received with awkward smiles.

Neither Kelly nor Barnes confirmed the sergeant's suspicion. Even here at the retirement party there was no need to open that can of worms in a room full of drunk cops. The fallout could be disastrous.

A blast of icy wind blew through the bar as the door opened. Kelly saw a face he hadn't expected as the door closed, and Paul Halstead entered the bar room.

Halstead had an easier time than Kelly in navigating his way through the crowd. It was as if he had some invisible force field pushing people away. He slipped his narrow frame through as the crowd parted, walked directly over to Sutherland, and shook his hand with an awkward formality.

"Dale, it's been an honor serving with you," he said rigidly. "Let me get you a drink."

Sutherland shook the man's hand and staggered slightly. "I think I'll let you do that," he slurred.

Halstead disappeared for a moment and came back with two beers, set them on the table, and then tapped the rim of his mug to Sutherland's. "To new beginnings."

Kelly and Barnes raised their glasses, and all four took a drink.

Halstead drank his beer rather quickly. Then, looking around awkwardly, he said, "I just wanted to come in and wish you well. You were a good cop, Dale, and I hope you have a good life after this job. I want you to know your team is in good hands with me."

"I didn't doubt it for a second," Sutherland slurred.

Halstead stood rigid. "I'm going to call it a night."

Sutherland bobbed his head and stared absently at the amber liquid in his mug.

"See you two in the morning," Halstead said, directing his attention to Kelly and Barnes.

And then, just as quickly as he'd arrived, Halstead slipped back out the way he had come. *One and done*, Kelly thought. *Impressive.* He'd come into a bar full of cops, made his peace with the man he'd be relieving, and then left. Smart move.

Halstead made something else very clear in his brief visit. He didn't want to be at their level. He didn't want to be their friend. He was assigned to their unit for one purpose and one purpose alone, and that was to be their supervisor, their leader, and to do that, he had to maintain his distance.

Kelly looked at Barnes. "It's going to be an interesting day tomorrow."

Her eyes seemed greener. The carbonation from the beer had watered them just enough to make them shine bright like mossy rocks at the bottom of a stream.

"It's Homicide. Every day is interesting."

"Kelly, you mind if I talk to you for a minute," Sutherland said. His cheeks were ruddy and blotched from the booze, but he wore a serious expression.

"Sure, Sarge. What's up?"

"Not here. Let's step outside for a minute."

"Probably a good time for me to check on Mainelli," Barnes said, taking her leave.

The two walked outside. A few other detectives were out smoking cigarettes and engaging in idle chitchat. The volume died down as the door closed behind them. It took a second for Kelly's ears to adjust to the quiet street, and soon the wind began to cut through his heavy coat.

"What's up, Sarge?"

"Listen, Mike," Sutherland said, squaring himself to Kelly. "I know you and I didn't see eye to eye on everything. Well, one thing at least."

Kelly knew exactly what he was talking about. Sutherland hadn't backed Kelly the way he thought he should have when he'd exposed an undercover who'd gone rogue. But this did not seem the appropriate venue for the conversation. Kelly, in fact, didn't think the conversation needed to take place at all.

"Listen, I know you've only been in Homicide a minute. A year is a drop in the bucket when it comes to working body cases. But I'll tell you this—in that time you've proven to be one of the best rookie Homicide investigators I've ever had the pleasure of serving with."

Kelly took the words in stride, not sure if this conversation was a drunken rant or had a purpose.

"I'm out of here. I'm cutting tail and starting anew. I just want you to know it still haunts me what happened. I should have been stronger and stood up for you. But I wasn't."

Sutherland looked down. In that moment, Kelly had a profound respect for the sergeant. He'd liked Sutherland. He was upset at the way he had handled things on the O'Malley case, but the sergeant had proven, before and after that, to be a decent boss compared to the many Kelly had worked with in his career. Humbling himself before Kelly was a rare trait amongst cops. Maybe it was the booze or the nostalgic flood of memories, but either way, Kelly respected him for trying to close this gap.

"Listen, Sarge, there were much bigger things in play on that one."

"I know." His gruff voice was thick. "I just wish I had played it better for you. You worked your ass off on that case. You put everything on the line, and when it came time to make the final push, I wasn't there. I hope you'll forgive me."

Sutherland looked up now. Kelly, a few inches taller than the man, met his gaze.

"We're good, Sarge. Now get in there and enjoy your damn retirement party. You only get one."

Sutherland stuck out his hand to give a hearty shake and a quick back slap. The ceremonious man-hug completed, the water under the bridge flowed again as he limped away.

Kelly took a moment to clear his head in the cool, crisp air.

Before reentering the bar, Sutherland called back, "You take care of yourself, Michael Kelly. No one else will."

18

Kelly's alarm was a jackhammer in his head. With each pulsating burst of its combination vibration and chirp sound, his migraine reverberated the cacophony within his skull.

He yawned, his mouth dry and cottony. He reached out to the nightstand and blindly crept his fingers along until they found the glass. Kelly swigged the last bit of water left in the cup. It was tepid but refreshing.

Kelly had allowed himself to sleep in yesterday. He wouldn't do the same today. Looking at the alarm, he realized it had been snoozed twice since first going off at 5:30 a.m. When he collapsed into his bed after navigating his way home from Finnegan's, he knew the three hours of sleep would do little to help him reset from the night's festivities.

As he sat up on the edge of the bed, the throbbing behind his eyes only worsened. He could still taste the sour remnants of the last shot. He couldn't remember who ordered it or what it was and doubted he ever would. The last hour of Sutherland's retirement celebration was hazy at best. All he could pull from memory was that he'd spent most of the time hanging out with Barnes, being close but not too close.

His conversation with Sutherland outside the bar was the last cogent memory before the rest of the night faded into a wispy fog. He rubbed his feet into the shag carpet underneath his bed. *At least I managed to get my shoes off before passing out*. A bleed-over from his married life. Nobody got into a clean bed with a dirty body. And definitely no shoes...ever.

Kelly staggered into the hallway, using the doorframe to steady himself. He wasn't wholly convinced a last bit of alcohol wasn't still floating in his system. His stomach sloshed with each step. The creak of the cold wood floor beneath his foot seemed to echo, or maybe the amplification was internal, caused by the migraine. Regardless, Kelly made his best effort to offset it, walking heel to toe, slowly rolling his feet along the outside edge of his foot to cut down on the wood's noisy reaction to his weight.

He passed by Embry's room. She was at her mother's. Habitually, he was drawn to open her door and peek in. There was something absurdly satisfying about seeing his daughter soundly asleep. He'd get no such gift this morning and continued his journey to the bathroom at the end of the hall.

Kelly ran the shower, letting steam fill the room before he stepped in. As the warm water rained down the back of his neck, he remained unmoved. Then he turned his head and opened his mouth. He filled, swished, and spat, then repeated several more times in an effort to clear the remnants of the taste left in his mouth.

After washing up, he felt a bit more alert but still sluggish. His only hope now was to get enough coffee to counteract the fatigue.

Today would be Halstead's first day on the job. Kelly wasn't about kissing ass, but he definitely wanted to make a good first impression on his new supervisor. He figured the better he did in that regard, the more likely it was he'd be able to carry forward with the Tomlin case. He was a realist and knew that arriving early would do little to change Halstead's decision about a case that had stalled out nearly three months ago, but it couldn't hurt.

He toweled his hair and put on a decent shirt, then grabbed his gear and headed down for his first cup of coffee. As he descended the staircase, his cell phone vibrated. Looking at the incoming number, Kelly recognized the three-digit prefix 538 registered for all BPD department-issued phones but not the last four numbers.

Kelly answered it as he pressed the brew button on the coffee maker. The grinds had been set the night before and the water tank filled to the max line. The cold pot buzzed to life, hissing as the first droplets of black gold struck the empty bottom.

"Kelly," he said. Speaking aloud caused his head to hurt.

"Detective Kelly, this is Sergeant Halstead."

"Morning, Sarge, you can just call me Mike."

Silence for a moment on the other end. "Detective Kelly, I need you to meet me at the bike path near Storrow Drive under the Mass Ave bridge. You'll see the cruisers."

"What do we got?"

"I'll brief you when you get here."

Kelly heard the chirp of a siren in the background, and the muffled voices of other men talking nearby. *Son of a bitch, he's already on scene.*

He'd become accustomed to Sutherland's way of doing business. His former sergeant, who was probably in a near coma after last night's abuse, used to just take the incoming by phone. If Mike's team was up on rotation, Sutherland would take the incoming call from a street supervisor, get the details, and then notify them. Rarely did he show up on scene unless requested, or it was a major one where he might be needed to run interference. Majority of the time he would review it from his office, keeping tabs on the case from the confines of the second floor.

Things were apparently going to be very different under Halstead's command. Kelly had heard rumors he was a micromanager, often running his own parallel investigation to his subordinates. Looked like he was validating that early on. He had gone to the scene before notifying the team. And with it, Kelly's effort to beat his new boss to the office had failed before the day had even gotten started.

"Be there in a few minutes." Kelly didn't have time for his normal routine. With the coffee still brewing, he exchanged his travel mug with the pot, filling it before returning the pot to its rightful place. He threw in a couple scoops of sugar for balance and extra cream to coat his stomach.

He was out the door less than a minute later.

It was cold. The air had a rawness capable of penetrating the outer layer of flesh and deep into the bone. The sensation was worsened by the dampness that only a New Englander truly understood.

Down by the Charles River, the wind skipped off the partially frozen edge of the waterway. The path around the river was a hot spot for joggers, and during warmer months crew teams from iconic schools such as Harvard and Boston College could be seen navigating its waterway. On mornings like this, the only people pounding the icy paving were the true die-hards. The woman who called in the body had told the patrolman she was out for an easy ten-miler when she found him. *An easy ten-miler? Not under normal conditions. And definitely not this morning.* Kelly was fit from his boxing and fleet of foot, but he had never been one for distance.

All the layers Kelly had piled on did little to mitigate the air's chilling bite. He shivered. The hangover was definitely adding an X-factor into the mix.

Kelly walked up to Halstead, who was standing by with Ray Charles and Trent Dawes, AKA Freckles. Everybody was there except Mainelli. Barnes had pulled up just a split second before him and was exiting her car.

She eyed him warily as the two met up, walking across the frozen tundra and down to their new supervisor.

"I guess things are going to be a bit different under our new commander," Barnes offered.

"Definitely looks that way."

They crunched their way down and stood outside the closed scene marked off by yellow police tape. In the backdrop they saw the tarp covering the body.

Halstead was expressionless as he looked at Kelly and Barnes. "Detective Mainelli said he'd be in soon, but I figured you'd want to get started as soon as possible," he delivered in robotic fashion.

The Iceman seemed to be a fitting nickname. Even more so in their current surroundings.

"You got a floater. He popped up this morning." Halstead thumbed in the direction of the body. "Early morning jogger saw. Patrol has her information. He washed ashore at some point."

"Isn't this Troop H's jurisdiction? The staties typically handle the waterway," Kelly said. Off in the distance, he saw the blue-gray shirt and blue pinstripes on the navy polyester pants distinguishing the Mass State

Policemen from the city cops. The sloop garrison hats nearly touched as they clustered together. One of them wore the chevrons of a supervisor.

"It looked like it was going to be theirs at first. That's originally why I came. No need to come in force if it wasn't going to be ours."

Maybe not as much of a micromanager as he thought. Halstead had come to determine whether the squad needed to be activated. He was prudent. Didn't want to expend resources where they weren't needed. Kelly sipped from his mug. The warmth of the coffee worked to thaw him somewhat.

"So, it's ours?" Barnes asked.

"You'll understand in a second." Halstead looked at Charles and Dawes.

"Water recoveries mess a lot with the pathology," Charles said. "But one thing's for certain, this isn't a boating accident. And the killing most likely happened off location."

"Just how long were you guys out here before we got called?" Kelly allowed a little bit of his edginess to show, partly from the hangover and partly from annoyance that he was playing catch-up on what would undoubtedly be his case.

"You'll see why." Charles gave a wry smile.

Kelly didn't like the games being played and knew Charles well enough to recognize that this was not his doing. He would tease, yes, but this holding back of information and bleeding it out slowly was not his way.

"Well, I guess we better get down there and see," he said, letting his annoyance rise to the surface.

Halstead was unfazed. His cobalt blue eyes turned toward the body. "Follow me," he said, slipping under the police tape.

Charles and Dawes shuffled alongside him while Kelly and Barnes trailed the small gaggle as they made their way down to the shoreline.

As the tarp flapped in the breeze, Kelly caught a glimpse of the body face down on the icy bank. Depending on how long the man had been submerged, there would most likely be bloat. What Kelly could tell from his brief visual snapshot was the dead man, in life, had been heavyset.

The patrolman standing watch over the body stepped aside and, at Halstead's direction, unveiled him.

The victim's hair was gray, whiter because of the frost coating it. His skin was a strange translucent, zombie-like color. The gaping hole in the back of his skull was covered in ice.

"Gunshot wound to the head. Exit appears to be to the rear of the skull," Kelly said to himself. He edged around the body, stepping carefully, and looked at the dead man's face, half buried in the snow. Even in the victim's current physical state, Kelly recognized him instantly.

He looked back at Barnes and then everybody else. "You know who this is?"

Halstead was deadpan.

"This is Turtle O'Toole," Kelly said, looking back down at the dead man. "Connor Walsh's number two man. This is his long-time running mate. These guys came up together. You're telling me somebody whacked the Turtle?" Kelly looked around at the people with him and the officers in the distance, half expecting to see Connor Walsh watching from the crowd.

"I'm familiar with Mr. O'Toole," Halstead said. "But that's not the whole reason our squad's been brought in on this."

Charles, again taking Halstead's cue, walked around and adjusted O'Toole's left arm. The ice crunched as he lifted it at the elbow, exposing the bagged left hand. "Take a look."

A knot formed in Kelly's stomach as he bent low.

Shielding his eyes from an icy blast of wind, he peered through the bag's clear plastic coating.

It took a second to see it. On O'Toole's left hand was the clearly visible cross carved in the web of flesh between his thumb and index finger. Kelly shot a glance past Charles and met Halstead's cobalt blues.

"Looks like your Tomlin case just got reactivated."

19

They spent the morning in the icy cold while processing the body and ensuring no other evidence was left behind before clearing the scene. Kelly had spent the remainder of the day working hand in hand with Charles, going over what little evidence they had collected. The ME's office took a preliminary look at the body on scene but offered nothing in the way of anything useful. No window of time for the murder, and stated a TOD was unlikely even after the formal autopsy was conducted.

Kelly doodled on his notepad while he waited. The phone was cradled against his ear as he scribbled a wavy line.

"You still there?" Best asked.

"Yup. Not going anywhere," Kelly said.

"Unlike our date," Best chided.

"Any amount of groveling going to get this to stop?"

"Not likely. Working around the dead is a bit boring. Thinking of new ways to give you a hard time is one of my favorite pastimes." Best laughed at her own joke.

"Glad I can provide such amusement." Kelly gave a moment's pause before shifting the conversation back to the reason for the call. "What's the definitive on the time of death?"

"It's anything but definitive. The window of time is adjusted for a multitude of variables, in this case the two most counterproductive being the temperature of the water and the water itself. Both retard the body's typical postmortem changes."

"Give me the layperson's explanation. I'm going to need to note this in my report." Kelly cradled the phone between his neck and shoulder and flipped to a fresh page in his notepad.

"The water temp was forty degrees with a slight variance over the last twenty-four hours. The shallow water was slightly colder, dipping just below thirty-two. After death, the body's temperature begins to slowly adjust to the ambient air surrounding it. In this case we're dealing with near freezing temperatures. Under optimal conditions, the human body lowers 1.5 degrees every hour. In pathology we use that to establish a baseline comparing the body's internal temperature to the external. Cold water, like where O'Toole was found, would accelerate the cooling process and thus throw off the equation. His core temp was taken rectally while on scene and registered sixty-five degrees. I did a test of his liver when he arrived here. The liver gives the most accurate reading. It read sixty-one degrees. I did some timeline extrapolation and have settled with sixty-three degrees as O'Toole's core temp at the time of the recovery."

Kelly tried to shorthand the information. If this was the layman's explanation, he'd hate to see the official calculations.

Best continued rattling off the information. "Applying the decreased body temp to the standard equation would make it appear the time of death to have occurred approximately twenty-four hours previously."

"So, the TOD is roughly twenty-four hours from the time the body was located?"

"No. I wish it were that easy. Like I said, the cold and the water change the game by speeding up the cooling process and slowing the internal changes such as lividity and rigor."

"Okay. Are we looking at more or less time?"

"Less. Lividity was clear and visible. Rigor mortis had extended to the arms and legs."

Kelly thought of the cracking sound when Charles had manipulated the dead man's arm to show him the mark on the hand. Part of the snapping noise was a byproduct of the ice. The other contributing factor was the rigor.

"That stage of rigor typically occurs between eight to twelve hours postmortem. Because of the submersion in the cold water, I'm sliding the number closer to the eight-hour mark."

Kelly scribbled the numbers.

"Taking the variables into consideration, I'm giving you a wider window for the time of death than I normally would."

"And that is?"

"Between six and twelve hours."

Kelly blew out a sigh.

"I know it doesn't give you much to go on. But it's the best I can do under the circumstances. Narrowing it further would be purely conjecture. And I'll leave that to you."

"Thanks, Ithaca."

"I'll be in touch once the formal autopsy is scheduled. We're flooded right now. Not sure when your guy will be up on the slab."

"Keep me posted. And thanks for breaking it down for me."

"Any time," Best said coyly.

Kelly ignored the innuendo and returned the phone to its cradle, then walked into The Depot and added the timeline notes to the whiteboard, marking the estimated time of death as occurring between 4:30 to 10:30 p.m. the night before the body was found.

Kelly was tired. The late night followed by the early rise, and those first few hours in the cold while his brain recovered from the night before, had proven exhausting. It took until mid-day before the dull, throbbing ache of the hangover dissipated enough so he could clearly function and think. And the all-consuming thought that came to mind was he was facing another red card on the board. But what he couldn't wrap his mind around was the victim. Why O'Toole? Why had The Penitent One come back three months later to put two bullets into Walsh's number two man?

He knew somebody who might have an answer to that question. He looked down at his watch. It was 6:00 p.m., and Bobby McDonough hadn't returned his phone call. Kelly was feeling sluggish, that end-of-the-day feeling when all of the effort, mental and otherwise, was put into a new case. With few leads, except for the cross on the hand, he was staring at nothing usable. Instead of cutting out early and getting a good night's rest, he decided the best thing for his brain and body was to head over to Pops'. He'd almost forgotten it was Thursday. Tradition won out, trumping fatigue.

He was up to spar with Bobby tonight. Kelly held out hope, even though his friend-turned-mob-enforcer hadn't been around in a while. He thought it might be a good time for them to catch up. Maybe he'd show since Kelly had called. Or maybe he wouldn't for the very same reason. McDonough was unpredictable at best. Kelly crossed his fingers as he shut down his computer and headed for the door.

It didn't matter how tired Michael Kelly was. The moment he set foot in Pops' gym, the energy of the place, the buzz of the ring bells, the thwack and hammering of heavy bags, the smell of sweat and blood refilled his depleted tanks. The gym had its own life force. And on his worst times, his best times, and everything in between, it fed Kelly and gave him a boost when he needed it most. And right now, he temporarily put O'Toole's body out of his mind, as well as the fact he was facing off for another round with The Penitent One. He suddenly felt refreshed.

Leaving his mental baggage at the door, Kelly stepped in. Edmond Brown and Donny O'Brien were warming up. They waved and smiled at him as he made his way over.

"It looks like your partner's not here," Brown said.

"He's been hit-and-miss, with more of it being misses lately," Kelly said.

"Well, you can jump in with one of us if you want," O'Brien offered.

"No thanks. If he doesn't show, you guys do your match. I'll just work the bag for a while. Blow off a little steam."

They knew not to ask unless Kelly offered, kind of an unspoken pact among the men. His cases and his work life had a tendency to take Kelly to dark places, and they knew the gym, his ring time, and his workouts carried him away from it. Pops's gym lifted him above the darkness for those moments, and they learned long ago not to drag him down unless he opened the door to that conversation, which he rarely did.

Kelly did want to talk to O'Brien and let him know he hadn't stopped searching for Father Tomlin's murderer. O'Brien had stopped asking after a month had passed without any progression. Since then, there'd been an uneasy awkwardness between the two. Kelly felt he'd let his friend down by not catching the person responsible.

Brown followed O'Brien as the two climbed into the ring. Kelly finished wrapping his hands. The wraps stabilized his wrists and added padding to his knuckles, essential in keeping his hands aligned when hitting the heavy bag. His wraps, no matter how he laid them out and dried them, immediately moistened as soon as he donned them. His years of sweat lived within the fibers. The familiar smell, repugnant to an outsider, carried an air of nostalgia. Like pancakes on Saturday morning, it brought him back to his youth, to his childhood. And it completely invigorated him.

Kelly warmed up, facing the 180-pound bag they had affectionately named Bessie because of its size and black-and-white coloring.

He dipped low, bobbing from side to side, warming up his hips. He twisted a little more each time, ducking a little deeper with each pass. Few knew true power came from the hips. The biggest man in the world couldn't deliver the full effect of his mass if he didn't shift his hip and put his body behind the blow. Anybody who knew how to effectively use the torque created from the midline was devastating, regardless of size.

It was second nature to Kelly, and his ability to put his body behind his devastating right hand had made him the reigning Golden Gloves champion in his youth. In a city chock full of fighters, Kelly had been crowned number one in the most competitive weight class. He was a lean middleweight. The weight class was the perfect balance of strength and speed, which also made it the most challenging competition.

Kelly let the first few snaps of his gloves, the six-ounce coverings over his wraps, smack loudly against the heavy bag. It rocked slightly. Force and its opposite reaction. Newton's Law of Motion in effect. Kelly hadn't begun to put the full force of his combinations together. He liked to ease into it. He used the ring timer chime to begin his three-minute onslaught.

He got into a rhythm, throwing combinations. Jab, right, hook. His footwork in sync with the strikes. He let loose his favorite combo—jab, left hook, right cross, left uppercut, overhand right. The final blast of his right hand was his signature knockout blow, his clean-up punch. When his overhand right clipped the bottom of another's jaw in perfect form, there was no feeling like it in the world. When delivered perfectly, it snapped the opponent's head, twisted his body, and sent him to the ground.

Kelly continued to unleash a flurry of combinations as the timer counted down. His mind could keep the three-minute round's countdown with near perfect accuracy, a testament to his endless time in the ring. The slap of each impact was timed with the movement of the bag. A synchronistic ballet, a pugilistic dance.

Three minutes later, the round buzzer sounded. Kelly dropped his gloved hands to his side and took several deep breaths as sweat poured out of his body. The remnants of whatever was left from the night before, the poisons and toxins, were forced out. He felt better than he had all day. Three minutes on the bag and he had crushed his invisible opponent. The mental strain of the day was now knocked out. His mind was reset.

Kelly made his way over to the water fountain as the gym's back door opened. Standing in the doorway, followed by a cold blast of wind, was none other than Bobby McDonough.

Kelly smiled at his friend. "Well, it's about damn time."

McDonough made his way over and dropped his bag of gear with the others, their claimed spot in the gym. Kelly and his crew were known as the Four Horsemen to the gymgoers. Not of any apocalypse, but of Pops' gym. Each a formidable boxer in his own right, but inseparability made them a force to be reckoned with. Anybody who knew them understood their friendship transcended the boundaries of race, upbringing, and circumstance. What made them truly unique was their ability to cross over the biggest boundary of all, the one that usually dissolved or destroyed even the tightest of friendships—the passage of time. Regardless of all those hurdles, the four maintained a connection as close as any bloodline could. Maybe more so.

Of the four, McDonough had proven to be the most wayward, the closest to the edge. Each, in their own way, worked tirelessly to keep him from falling off and disappearing forever. His chosen profession notwithstanding, Bobby McDonough always had a dark cloud overhead. The other three saw it as their duty, their responsibility, to bring him into the light.

No one bore that responsibility more heavily than Michael Kelly. Seeing his friend here now alleviated some of the stress he'd felt all day long. Kelly had been worried ever since this morning, when he saw Turtle O'Toole face down with a bullet hole in the back of his head and the assassin's mark on his left hand. He called McDonough multiple times in an effort to get some insider scoop on what might've happened. When he received no call back, Kelly became concerned there might be another body out there in the form of his best friend.

Seeing McDonough, he wanted nothing more than to drill him for answers. But Kelly knew better than to bring it up now, here amongst the many ears and eyes in the gym.

"You ready?" McDonough wanted to know, reaching into his duffle bag.

"Six or ten today," Kelly asked, referring to the ounces of the gloves. Both were relatively lightweight when it came to sparring, but six-ounce gloves were basically only padding for the knuckles.

Mike Tyson had made it a requirement in his fights that the glove weight be light. He didn't want a pillow fight. He wanted his opponent to feel the devastation and the impact of each blow.

"I'll take the six," McDonough said.

By picking the lightweight gloves, Kelly knew his friend wanted to bang it out. This was going to be more of a fight than a sparring match. The two had been at odds for months. Maybe a good hard fight was what they needed. The etched sign above Pops's door spoke volumes—*Fighting Solves Everything.*

Kelly smiled. "I already got 'em on."

The two got into the ring as Brown and O'Brien slid out.

"You don't want to warm up first?" Kelly asked. He felt he had an advantage having just done a round on the heavy bag.

"Nah," McDonough said, swinging his shoulders, rolling them back and forth while twisting his trunk. "I'm good to go if you are."

Kelly was already in a full lather of sweat. His muscles felt good, loose, the way you wanted them when you fought. No rigidity in his movements. Smooth, quick, and with plenty of power.

They touched gloves just as the buzzer sounded its three-burst, mechanical chime. They danced around a little bit, getting a feel for their distancing.

The mind needed to get acclimated to violence. The two sought their range with quick, light jabs. They'd get harder as the round progressed.

Kelly ducked a stiff jab, avoiding taking the brunt on his chin and opting to absorb it with his forehead. It stung but in a good way, like when a football player slaps his teammate's facemask. It wakes him up, shocks him, and gets him ready for battle.

Kelly felt alert now, keyed in. He returned with a double jab of his own, the second one snapping at the bridge of Bobby's nose, grazing off the top of his glove as McDonough tried to deflect it. Bobby's head shot back.

Kelly slid in quick, and instead of chasing the head, twisted his hips hard and slammed several body blows in a barrage of upper cuts and short half hooks. The punches landed with solid thwacks of leather on skin, angling in between his friend's elbows.

He beat the body hard, the six-ounce gloves leaving their sting. Bobby winced as the hail of punches reverberated along his ribcage.

Bobby's hands began to lower as Kelly brought his assault up to the head. Bobby was already against the ropes.

Kelly moved in, following up with a devastating overhand right, catching McDonough square on the chin. A retaliatory uppercut clacked Kelly's teeth together and, even though he was wearing a mouth guard, sent a shockwave through his head. Dizzied, Kelly staggered backward.

His friend launched off the ropes, pouncing like a cornered stray, and began swinging wildly.

Kelly brought his gloves up as his head cleared, trained instinct protecting him. His gloved hands were now in front of his face, shifting slightly to block his temples as a flurry of blows rained down from all sides. Kelly had a good guard, a tight guard, rounding his shoulders forward, tucking his chin deep. He absorbed the punishment, biding his time.

McDonough was head hunting, not wasting any time on the body. This worked to Kelly's advantage. He was able to raise his elbows and deflect the majority of the attack through his forearms.

Through his defensive posture, Kelly saw McDonough's eyes, wild with rage. He was fighting like he was on the street, like he was drunk, and Kelly wondered if maybe he was. His punches were sloppy and uncharacteristically wild.

Kelly saw a window of opportunity as McDonough's energy waned. The wide-angled swing was telegraphed.

Kelly slipped inside his friend's punch, catching it with his left arm at his elbow joint, dissipating its effectiveness. McDonough's glove grazed off the side of Kelly's head. With lightening quick speed, Kelly unloaded his right hand, driving an overhand right that clipped the bottom end of McDonough's chin at the cleft.

Instead of spinning his head, it drove it downward. Kelly shot an uppercut that caught him in the eye. McDonough fell flat on his back, not unconscious but certainly dazed.

Kelly backed off and walked to a neutral corner just as the buzzer sounded.

McDonough sat up, pulled his mouthpiece out. "Didn't see that coming!"

He smiled. There were no hard feelings in the ring.

"Think it's time we grab a beer?" McDonough offered.

"The way you were swinging, it looks like you've already gotten a head start," Kelly fired back as he walked over and reached out his gloved hand. McDonough grabbed it and Kelly pulled him up.

"Maybe I have." He laughed.

McDonough didn't live by their rules. He didn't have a normal day job. Working for the most dangerous mob boss in Boston meant you didn't have to live like regular folk. It'd been a long while since McDonough dared enter Pops' gym with a little bit of booze in his system. The father figure permitted them to drink out back, but he didn't tolerate it inside the gym, and he definitely didn't tolerate it from somebody in the ring.

"Let's head out back."

The group grabbed their gear bags and made their way out into the cold, throwing on hooded sweatshirts. The biting cold air actually felt good against their body heat.

They sat on the back stoop and waited while Brown grabbed the cooler from his trunk and served up the cans. Kelly looked at the label's design, a patterned swirl of purple spiraling out from a sunglass-wearing ghost in orange. He didn't recognize the brand, Kasper's Ghost IPA, but it seemed as though a new microbrew popped up every day.

He popped the top and took a long sip. The carbonation coupled with the bitterness burned the back of his throat.

McDonough took a seat next to Kelly.

"You and I need to talk before we're through here tonight," Kelly whispered just loud enough for him to hear.

McDonough cracked open his beer and took a swig. Kelly knew his friend heard him, but he offered nothing in return.

"Seriously," Kelly said. "You're not leaving until we talk."

"Yeah, I figured as much."

20

The cold bite of the air had cut short their post-boxing commiseration. As Brown and O'Brien headed to their vehicles, Kelly lagged behind with McDonough. Each had an unopened IPA in hand. Brown had handed them one before leaving.

"Bobby, got a second?" Kelly called over to his friend.

McDonough turned, his face pained, knowing very well the topic of conversation. "I'll give you a minute or two, but I can't stay long, Mike."

"Fair enough." Kelly double-tapped the key fob unlocking the doors to his Caprice. McDonough eyed him. "What? It's cold. Besides, it's not like you're sitting in the back seat."

Kelly entered the unmarked detective car as McDonough slid into the front passenger seat and closed the door.

McDonough cracked open the can of beer. The fragrant fruitiness of the Kasper's Ghost IPA filled the compartment. "First time getting to drink beer in a cruiser. Feels good."

Kelly laughed, glad his friend's sense of humor was intact, then opened his can and took a long slow sip. It had a bitter aftertaste, but Kelly's taste buds had adjusted to the unique flavor, and he was starting to enjoy it.

McDonough slurped, and then turned to look at his friend. "All right. So out with it. What gives? And feel free to kick on the heat anytime you want. It's only twenty degrees out."

Kelly started the engine, responding to his friend's request before jumping straight into the topic.

The gym session hadn't been as long as normal, and since the car's engine was still relatively warm, the heater soon started to work its magic.

"You know where I was this morning?"

McDonough rolled his eyes. "I can only imagine."

"Can you, Bobby? Can you? Because I was standing knee deep in a frozen tundra, looking down at the dead body of Turtle O'Toole."

Bobby took another swig of his beer.

"I can see by your utter shock that the news has obviously circulated through your ranks...probably before I was even called to the scene."

McDonough shrugged. "Not sure what you want me to say, Mikey." He didn't make eye contact, instead choosing to stare down into the can.

"I need you to say something. One of your own ended up on the side of the Charles River, with a hole in the back of his head. If I didn't know better, I'd say somebody's sending your boss a pretty serious message." McDonough's silence was irking Kelly. "O'Toole was Walsh's number two. Doesn't bode well for you or anybody else in the crew."

"Somebody is always trying to knock off Walsh. Nothing new there, Mike. It's always been that way. When you're at the top, somebody is always gunning for you."

Kelly knew his friend's simplistic viewpoint was actually spot-on. As soon as you're in a position of power, people who want what you have will do whatever it takes to get it. And Connor Walsh had a bigger target on his back than anybody. He was at the top of the criminal food chain, at least for now.

"I get it," Kelly said. "But I'm going to tell you something that nobody outside of the investigation knows, and the reason I'm doing this is because A, I'm worried about you and your safety, and B, you may be the only person I can reach out to on this who'd be able to point me in the right direction."

Bobby sipped his beer noisily as if trying to drown his response.

Kelly hesitated for a moment. When he'd worked the case with Gray a few months back, he'd learned the shocking news that the FBI had been working to capture this killer for over fifteen years. They had never released information on the wound on the victims' hands to avoid copycats muddying the water. They didn't want the killer to change his MO, his calling card, and make it more impossible to link the cases than it was now. Yet here Kelly sat, preparing to confide that tightly kept secret with a mob enforcer. *Fifteen years and nothing more than a whisper. No suspect, no ID, no person of interest ever established besides the list made by the BAU analysts.* He needed to get the upper hand, and Bobby McDonough potentially had the ability to give him that insight.

"You remember when I reached out to you about trying to find Phillip Smalls when I was looking for the killer of that young girl?"

Bobby nodded slowly.

"Remember how he killed himself? Then you told me not to look too deep into it."

Bobby raised his hands. "Whoa, whoa, whoa. Don't put me there. I just told you where to find him, and I told you what he knew. I'm not saying how I came about knowing it. And if I recall—the information I gave you helped save a couple girls."

Kelly knew his friend was right. He'd asked for help and Bobby delivered.

"Well, the same mark on Smalls's left hand matched the one on O'Toole's today, also many others—including the priest at Saint Peter's."

McDonough's eyes flashed with surprise. Kelly had said something that unnerved his friend, a nearly impossible thing to do. It took a lot to frazzle a kid who grew up in the rough section of the neighborhood, a kid who had it tougher than most, and then, at an early age, had proven himself for the most dangerous man in Boston and risen in the ranks over the years to become his top enforcer. McDonough either didn't know about the mark on O'Toole or was shocked Kelly did.

Kelly saw something in his friend's eyes, a look he hadn't seen in a very long time. Fear. That fear registered the moment Kelly told him about the cross on O'Toole's hand. *He knows something. He's holding out.*

"Bobby, this is where you open your mouth, and the words start coming out," Kelly said. "This is where you prove to me our friendship means more than the alliances we keep to our employers. After all we've been through— you owe me."

The surprise in Bobby's eyes flashed over to anger like fire when fresh oxygen was breathed on it. "I'd call us pretty damn even," Bobby snapped.

Kelly knew he was right and regretted trying to lay that card on the table. McDonough had saved his life when Kelly was staring down the barrel of a gun. And in turn, Kelly had saved him from the law enforcement manhunt that followed.

"Look, I'll check it out, and if there's something I can tell you, I will," McDonough said.

"Every minute we waste playing this game, Bobby, puts people's lives at risk. Maybe yours."

"My life's been at risk since the day I was born."

Kelly had mulled over his friend's lack of cooperation the previous night as he sat up in bed just before dawn broke. His routine was back in place after the last two days had thrown things out of whack, and he was on his way out the door a few minutes ahead of schedule.

He liked the quiet of the morning commute and rarely, if ever, listened to the radio on his way into work. Kelly drove in silence from Dorchester to downtown Boston, replaying the last thing McDonough had said to him before leaving. *Maybe I'll find him before he finds me.* His friend was way out of his league on this one.

Kelly pushed the thought from the forefront of his mind and began plotting out his shift. It wasn't long before his mental day planner was rapidly filling up.

He'd shot a text message to Gray yesterday, letting him know there was a new body, and it looked to be their guy. Gray had called back almost immediately, asking for the detailed case file to be sent his way so he could bring it up to his supervisors and petition to assist. Kelly hadn't heard back from him since that conversation, and as quickly as they had pulled him out last time, he wasn't expecting much in the way of support.

He pulled the Caprice into the gated lot of One Schroeder Plaza, then took the side entrance and climbed the stairs to the second floor. As he entered the hallway from the stairwell, the motion light activated, illuminating his path to the doors of Homicide. *First on the floor. Routine restored.*

As he fobbed his way in, he saw the light inside was on. Somebody had arrived a while ago, long enough for the motion sensor lights in the hallway to deactivate. *So much for first in.* Kelly assumed it must be Barnes. She too would want to reclaim her sense of routine.

He entered and looked toward his squad's cubicle area but didn't see Barnes. To his surprise, FBI Special Agent Sterling Gray was seated at the vacant desk.

He smiled and held up the blue coffee mug in mock cheers.

"Didn't think you'd get here this quick, if at all," Kelly said.

"Neither did I, but when I showed them that picture of O'Toole's hand and told my boss the connection the dead man has to the Irish mob, they immediately authorized my temporary reassignment to the case."

"How'd you get in?"

Gray pointed his mug toward the sergeant's office, where Halstead was already seated at his desk. *I guess beating the boss to work is a thing of the past,* Kelly thought with a grimace.

"Well, I, for one, am glad to have you back, and like I said when we talked yesterday, I haven't moved forward much in the way of the Tomlin case. So this new body just means more work. I would say based on the way he was found, where he was found, the fact that he was submerged in the Charles River for an unspecified time period, and knowing how clean our perp is, the likelihood of this being much of an adrenaline boost to that dead case isn't hopeful."

"Hey," Gray said, leveling his eyes at Kelly. "Every time a body drops it gives us a window in, small as it may be. Although we've been unsuccessful so far, you never know what this case will give us that the others haven't. Maybe it connects in some way that will help make order out of the chaos. You've got a dead priest and a dead mobster. That to me is a strange pairing if I've ever seen one, and from my experience and study of The Penitent One, he typically does not kill so close together, and to do so in the same area is also a red flag."

"Maybe he's slipping," Kelly said wishfully.

Gray cocked his head. "Not likely. But every case gives us new potential to find him."

"Let me grab a cup from the back and I can get you up to speed on the O'Toole case before everybody gets in." Kelly tossed his coat on the back of the chair and made his way to the break room. He topped off his travel mug and returned to Gray.

"Before we get into the O'Toole case, I wanted to show you something that has really been nagging at me with the Tomlin case."

Gray's interest was piqued. "Sure. What do you got?"

Kelly opened the drawer and pulled out the thick Tomlin case file, the same one he'd mulled over every day since it landed on his desk the Sunday before Thanksgiving of last year.

He rifled through the file and removed a small stack of papers. It was the dead priest's work history or, more accurately stated, lack thereof. He'd called the church where O'Brien thought he'd heard him mention he worked, which turned out to be a dead end. Then, when reaching out to the archdiocese, he'd continually been met with red tape. Nobody seemed willing to share, or was able to find, any record of Father Tomlin's work history.

"What am I looking at?" Gray asked as Kelly slid over the stack of papers with notes scribbled in the margins.

"That's it. You're not really looking at anything. This right here is Father Benjamin Tomlin's work history, what little I could gather."

Gray looked down at it, thumbing through the few pages in the stack, most of which were in Kelly's handwriting.

"Nothing there. That's my point. The only proof we had that he was ever a priest was the collar he wore at Saint Peter's. Prior to that, he was like a ghost. Everything I've checked doesn't seem to match. I can't find anything on a Father Tomlin anywhere."

Gray stopped shuffling through the papers, reorganized them, and handed them back to Kelly, looking pensive.

"Something you want to say?" Kelly asked. "I mean, because I'm all ears. I've been staring at this case file, losing my mind, losing sleep, and letting everything else in the world fall down around me trying to put this one to bed. I'm grasping at air. And now, with another body on my desk related to this, I'm not sure what I'm missing. But something's off. I've got four red cards on my murder board, and the doer is the same for each. I'm at a loss."

"When I came here in November, I was under strict oversight. Any information I was to disseminate needed the approval of my supervisors, who are extremely tightlipped about what information can be released. Even with an ongoing active investigation into a homicide."

"You've been holding back?" Kelly set his mug down and focused his attention on Gray.

"This case has been at the forefront of the FBI's list for years. The fact that they can't put a wanted poster with a person's face on it has not gone unnoticed. And at the higher levels, it's become this administration's personal bout with the Jackal," Gray said.

Kelly understood Gray's reference to Ilich Ramírez Sánchez, better known as Carlos the Jackal, the elusive, legendary terrorist of '70s fame fictionalized to stardom by the author Robert Ludlum's Jason Bourne series. The Jackal had managed to elude capture for nearly twenty years after numerous international manhunts failed. The fact the FBI's upper management were making comparisons didn't bode well for his case closure.

"Okay," Kelly said. "So he's public enemy number one to the FBI, and they're super guarded with what they release, but I thought last time you were here, you were given the green light to share everything with our squad."

"I was—to a degree," Gray said.

Kelly didn't like that answer.

"And everything I was able to share with you at that time, I did."

"But," Kelly said, knowing there was more.

"But there was a piece of Tomlin's death that I couldn't share, and it was one of the reasons why I was first assigned."

"I hope I'm not going to have to wait a few more months to hear the answer to this."

Gray offered a sheepish smile. "Like I said, I was following orders, and since they came from the top, I didn't have much wiggle room to break them."

Kelly also knew the dynamic Gray spoke of. He'd been privy to knowledge about a rogue cop, and he had been threatened from on high of the danger in exposing that. Not only to the PD, but to Kelly and his family.

He understood when weighing the balances of justice and your own personal survival, sometimes the latter won out. So yes, Kelly understood the politics at play in any case, especially a high-profile one. Apparently the Bureau played by the same rules. Guys like Kelly and Gray were just pawns in a much bigger game. Although even a pawn can kill a king if the timing and position are right.

"That work history file, or lack thereof that you've been searching for regarding Tomlin, there's a reason it didn't exist."

Kelly felt himself leaning forward, literally on the edge of his seat.

"The reason it didn't exist, the reason you couldn't find anything on him, is because he wasn't a priest."

Kelly shook his head, his subconscious coming to the forefront and battling with his conscious mind. It didn't make sense. *He was a priest at Saint Peter's Church. Donny had served with him.* "What do you mean, not a priest?"

"He was an undercover FBI agent. He was set up at Saint Peter's Church to eavesdrop and monitor Connor Walsh. It was a major play by the FBI's Organized Crime Task Force. They seized a window of opportunity. One of many that have been deployed in an effort to gather usable information capable of putting Connor Walsh away forever."

Kelly let out a breath he hadn't realized he'd been holding.

21

Inside The Depot, Kelly watched his squad's faces as Gray laid out the truth about Father Benjamin Tomlin: that he was an agent with the FBI, assigned to Organized Crime, and was working undercover in an attempt to gather intelligence and information to dismantle Walsh's criminal organization. He followed his briefing with an apology for holding back the information.

Mainelli, who seemed the most hurt by it, had his arms folded and was wearing a pouty face. "So, how are we supposed to expect that you'll be on the up-and-up with us now? I mean, maybe that information would have been pretty important back at the time. Maybe we'd have leaned on some of Walsh's guys, put the heat on them, maybe some of our snitches could've worked their magic."

Halstead interrupted Mainelli's angry rant. "I understand your frustration, Detective Mainelli, but Agent Gray was operating on orders and following them explicitly. He told you what he could at the time." He looked to Gray. "And he's here assisting us again, and from my understanding we are privy to all pertinent information regarding Tomlin's death. No more red tape. Hopefully his partnership will shed light on O'Toole."

There was a finality in his tone, unlike his predecessor, Sutherland, who would engage Mainelli in a back-and-forth repartee. It had served as comic relief for Kelly on a frequent basis, but he saw that Halstead would not be engaging the members of his squad in that manner.

"Nothing saying we can't take that approach now," Kelly said. "Jimmy's got a good point. We know now that there's a tie-in to the mob and that Tomlin was there to eavesdrop. Now we've got one of Walsh's top crewmembers dead. I think we can definitely say there is some correlation that needs further scrutiny. Let's rattle some cages and see what falls out."

"I couldn't agree more," Halstead concurred. "Make sure you let me know your plan of action. And keep me posted on your progress with this investigation. I'll be stopping in from time to time. I don't know what you've heard about me from your friends in the department, those who have worked under me or with me. But I think you'll soon come to find that I support the men and women I serve with, as long as I know what's going on. I don't want to be caught out in left field where somebody above me or beneath me knows more than I do. I want to be the one who holds all the cards. That way I can protect you and, at the same time, protect this unit. Are we clear?"

"Crystal clear," Kelly said.

"All right then, I'll leave you to it."

With nothing else said, Halstead left The Depot and closed the door behind him.

"Crystal clear, sir." Mainelli gave a mock rendition of Kelly's response.

"He makes a good point. If he's privy to everything we know while we're working a case, he can best protect us against people trying to one-up us. He just wants to be in the loop. I don't see a problem with that."

"Yeah, well, Sutherland just let us do our thing. He didn't hassle us along the way. We gave him results. He trusted us. We kept working. He knew we were handling our caseload. Life went on."

"Well, obviously we're under different management now. To continue making comparisons to how things used to be seems a complete waste of time. You either adapt and overcome or you get run over. I don't have a problem with keeping the boss informed. I mean, he's going to be the one running interference," Kelly retorted.

"I personally don't want to have to face the lieutenant, or worse, Acevedo, if he decides to pop in. I like that he wants to run a good, clean defensive block for us, should the need arise," Barnes offered, throwing in her support.

"Of course you'd agree with him," Mainelli said, rolling his eyes.

Kelly was grateful Mainelli didn't finish his thought and make an overt comment about their dating relationship, especially in front of Sterling Gray. He didn't want Gray to think the unit had gone all amateur hour in the few months since he had been with them.

"Ideas on how we attack this now that everything's on the table?" Gray asked, redirecting the conversation back to the subject, which Kelly appreciated.

"I can reach out to a couple of my girls," Barnes said. "A few of them are regulars, go-to girls, for Walsh's guys. I can see if they've heard anything. Maybe there's some talk on the street."

"I'll make some calls, check with Organized Crime and see if they've got anything on Tomlin. Maybe somebody got wind there was a plant in the church. Maybe they put a hit out on him, hired this killer. Who knows?" Mainelli offered.

Kelly thought of McDonough and the conversation they'd had the night before, and the lack of information and cooperation he offered. Now with everybody grabbing intel from multiple sources, Kelly realized he needed to push his friend a little harder.

"I've got something I can look into. It's more of a long shot, but I've had results in the past," Kelly said, intentionally vague.

Barnes shot a glance at him. "I can come with you, Mike."

"It sounds like you're heading out to see some of those prostitutes," Gray said, "so maybe I could take a ride with him. We divide our resources up, maybe we get more done, and when we reconvene, we'll have something to push forward with."

"It's settled. Let's go," Kelly said.

Kelly and Gray sat in his unmarked Caprice about a block and a half from JW's Pub, Connor Walsh's hangout. For lack of a better term, it was the mobster's clubhouse. But Kelly wasn't there for Walsh.

Bobby McDonough's beige Ford Taurus had pulled up, parked in the back lot, and remained unmoved for the last ten minutes. Kelly waited. The lot was about half full, but nobody had come or gone in since McDonough's arrival. Kelly figured his window of time was running out, but he wanted to give enough time from when his friend went in to make sure he didn't pop back out. Ten minutes seemed reasonable.

"So, this guy's a friend of yours?" Gray asked.

Kelly gave him a reader's digest version of his and McDonough's long-time friendship, leaving out many unique aspects that had made things more complicated in recent years.

"Why don't we just talk to him?" Gray said.

"I tried that last night. He's holding out. I can tell. And to be honest, I don't want to wait until another body or two drops before he decides to talk to me. He's as stubborn as they come. I've known him the better part of my life, and there's a good chance he may never speak to me about it."

Kelly fiddled with the magnetized device in his hand. It was the size of a pack of gum and weighed about the same. He pressed a small rubber button, activating it, then checked on his phone to ensure the tracking device was synced to the mobile app. He'd used them in Narcotics. He'd ordered a couple online and kept them in his drawer at the office. Until now he hadn't used them since coming to Homicide. "Now's as good a time as ever," Kelly said, mostly to himself, as he opened the door.

Kelly made quick work of his approach to the bar's alleyway, which led to the lot where McDonough had parked.

He hustled around the corner, ducking as a nasty gust of wind lashed at his back. Kelly wasn't dressed in his normal BPD windbreaker or jacket, trading them in for a more subdued look of jeans, a hooded sweatshirt, and a puffy overcoat. He had a baseball cap pulled down just in case anybody looked outside. The hood was up, and his face was as obscured as his wardrobe would allow.

He walked along the row of cars, stopping near McDonough's as he pulled out a cigarette, another throwback to his Narcotics days. A cigarette went a long way in adding to his subterfuge. He always kept the pack with him should the need arise for Kelly to hide in plain sight. Cigarettes gave a reason for a person to be standing about, but also aided him in the next step of his plan.

Kelly put the cigarette in his mouth but didn't light it, instead intentionally dropping the red dime-store lighter on the ground. It bounced once and landed near the right rear tire of McDonough's Ford. Kelly then bent down to pick it up. In one deft move, he slapped the magnetic backing of the transponder to the dirty undercarriage of the Taurus. He gave a quick tug, making sure it adhered to the metallic surface. It held.

He stood with the cigarette still in his mouth. Completing the ruse, Kelly lit it with the cheap red lighter. He took a quick puff for anybody who might be watching, either with plain eyes or on the security cameras undoubtedly covering the lot. He then walked out of the alleyway and back toward Gray.

Kelly paused momentarily before getting in to scan the street. It was desolate. Flicking the cigarette out onto the sidewalk, he climbed inside, then checked the mobile app one more time before driving down the block, passing JW's Pub.

He drove in a doglegged pattern, pulling into the back lot of a McDonald's a couple blocks away to begin the waiting game.

"It's pretty accurate. Should be able to keep tabs without having to be in visual range."

"And what do you hope to accomplish by following your friend around all day?"

"To be honest, I have no idea. I just thought it might be a good idea. He's definitely shaken by this, and I'd imagine so is his boss. Knowing McDonough the way I do, and his role in Walsh's crew, I'd imagine if somebody is killing their people, then my friend will be assigned to eliminate that threat."

"I don't want to get tied into some murder conspiracy," Gray said. "As nice as it would be if the mob could kill off the TPO and save us a whole heap of paperwork, it's still not how we're doing business. Agreed?"

"Never crossed my mind. My hope is Bobby can draw him out of hiding. Right now, I don't see any other option. I mean, unless Barnes gets some intel, I have little to no hope that whatever Mainelli's doing is going to result in much."

"Let's see how this idea of yours plays out. Can't hurt. Besides, it's been a while since I've had a good stakeout. Bureau life has had me tucked inside an office for the last couple of years. It's nice to be out amongst the people. Even if those people happen to be mobsters and killers." Gray laughed at his own joke.

They idled in the back lot for a little over an hour as the smell of the deep fryer wafted out and penetrated the inside of Kelly's Caprice. None of the patrons paid any attention to the two investigators as they sat in uninterrupted relative silence while they waited for McDonough's next move.

The app on his phone chirped an alert followed by the message: MOVEMENT DETECTED. Kelly tapped on the notification and a map filled the small digital screen similar to a Google Maps display.

McDonough's vehicle was indicated by a small red blip. When in motion, it pulsed. Kelly's position was indicated by a blue arrow. Simple enough.

He waited, knowing the GPS had fairly excellent accuracy. When he'd used it in the past, the transponder had been accurate to within ten feet of the target. Knowing this, Kelly allowed McDonough to get some distance between them before giving a very loose tail. It wasn't long before McDonough's blip showed he'd gotten on the Mass Pike and was heading out of the city.

He had known Bobby McDonough for the better part of his life, and if he knew one thing about his friend, it was that he rarely, if ever, left the city. Bobby said he never felt comfortable outside of the neighborhood and sought to avoid leaving it at all costs. He didn't take vacations and only traveled when directed by his employer. Seeing him leave now, after whatever meeting took place at Walsh's clubhouse, caused Kelly concern.

"Well, this should be interesting," Kelly said.

"Why's that?" Gray asked.

"Because Bobby McDonough doesn't leave Boston unless he's under orders."

They closed the distance on the highway, fluctuating between keeping half a mile to a mile away from McDonough. After driving west for the better part of an hour, the two had stopped playing the guessing game of trying to figure out where he was taking them. The thought had entered Kelly's mind that his friend had somehow figured out he'd been tagged and was leading them on a wild goose chase just to screw with him.

They turned onto US 5N and snaked down the long offramp into the City of Agawam near the Connecticut border. Kelly had only driven through it when taking his daughter to The Big E, Eastern States Expo, held mid-September to early October every year.

Passing the turnoff street he typically took to the expo, he thought back to his and Embry's favorite tradition. All six New England states were represented in these massive, house-like vendor havens. The expo was set up like a carnival, and the food was legendary. Embry fell in love with the Maine house's loaded baked potato. Every year they went, Kelly stood in line with his daughter for the hour-long wait it took to get one.

The price was worth it, both in time and cost, when he saw the look on Embry's face. Her eyes would light up as she took her first spoonful of the baked deliciousness.

"Your buddy got connections out here that you know of?"

Gray's voice snapped him out of his thoughts. Kelly shook his head. "No, not that I know of. Like I said, everything McDonough knows is in Dorchester. He'd maybe branch out into one of the other neighborhoods, but not this far away. He's not a suburbs guy. He's got to feel crazy out here. Makes me wonder where he's going."

As if he were somehow telepathically communicating with his friend, the red dot stopped moving. Scanning the map, they could see he had pulled into a commercial lot containing a hardware store and weed shop.

Kelly pulled the car to a stop on the adjacent street, parking on the road with a good eye on the lot's entrance.

McDonough's vehicle didn't move. A few minutes passed.

Kelly considered doing a drive-by of the lot to see if his friend was meeting with somebody, and was about to take his foot off the brake when a white panel van nosed out from the lot and waited to turn west onto the street. Ray's Electric was stenciled on the side, and at the wheel was none other than Bobby McDonough. He turned left without looking in their direction.

"You think he saw us?" Kelly asked softly.

"No, I don't. Your friend moonlighting as an electrician?"

"I hope," Kelly said, but he knew better. There was no reason why Bobby would be driving an electrician's truck.

"Do you think he knows about the tracking device? He's ditching us?"

Kelly shook his head. "I don't think so. That doesn't make sense. I mean, why go through the trouble of grabbing a different van and coming out the same way he had gone in? No. If he thought we were tracking him, he would have done something else to ditch us long ago. He would have stuck it on another car. He wouldn't have let us wait for him as he came back out in a different vehicle. No, this is all him. I just don't know why he's doing it."

They now had to contend with a much more complicated tail, and Kelly had to apply his Narcotics experience. At least Gray had dialed down his look and wasn't wearing the full suit, trading it in for a business casual look and windbreaker. The good thing about following a panel van was that it stood out amongst the crowd of other cars. It wasn't like Bobby was driving a blue Honda Accord, blending into the scenery. Kelly tried to keep three cars between them and the van.

McDonough continued driving, appearing to be unaware of their efforts to follow him as he navigated Agawam's side streets.

Then the vehicle took a right into a quiet neighborhood. The map showed the street to be a dead-end cul-de-sac. Kelly pulled to a stop just past the street, giving Gray the best vantage point of the parked van.

"Your friend hasn't left the vehicle. Scratch that—door's open. He's stepping out. He's wearing a gray overall suit and hard hat. He's got a rectangular, heavy plastic case in his right hand."

Kelly's pulse pounded. If this was a hit, he wouldn't be able to protect his friend. If Bobby did something now that was witnessed by the FBI, he'd be done. Kelly thought about pulling away, saying it was too hot, too dangerous, all in the veiled effort of protecting his friend, but Gray would see right through it.

He knew there was no way around it. They had to see what he was up to.

"He's crossing the street and going behind that yellow house. Your call," Gray said, focused out the window.

"Let's move," he said, opening the car door and hopefully not closing the chapter of his lifelong friendship with McDonough.

22

Kelly's mind raced at almost the same pace at which he and Gray were approaching the house where McDonough had just slipped around back. Whatever he was there to do, it was not good, and neither was what was in that case.

Kelly hoped, if nothing else, he would manage to get there quick enough to intervene before whatever was about to take place actually did. He might not be able to save Bobby from a prison sentence, but maybe he could save his life.

The fact that McDonough was wearing gray overalls and had ditched his car for a fake electrician's van left Kelly with only a few possible scenarios. Moonlighting as an electrician wasn't an option. This was definitely a hit. The who was still up for debate. Walsh had a lot of enemies. The Penitent One was now one of many on a very long list vying for Walsh's head.

Why here? Why in the middle of suburbia? None of this was making sense. But ever since touching the Tomlin case, nothing in Kelly's investigative world seemed to add up.

They were one house away when they slowed their pace from a sprint to a jog. They no longer had a visual on McDonough, the house's back corner shielded from view by a large pine bush.

The neighboring houses looked to have been built in the '70s, relatively new by Massachusetts standards. All of the houses looked dated, except the one McDonough had picked. Kelly banked to the left, skirting the space between it and the neighboring house.

In warmer months, the backyard would have provided ample cover to conceal their movements. Big trees and shrubs lined the rear, but most were completely barren. They crouched low and moved along the ice-covered grass to the poured-concrete patio tucked behind an oversized do-it-yourself fire pit. Kelly peeked around.

McDonough stood facing the back of the house. He knelt down and opened the case, withdrawing a handgun and screwing a gray cylinder onto the barrel. A silencer. The possession of those two items alone could land his best friend in prison for a cool ten.

Kelly cursed to himself. *Did I just betray my best friend to the FBI? Have I severed a lifelong connection in the sole hopes of solving a case?* The lines of his investigative career, his need for the truth, for justice, had never been so blurry as they were right now. He wanted to scream to his friend and tell him to run.

But how would he explain to McDonough why he and an FBI agent were there?

Gray took the lead.

"Let's see what he does. He's got a reason for being here. I mean, if what you told me is true and he is their top gun, maybe this is where The Penitent One lives. We may be closer right now than we've ever been."

Kelly looked over at his federal counterpart, who was almost salivating. The drive, that invisible force that pushed Kelly forward on his cases, Gray had it too. His eyes narrowed, as if trying to see through the walls of the house.

Bobby stood with the silenced semi-automatic handgun down by his right thigh, making no attempt to conceal it. At this point, he was committed.

"You think this is our guy? You think this is The Penitent One's house?"

Gray shrugged, still staring at Bobby and the house he'd targeted.

For Kelly, it seemed like time was as frozen as the landscape around them.

"The guy's got to live somewhere. I guess here is as good as any," Gray offered. "We've got to get closer. We've got to be able to see in. If we're wrong and we just walked up on a regular old mob hit, we've got to stop your friend before he pulls the trigger. Otherwise, he's going to be looking at a heavy sentence. Nothing either of us will be able to do to help with that."

It was like Gray had read his mind. Here he was, a fed, out of his area, but somehow he understood the level of connection Kelly had with McDonough. It must have been the military in him. He understood brotherhood at the take-a-bullet-for-a-friend level. And Kelly was impressed Gray was at least willing to help stop his friend before he did something stupid and irreversible.

The two pushed themselves up, using the fireplace for balance as their feet slipped on the iced-over patio slab.

McDonough stepped closer, disappearing behind a shed protruding from the back corner of the house.

Kelly and Gray were now moving quickly, or as quickly as they could while trying to maintain noise discipline over the crunch of each step. Both withdrew their duty weapons, keeping them low.

Kelly didn't like the thought of having to point a gun at his best friend, but it wouldn't be the first time the two had been in a standoff together. The last time, Bobby McDonough had pulled the trigger to save Kelly's life. Even though Kelly had worked hard in the aftermath to conceal his friend's involvement, a life debt is one that is never truly repaid, and Kelly knew that. Now, here he was, sneaking up on his friend with a federal agent on his heels. Not the debt repayment he intended.

At the invisible, fenceless border between the yards, they tucked in behind the twisted trunk of a maple tree and peered out from alternate sides.

Kelly had an angle from which he could see McDonough, who was hunched over at the door, working to disable the locking mechanism. Watching him pick the lock, Kelly wondered how many other skills his friend had accumulated over the years of service to one of Boston's most notorious.

"It looks like he's picking his way in," Kelly whispered. "When do you want to move in?"

"You got eyes on the door?" Gray asked.

"Yeah."

"Well, let him get it open. Maybe we'll get a look at our guy."

There it was again. Kelly heard it in Gray's voice. The hunt was on, and Gray could taste how close he was. He was willing to forgo stopping this crime in progress for the chance of seeing The Penitent One's face.

A second later, McDonough stood erect.

"I think he's got it," Kelly said.

McDonough peered through the window of the back door. Kelly could see his friend's hands were gloved, obviously the work of a seasoned professional.

"He's in," Kelly relayed, watching his friend disappear through the open door.

McDonough left it open a crack. Most likely to make for a quick and easy egress should the need arise.

Kelly and Gray left the cover of their tree trunk, making a hasty crossing of the short distance between the two yards.

They slowed as they neared the door, guns up. No sign of McDonough. Each closed in on the door, Kelly peeling to the left side and Gray to the right.

Kelly nodded at Gray, who nudged the door open wider without making a sound.

Kelly stepped into the opening quickly, filling the void—the fatal funnel, as it was known in tactical circles—and entering the home of the unknown person. Gray was tight on his six.

They were in an indoor/outdoor hallway separating a two-car garage from the house. It was basically an elongated mud room but unlike any Kelly had seen. It was immaculate. The floor was spotless, except for what the intruders tracked in.

A door ahead and to the left led to the house. Still no sign of McDonough.

Kelly took the lead as the two closed the distance to the door. It was open and ajar. Kelly stopped at the frame. Gray stacked up behind him.

Gray tapped Kelly on his shoulder, indicating he was ready to move. Kelly pushed the door wider and visually cleared what he could.

Kelly stepped into the kitchen. Light flooded through a window above the stainless-steel sink. The kitchen had a U-shaped layout with a large marble-covered island in the center. McDonough was nowhere in sight. Kelly moved in slowly. He heard something in the hallway and ducked behind the island, Gray wedging in beside him. Footsteps, those of somebody attempting to step lightly but failing miserably, could be heard approaching from the front hallway.

The footsteps grew louder. Whoever was making them had just entered the kitchen area. Kelly heard the transition of sound from the hardwood to the kitchen tile.

Kelly coiled like a rattler ready to strike. Gray gave the ready tap, just as he did in the hallway.

Kelly took two quick breaths and a slow exhale, preparing himself, then sprang upward with his department-issued Glock pointing toward the sound.

Gray moved in synchrony with Kelly as he stood.

McDonough had his hands on a doorknob, his gun tight to his ribs but pointed out toward the closed cellar door. He spun on his heels, now facing Kelly and Gray. The silenced pistol followed his body's turn and was now directed at them, McDonough's left hand still clinging to the doorknob.

Kelly felt sick. He was looking at his best friend down the sights of his gun. The silence that followed could have been measured in milliseconds but to Kelly felt like an eternity. Not a word was spoken. No commands were given by either side.

McDonough released his grip on the door and slowly moved his hand toward his face. He pressed his index finger to his lips, signaling them to be quiet, and then shot a glance at the closed door to his left.

Kelly reached out with his left hand, silently pleading with his friend to lower his weapon. McDonough did, but just slightly. Kelly could see the tension in Bobby's face.

Neither Kelly nor Gray lowered their weapons.

"Get your friend under control," Gray whispered.

"I'm trying," Kelly said.

Kelly lowered his weapon slightly. Bobby did the same. Gray slowly dropped his weapon, but not completely.

McDonough reached for the door again.

Kelly waved McDonough off and shook his head, but he turned the knob, calling Kelly's bluff. McDonough knew Kelly couldn't pull the trigger.

The open door momentarily shielded McDonough from view.

Kelly heard a strange mechanical thunk, out of place in the silence.

They stepped wide to the left, slicing the pie and trying to reestablish visual with McDonough.

Just as Kelly caught sight of McDonough standing at the top of the stairs leading to the basement, an explosion erupted, sending a fireball up the stairwell. McDonough was launched through the air, bouncing off the countertop before disappearing from view.

The house shook violently, as if every bit of the frame buckled at once. The impact knocked Kelly to the tile. Gray slammed down on top of him. Flames flashed over the kitchen island as they fought to regain their footing.

The heat was intense. The kitchen cabinets and walls were already fully engulfed by the ravenous flames. Kelly and Gray stayed tucked behind the kitchen's sturdy island as flames ripped and tore at the walls, the fire burning faster and brighter than anything Kelly had ever seen. It was like the house was designed to burn.

Gray coughed and said, "Got to get out of here!" He darted back in the direction they had come, through the open door and into the hallway, disappearing behind a wall of fire.

Kelly looked toward his one chance of escape as the opportunity quickly dwindled. Survival instincts kicked in as he prepared to follow, but even in the midst of the inferno, Kelly couldn't leave his friend behind.

He snapped out of his desperate need for flight and scanned for any sign of McDonough. Through the smoke and fire, Kelly saw his friend's foot sticking out from behind a cabinet on the far side of the kitchen.

Kelly sprang into action, crawling fast and low across the shattered tile floor. Bits of the damaged ceramic slashed at him as he moved. He put the pain out of his mind and pushed forward. He rounded the corner and found McDonough crumpled in a heap, the gray suit covered in black, a portion of it near his shoulder still on fire. Kelly swatted at the flames, dousing them.

He reached over and grabbed his friend by the collar, pulling him close. Nothing, no movement. No time to check for vitals. Either way, dead or alive, Kelly wasn't leaving his friend inside. Without question, Bobby McDonough would do the same for him.

Kelly yanked and pulled his friend across the floor, staying low. McDonough's dead weight made for an incredibly slow go of it. Kelly had pulled his sweatshirt over his nose and mouth, trying to keep himself from being taken out by the smoke blinding his vision.

Near the refrigerator, Kelly banged his forehead into the corner of a cabinet. Had he not been in a dire situation of life and death, he might have yielded for a moment to the pain of the sharp edge. He felt it immediately, the warmth of his blood trickling down into his right eye, blinding him further.

Kelly persevered, taking each inch forward as a small victory. He was beginning to lose steam. The smoke was filling his lungs. The more he exerted, the more he coughed. The flames swirling overhead intensified as Kelly's vision faded into a haze. He'd lost sight of the door. His head began to spin, and he knew it was now or never. The hard ten, Pops called it. The last ten seconds of a round when a boxer unloaded with everything left in the tank. Kelly heard Pops signaling him to move, to unload. Problem was, he had nothing left to give. Kelly's head dipped. He felt a jagged piece of tile gouge at his cheek.

As the bright fire dimmed and his mind battled for strength, Kelly felt something grip his shoulder. He was moving, but not of his own accord. His brain was mush and couldn't complete the thought and make the connection.

He was met with a whoosh of air. Kelly's vision and mind cleared enough to realize he was back in the mudroom, which hadn't been fully ravaged by the fire yet. Kelly instinctively reached for McDonough and panicked when he realized his friend was not with him.

A split second later, Gray appeared from the kitchen door, dragging the unconscious McDonough behind him.

Kelly stood. His lungs burned, but he'd regained enough strength to help. He grabbed McDonough under the armpits and started to drag him, his academy training kicking in.

Gray jumped in to assist, picking up McDonough's feet. The two lawmen moved in tandem to carry the mob enforcer to safety.

Kelly slipped and fell, coughing wildly. His lungs had filled with the black smoke and his eyes still stung.

Gray helped Kelly up, and they grabbed McDonough by the wrists, pulling with all their strength as they dragged his limp body out of the mudroom and into the house's hard-packed, iced-over yard.

They didn't stop once outside. Kelly and Gray continued hauling McDonough's dead weight as they put as much distance as possible between them and the burning house.

About twenty feet away from the house, a secondary series of explosions erupted from inside as Kelly and Gray collapsed in total exhaustion.

Not a portion of the house wasn't totally consumed by fire.

Kelly and Gray wheezed and coughed as McDonough remained unmoving where they dropped him.

23

"Explain to me one more time why you and our guest here happened to be at a house in suburban Agawam that's fully engulfed in flames. To boot, we've got one near-dead mobster unconscious at the hospital. Worst of all, I'm only hearing about this after the fact. I thought I made myself exceptionally clear when we spoke earlier today." Halstead's face held no line of tension. And though the message conveyed was one of both outrage and disappointment, none of it could be discerned in the calm, steady manner in which he delivered it. Cool and calm, somehow containing the rage bubbling just beneath the surface. The Iceman.

In little more than twenty-four hours with his new boss, Kelly felt that he'd made an unusually poor first impression. First, showing up at the O'Toole murder scene reeking of Sutherland's retirement party while nursing a vicious hangover. Then upping his game the following day by being on-scene at a blown-up house after following little more than a hunch while managing not to keep Halstead informed after being explicitly told to do so.

"This may be my fault," Gray interjected, his voice crackling like that of a lifelong smoker.

Halstead turned his attention to the agent.

"Kelly was telling me a little bit about Walsh's gang and said he had some intel on one of their guys who runs the muscle. He mentioned if we expect a retaliatory reaction from Walsh, he's a good guy to watch. So that's what we did. We went over to the bar where we found his car. He took off and we gave a loose follow. We didn't want to waste your time until we had more to offer."

Halstead then looked over at Kelly.

"It's Bobby McDonough from the neighborhood. We grew up together. And yeah, I had a feeling if we kept an eye on him, we might get lucky."

Halstead pointed to the smoldering house in the backdrop. "You call this getting lucky? I'd hate to see what bad luck looks like to you."

Kelly ignored the comment. "We thought we might get a lead on our perp. Walsh's people are more connected than the police. They have a better network of intelligence. The rules don't apply to them."

"And you figured what?"

"I don't know." Kelly shrugged. "But I figure if you whack one of Walsh's guys, there's going to be some type of retaliation. And who better to follow than his number one enforcer?"

"Why wasn't I privy to this?"

"Like Agent Gray was saying, we wanted to have something to show when we let you know."

"If he was driving out here and it turned out to be nothing, it would've been a waste of your time and a bigger waste of ours. I'm not in the habit of wasting my supervisor's time." Gray stepped in front of Kelly and folded his arms as if defending him from a schoolyard bully.

Kelly was thoroughly impressed. The FBI agent who'd spent barely a week with them back in November had just taken up for him. He was glad to have him on the team. In that moment and the moments inside the inferno, Gray had proven he was a brother in blue, regardless of the team they played for.

Halstead looked back at Kelly. "This won't happen again, you understand me? I won't be kept out of the loop. I'll be the judge of whether something is or isn't worth my time."

"Fair enough," Kelly responded.

"With that unpleasantness out of the way, I guess you best get started," Halstead said.

"Get started with what?" Kelly was confused. Maybe he was referring to the mountain of paperwork that would no doubt be associated with this debacle. He thought about McDonough, who'd left by ambulance nearly two hours ago. He wanted to check on his friend and be by his side if and when he woke, but he knew that would have to wait. There was something Halstead needed done.

"What do you need us to do, Sarge?"

"Work the scene."

Kelly looked at Gray, who seemed just as baffled.

"Well, you caught it, you bought it. Agawam doesn't want this case, and since you're saying this house may be linked to our guy, I'm making it our scene to work." Halstead stepped closer and spoke more quietly. "This may be the best chance we have of getting any inkling as to who this Penitent One is. Don't screw it up."

"We won't," Kelly and Gray said in near unison.

"Agawam PD will remain on scene and hold the perimeter, but you guys are going in. We'll forward them a copy of our report later."

"When's tech going to get here?" Kelly asked.

"I notified them as soon as you called me. They should be here shortly."

Then, to his surprise, Kelly saw a pitch-black Suburban with heavily tinted windows pull to a stop outside the crime scene tape and sea of fire trucks and cruisers maintaining the wide perimeter of the scene.

Superintendent Acevedo stepped out of the passenger side and stood by the vehicle.

Halstead looked at the investigative unit's commanding officer and then back at Kelly. "You better make this count. You better get me something on this one, you understand me, Detective Kelly?"

Kelly nodded.

Halstead began walking away, then looked back and said, "I'm stepping up for you on this one, Kelly. Better make it worth my while."

Halstead had proven himself correct when he said he stood up for his guys, even after being kept out of the loop. *Pretty ballsy.* As the new supervisor of their squad, running interference with the top brass took some intestinal fortitude.

With Halstead running his interference, Kelly turned his attention to Gray. "Hey, you didn't have to do that—putting yourself out there like that to protect me."

"Look, I was pushing the envelope just as much as you, I think more so toward the end." Gray rubbed the cold from his arms. "You know how long I've been looking for this guy? Do you know how many people have failed before me? This is the FBI's white whale. And I want to be the fisherman who hauls it in."

Kelly realized Gray's drive didn't only stem from a need for justice but also for the accolades that came with serving it. And in a case like this, Sterling Gray would be a legend within the Bureau. Maybe he saw this case as his ticket to the next level, or a way out of some crappy unit? Or maybe he just enjoyed the sheer rush of bringing down somebody that everybody else had failed in doing.

Either way, Kelly realized at that moment that they differed slightly in their approach to law enforcement. Not that his was any better, just different.

"How do you typically like to attack a scene?" Gray asked. "Everybody has their way of doing things, and this is your baby, so I don't want to step on your toes."

"I appreciate that. A lot of guys wouldn't have asked, but since you did, I kind of like to see it for what it is. An initial walk-through, usually with a camera, and then I come back through and do a more thorough piece-by-piece investigation. It helps me organize the evidence and come up with a plan of attack before I go in. You can get into the weeds on these things, focusing too minutely before seeing the big picture."

"All right. Do you want to wait for Crime Scene or get started now?"

Hard for Kelly to tell if Gray had a preference or was just asking for the sake of it.

"I say we get started now. We can do the preliminary walk-through while we're waiting," Kelly offered.

Both men slipped on a Tyvek jumpsuit, booties, and double-gloved each hand with sterile latex gloves before making their way into the crime scene that was now a smoldering wreckage of a house. No door to open this time, and no fingerprints likely left on anything in the house.

The smell was horrid. Smoldering ash was everywhere. Kelly coughed. The vapors were activating the tingle in the back of his throat, already irritated from his earlier bout with the fire and smoke.

The two now stood where the island in the kitchen had been, the same island that had worked to shield them from the initial blast wave that rocked McDonough. There was little left. The studs at the base that kept it rooted to the floor were all that remained of the charred ruin.

The tile floor was covered in soot, thick and pasty from the deluge of water dumped from the fire department trucks. The evidence eradication team had flooded this fire. They had done their bit, it seemed, to run every bit of water in the State of Massachusetts through their hoses.

Kelly treaded lightly, although there was no way to enter a scene like this without leaving your mark. Thankfully they could follow the path left by their shoes on their way back out. He walked over to where the access door to the basement had been, now nothing but a gaping hole. The stairwell led down, but many of the boards were burnt or missing altogether. The FD had managed to water the slab fairly well, flooding much of the lower few feet of the poured concrete basement.

Kelly stood on cracked tile in the kitchen and scanned the ground where he'd found McDonough. Wedged between an exposed pipe in the splintered baseboard was the silenced pistol they'd seen McDonough carry and, for a brief moment, point at them.

Kelly pointed to it. Gray nodded and then looked around. "Doesn't have to be his, you know. I'm sure if what you say is true and he is the enforcer, then there's going to be no tie between that weapon and anybody in their crew. And you putting a gun in his hand regardless of the house, well, that's a lot harder to explain than somebody doing a little recon. The intent to kill comes off and it just looks like a break-in. I'm pretty sure the owner of this house, if it's who we think it is, isn't filing any complaint charges."

For the second time in barely twenty minutes, Sterling Gray had proven himself loyal beyond Kelly's wildest expectations. He was jumping headfirst into the faded gray of the world Kelly had found himself in since putting on the shield.

This second go-round with Gray, he'd begun to see him more as an equal. In November, Kelly saw the agent as somebody sent down from on high for the sheer amusement of some supervisor's whimsy. A face for the press with little to offer. But it appeared he'd been wrong, completely misjudging both the man and the mission. There was more to Gray than met the eye, and

Kelly was glad to have him here now. His trust for the fed was growing exponentially.

"Feel like getting wet?" Kelly offered.

"It is a little bit balmy today. Wouldn't mind cooling off." Gray laughed.

Both men were making light of the fact that they were about to plunge into the cold water that had filled the basement when the external temperature hadn't yet hit thirty degrees. The thought of submerging themselves in the frigid pool was less than appealing.

Kelly took the lead, navigating the functional steps and using the wrought iron railing that had survived the fire. With a few steps to go, Kelly felt the water penetrate through the Tyvek suit's paper-thin material and into his pants. It was shockingly cold, nearly taking his breath away. Regaining his composure, and with the quick numbing properties of the water adding to his ability to compensate, he stepped onto the concrete floor into knee-high water.

The basement was like something he'd expect in a horror movie—aisles of religious memorabilia, neatly organized and in glass cabinets, most of which were either shattered or melted. It was like a wax museum lit ablaze. Gallons upon gallons of water and fallen debris littered the space. Even through the damage, Kelly could see ornate items of religious significance, crosses and bits of stained glass, that looked handmade, along with stones labeled with the names of the holy places of their origin. A shrine filled with religious accoutrements was not what Kelly had expected to find when he first hit the icy water.

"Jackpot," Gray said. As cold as he looked, there was excitement in his eyes.

"Looks like we found our first potential lead in figuring out who this guy is," Kelly muttered.

Kelly's interest was piqued by something he saw in the corner–a kneeler set against the wall. It was lacquered wood and looked as though it had been cut out of a church confessional. That was until he looked up. Heavy gray shackles hung above it, and a small circular mirror the size of a quarter was centered where someone's head would be if they were in a kneeling position. Kelly had seen this before. Or read about it somewhere. Small mirrors like this were used by some for focused meditation for critical introspection.

"What do you make of this?" Kelly said, looking at Gray.

The two got closer. Etched in the wood just above the mirror were the words: *Then He will also say to those on His left, "Depart from Me, accursed ones, into the eternal fire which has been prepared for the devil."*

"Tell the guys at BAU they nailed it. I guess The Penitent One was an appropriate nickname after all," Kelly said.

He was transfixed by the kneeler. *Punishment.* The pain of his upbringing morphed into his calling card.

Kelly moved on, scanning the basement without touching anything. Observations only at this point.

No photographs hung on the walls. At least none of any non-religious images. The shackles might be beneficial in gathering some potential DNA. He made a mental note to relay that to Charles or Dawes. The rest of the house was destroyed, and the basement would be their best chance of finding any clue. Once they drained it and Charles had a chance to go through the scene, they might be able to find something usable.

Kelly was standing still, momentarily lost in thought. The water drew his attention. He looked at the water line just below his knee, now approximately two inches lower. Either the ground wasn't level and he'd walked up an incline, which was common in New England homes, or it was draining. A second later he had his answer.

The water was moving, flowing in one direction. Kelly followed a small bit of floating wood.

"Hey," he said to Gray, pointing at the little ripples of moving water flowing toward a wall across from the kneeler.

Kelly pulled his pistol and slowly began following the flow of the water to the wall. Gray followed.

He reached the wall and started running his finger along the edge, soon finding a small, hair-like seam. Had the basement not been flooded it was unlikely he would've found it.

"Get me something to pry it open."

Gray trudged over to a tool bench, sloshing his way through the cold water. He returned a few moments later with a crowbar. "Think this will work?"

Kelly took the beveled edge and slipped it into the crack. He worked it into place and began pushing and pulling, working it deeper. After several minutes, he heard a loud cracking sound. Whatever mechanism opened and closed the door had snapped.

One massive effort, with Gray assisting in the final pull, and the hidden doorway budged. As soon as it did, the water in the basement flowed out. Kelly slammed the crowbar in tight, fighting to keep it open as the water pushed hard against it.

It took a few minutes until the water pressure weakened enough for them to pry the door wider. Once opened, they traded the crowbar for their guns.

The two pointed their guns down the dark tunnel as the water's surge echoed loudly along the tubular walls.

They edged forward with Kelly in front. One hundred feet or so ahead, they saw the gray light of day illuminating the other end. They moved quickly, their heads ducked low and their weapons at the ready. Where the tunnel ended, they were met by a locked iron gate.

Peering through the bars, they saw a small dock like that of a personal boat launch. No boat was tethered to it.

"You know what this is, don't you?" Kelly asked.

"An escape hatch."

24

"Can you believe this?" Mainelli huffed. "We get stuck on guard duty for the crime boss of Boston. All because some nut job is planning on taking him out! Seems like it'd be doing the taxpayers a favor if we were to drive around the corner for a bit. Maybe grab a bite to eat. There's a great deli down the street with the best mozzarella you'll find outside of the North End. And if we get back and happen to find Walsh dead, would that be so bad?"

Barnes had been listening to Mainelli's tireless rant, or some variation of it, for the better part of the last four hours. Sadly, that meant they were only halfway through their security detail.

Positioned outside in an unmarked cruiser was not exactly what the BPD brass had in mind when they offered up the protection. Walsh had thrown a fit Barnes had only caught one end of as Halstead worked to broker the deal. Cooler minds prevailed. Halstead, the Iceman, prevailed. Walsh agreed to have unmarked units present outside of his home if BPD felt so inclined. Which, of course, they did. And so, Barnes and Mainelli had been assigned the first rotation.

"And would you look at that place? I couldn't afford that house in three lifetimes. Maybe more."

Barnes had been staring at the house for the past four hours. Mainelli's comment wasn't lost on her. The *Herald* had done a piece on the converted multi-family in the lifestyle section a few years back. She couldn't remember the cost, but it was in the millions. It stood out amidst the other neighboring buildings. It was a corner lot at the intersection of Dorchester Avenue and Harvest Street.

Not only was the burnt orange paint distinctly different, the contours were sharp when juxtaposed with the older surrounding structures. Barnes remembered one quote from the article. The interviewer had asked Walsh why he'd spent so much money converting the old triple decker when he could've spent the same elsewhere, like the Carolinas, and gotten triple the luxury. His answer was simple. "This is where I was born. And this is where I'll die." Looking at the front door now, she just hoped it wasn't tonight. And wasn't on her watch.

"Ya know, Jimmy, us being here providing security really isn't about him. We're not doing it for Walsh or any of his cronies. We're doing it for the other victims on the list. The ones who deserve better, like Rourke and Tomlin. And if we're lucky enough to grab the son of a bitch responsible by using a floating turd like Walsh as bait, then I'm all for it."

Mainelli nodded. Barnes was shocked he was actually listening. Most of the time the gruff Italian only waited to talk and rarely listened to the words that came out of anybody else's mouth.

"But still...you've got to admit," he said with a smile. "It'd be pretty damn great if Walsh got taken out by this guy and then we caught him right after the act."

"It'd definitely be two birds with one big stone. And it would save us a ton of paperwork."

Mainelli's smile edged up unevenly across his face, as if his left and right cheek were in an invisible tug of war. "Exactly."

Anybody who'd worked with Jimmy Mainelli for more than a minute knew how much the salty detective loathed paperwork. Barnes knew she'd found his sweet spot.

Then the conversation faded back to an awkward silence.

Barnes was comfortable working with him. Not that they were close or overly friendly. It was strictly a working partnership, and not an unpleasant one. She'd come to know and like the portly detective, although his professionalism was lacking at times, as was his hygiene. Both were tolerable and both made him an acceptable, not exceptional, partner to have on a case.

What Mainelli lacked, Kelly made up for in spades. Among the three of them, a healthy investigative balance had been struck. But not lately.

Barnes had noticed that ever since she and Kelly had begun a dating relationship, or at least once Mainelli had picked up on it, his idle chitchat with her had dropped off. It was worse when they were alone. He'd become much more guarded and awkward.

She figured talking about it would be equally as awkward. Probably more so. Barnes had no intention of spending any portion of this eight-hour security detail discussing the ins and outs of her relationship with Michael Kelly and the effect it was having on Mainelli.

Barnes braced herself as Mainelli adjusted himself in his seat. It was his telltale sign he was about to pontificate. Again. She crossed her fingers and hoped that it wasn't on why they should be paid more, or how the cruisers needed to be updated. Those were his two go-to topics in times of strained silences.

"It's Gabriella," Mainelli said softly, looking down toward the steering column and not making eye contact with Barnes. He was intentionally avoiding looking at her.

Barnes leaned in, dipping her head in an effort to meet his eyes. "Is she okay, Jimmy? Is she sick?"

Mainelli went quiet for a moment. "No. She's leaving me." His voice was barely a whisper.

"What?" She knew he and his wife had a tumultuous relationship. She figured he was trying to live up to some stereotypical Italian way. The loud arguments he'd have over the phone at his work cubicle seemed more for show. And to Barnes, they'd been comical. All of their flareups appeared superficial and she never thought much of it. With three kids running amuck, who wouldn't have a bit of stress? But was the marriage the disintegrating kind?

What happened? was the first question that popped into Barnes's head. But she was a cautious speaker and knew better than to lead with that. She decided to just wait out Mainelli, and in time, he'd fill in whatever gaps he was comfortable with.

"That's why I've been a little bit late and looking like I slept in my car these past couple of weeks."

Barnes wanted to tell him he always looked that way but opted for a softer approach. "How long has this been going on?"

"I found out she was cheating on me with another guy. Get this. It was her personal trainer. The one I set up for her on her birthday." Mainelli looked down at his midriff and gripped his girth with two hands, shaking his belly fat. "Guess I never had a chance. I knew I should've got a crockpot instead."

"What are your plans? Can't keep sleeping in your car." That was Barnes's way—stick to the practical, steer away from the emotional. She didn't need to deal with the unloading of that closet full of problems. She was no shrink. God knows she had enough things to deal with without adding Mainelli to the list. No, Barnes knew herself well enough to know she was much better at planning and strategizing than offering personal advice. And if someone was facing a divorce, what better time to do a little bit of life planning? They had plenty of hours to kill. She figured she'd give it a shot.

"She said she was going to go live with a sister in Revere, but I don't know. It's just, it happened so fast. It really is a lot to figure out. Just worried about my kids. I guess I could have done more."

Mainelli's voice was soft, softer than Barnes had ever heard him speak, and she found herself struggling to make out his mumbled words. It appeared, asked for or not, Mainelli was preparing to unload his emotional burden on her. Barnes sought to sidestep this, racking her mind for a change of topic. And the answer to her prayers arrived in the form of a florist truck.

It pulled to a stop in front of Walsh's home. The side was embossed in bright red and gold lettering that read Amelia's Flowers. Tulip petals surrounded the words.

Walsh had a six-man, handpicked security team. Two covered the front door, while the remaining four were staggered at various points within the home. Walsh's men. Walsh's rules. The two men outside did not display any firepower, but Barnes knew they were armed. The larger one's shirt bulged under his left armpit from the gun shoulder holstered underneath. She had watched him slip his right hand inside his coat to fondle the butt of it every few minutes since they'd arrived four hours ago.

The two guards approached the van, disappearing from view behind its high sides.

"Should we move?" Mainelli asked.

"Give it a second. If this really is a florist and our guy is watching, then we'll blow our position."

"It's not like we're invisible in the Caprice," Mainelli said, apparently back to his normal doom-and-gloom meanderings.

The driver of the van got out and walked around to the back. He wore a white jacket with a matching white baseball cap pulled down tight over his head. Barnes raised her binoculars to get a better look. It was a little past 4:00 p.m., but the weak winter sunlight had already begun to shift to night. All she could make out before the deliveryman turned away from view and opened the double rear doors was the pair of silver wire-rimmed glasses he wore.

He bent forward, the white jacket disappearing as he leaned into the back of the van and reappeared a second later holding a rectangular glass vase of green roses.

The deliveryman closed the door, and Barnes caught a glimpse of the smaller of Walsh's external security team. The florist nodded and approached. Both men then disappeared from view again.

The seconds ticked by like minutes. Barnes's eyes watered, but she refused to blink as she stared through the binocular's amplified lenses.

Green roses? Something familiar fluttered on the outer edge of her mind, just out of reach. There was a connection. Then it hit her like a wave. *Shit! Green roses...Walsh's calling card he left on his dead enemies.*

"Move!" Barnes unholstered her duty weapon as she stepped out of the car.

Mainelli squinted toward the van and then back at Barnes.

"It's him!" Her voice was forceful enough to convey the message without being so loud as to alert the perp of their impending approach.

The deliveryman came into view again, still cradling the vase in his left arm. He was holding something in his right hand, but Barnes was too far away to make it out.

The man stood calmly in front of the main entrance to Walsh's home. Neither of the two security team members were in sight. It dawned on her what he was doing at the door and what he held in his right hand. The keys.

A second later, the man disappeared inside.

Mainelli's eyes were wide as he scrambled for the unmarked's radio. The message he relayed to dispatch was a frantic, "Code 99. Mainelli and Barnes need assistance at our location. Dorchester and Harvest. Suspect on scene. I repeat, Code 99!" Mainelli's voice was uncharacteristically pitchy.

Anybody on the receiving end of that transmission would be racing their way. A Code 99 was BPD's critical incident designator.

Barnes heard sirens in the distance as she sprinted across the intersection in a beeline for the door. Mainelli did his best to keep up.

She rounded the back of the van and saw the two mobsters. Their bodies lay side by side on the sidewalk near the curb, each with a single gunshot wound in the forehead. A green rose lay on each of their chests.

They were in a dead sprint for the door, weapons at the ready. Barnes grabbed her radio as she moved to the door. "We've got two down by a florist van in front. DRT. Hold medics. Send tactical. Active shooter. We're going in!" Her voice was steady. She slipped the radio back into its holster and prepared to make entry.

The shift had been made in law enforcement many years back with regards to nationwide protocols when it came to active killing events. Whenever police encountered such a threat, regardless of the number of officers on hand, there was no waiting around for backup. There was no waiting for a tactical deployment of SWAT when active killing was taking place. The only option, and one officers were indoctrinated to do, was the completely counterintuitive decision to head toward the sound of gunfire.

Barnes pressed herself against the door and checked the handle. Still open.

"Let's do this," Mainelli said.

Barnes yanked open the door and they pushed inside, their Glocks leading the way. The first floor was huge. Not much had changed from her memory of it in the photo spread from the *Herald*. It was quiet. Too quiet.

The stairwell was redesigned from the original triple decker, but it was still near the foyer entrance. Barnes paused at the bottom of the stairs and listened.

Mainelli cursed under his breath. Walsh's private suite, a massive bedroom and living space with a full-length bar, was on the third floor.

Barnes was preparing to clear the first floor when she heard three loud gunshots from upstairs.

No time to waste, Barnes sprinted up, taking two steps at a time. Mainelli did his best, but was already one floor behind her, spitting and huffing as he went. She couldn't wait for him, could only hope he would catch up. She worried he'd have a heart attack before reaching the third floor.

Seconds later, her shoulders were pressed against the outer wall, near the access door to the hallway leading to Walsh's suite. She turned the handle and it opened. Barnes pressed her weapon forward, jamming her left hand into the door and pressing it wide. She stepped in. A soft, intricately woven rug runner led the ten feet to the door. The rectangular enclosure was bright white, with a black orb surveillance camera set at eye level on the right-hand side of the door. Beneath it lay a dead man. He had multiple gunshot wounds, several in the chest area and one in the skull that was slightly off-center above the right eye. He had a revolver in his hand. Barnes looked behind her and saw three shots in the wall near the door. *At least he got a couple off before going down. Maybe he got lucky and the killer is bleeding out on the other side of the door?* Wishful thinking, she knew.

Walsh had bragged to the *Herald* that nobody could get to him in his penthouse, not even the cops. It looked like that theory had just been proven false.

Barnes paused for a moment, tensing and relaxing her muscles. Adrenaline pumped through her veins. She could feel the thump of her heartbeat.

She willed herself forward, staying low until she reached the crumpled heap of the bodyguard. She ran her hands along his body.

Mainelli came up from behind, wheezing and grabbing his side. "Personal trainer. I should've been the one who got the trainer." He shook his head, hands on his knees, department-issue Glock pressed between his meaty hand and thigh. He looked at Barnes. "I don't think you need to check him for a pulse."

Barnes found what she was looking for. She held up the fob access card. "We're gonna need this to get in."

"Are you ready for this?" Barnes stood, extending the retractable lanyard attaching the access card to the dead bodyguard's hip. It was just long enough to reach the panel without having to move the body.

Looking nervous, Mainelli glanced down at the dead man at their feet. Sweat emptied from his pores, activated by his momentary exertion up the stairs. "Do I want to rush in and get killed protecting a mob boss? Not particularly. But there ain't no way I'm letting you go in alone."

"Thanks," Barnes muttered, not realizing Mainelli was even considering that as an option.

She held up the fob to the access panel. The red light changed to green and she heard a mechanical pop just as a hail of gunfire rang out from within.

25

Kelly pumped the soap from the dispenser, vigorously rubbing his hands together to create a thick, foamy lather under the warm water. It was the third time he'd washed his face, but he couldn't seem to get the acrid smell of the burnt house out of his nostrils. At least it wasn't the smell of death, but this wasn't much better. The smell of latex overwhelmed the soap's fragrance, the long hours of wearing the form-fitting gloves melding their clinical scent into his skin.

He dried himself with paper towels and left the bathroom. Gray was in The Depot going through the crime scene photos given to them by Charles. The assorted images were spread unevenly across the table. Gray was systematically and meticulously going through the crime scene again, the second time since they'd returned from the house.

Kelly walked into the room, feeling slightly refreshed from his sink shower. "Any luck?"

Gray barely looked up from the photo he was staring at. "Not anything since the last time you asked."

Between nearly dying in a fire earlier in the day, and then spending the next several hours working the scene and processing what was left in the way of usable evidence, both men were physically and mentally taxed. The emotional wear and tear left them depleted. And seeing his best friend hauled off on a stretcher added an invisible weight to Kelly's shoulders.

He focused his energy on the here and now, deciding the best thing he could do for Bobby would be to find the person responsible. Kelly stepped away from the conference room and went over to his desk. He picked up the phone and dialed the extension for Raymond Charles, who picked up on the third ring.

"Did you hear back from the lab?" Kelly asked.

Charles exhaled. It was more of a wheeze, the rasp of his throat attributed to his lifetime of smoking.

"I called in every favor I had over at the state lab. The fastest turnaround they can do on those DNA swabs that we took from the shackles—and I'm talking the absolute fastest, meaning everything else in the state lab gets dropped and everybody works hand in hand—was a couple days at best. They said sixty hours is the fastest they could turn it around, and that's under the most optimal of conditions. More likely even with the rush, it'll be three days to a week before we get any definitive answer on whether we even attained any DNA from our potential doer."

Kelly sighed. When Gray had seen the shackles, Kelly first thought they were used as some type of torture device. And in all respects, they were. But not for random victims. No, those shackles, Gray theorized after a brief call with the Behavior Analysis Unit down in Quantico, were most likely used for self-inflicted abuse. The conjecture being that The Penitent One had masochistic tendencies, probably stemming from his childhood. A reliving of past trauma. The shackles and kneeler were for his own private penance.

Charles had swabbed several of the deep grooves in the metal, hoping that even if the TPO attempted to remove his DNA, there might be enough trace left for them to get a hit. Kelly still held out hope that was a possibility but was disheartened by the fact that even with pressure and favors called in, it would still take nearly a week to get the results. They didn't have a week, especially now that their killer knew they were coming for him. The window of time before The Penitent One dropped off the radar altogether was closing, and Kelly could feel it.

It had been Gray's fear all along. He had said during the initial workup done by BAU that if this guy felt the pressure, he would drop off the grid, and any chance of finding him again would be nearly zero. Kelly couldn't let that happen. Looking back into the conference room, he could see from the lines of frustration squiggled across Gray's brow that his federal counterpart felt the exact same way.

"All right, Ray. Well, thanks for trying. And let me know if you find anything else."

Kelly walked back into The Depot. "Bad news," he said.

"Great, can't wait to hear it." Gray set down the photograph he was looking at.

"Charles said there's a rush put on the DNA swabs he took, but the likelihood of getting a response anytime soon is going to be hard to come by. Best-case scenario, we're looking at close to three days. With the worst being much longer."

"Well, not to add insult to injury," Gray said, "but I've run the name that the house was purchased under, a Clint Vesper. Everything I can find matches the info from the mortgage company. I crosschecked it using Accurint. Clint Vesper bought that house five years ago."

"What's the problem?"

"I can't find a Clint Vesper anywhere in the system. Not that I thought it would be that easy. It was a longshot that a killer who had been able to cover his tracks for the last fifteen years would use his real name to make a purchase. A guy who's rigged his house to blow up is not likely to make such a mistake. But still, I was hoping it would give us something to go on, maybe a dead relative or friend. But as far as I can tell, Clint Vesper doesn't exist."

"I feel like we're starting at square one all over again. The closer we get, the further away I feel from catching this guy," Kelly said, venting his frustration out loud. He normally internalized his angst when it came to a case, but he felt that he and Gray were synced, that they got each other. They both had the same drive. If not for the same motivations.

Just then the radio crackled to life, and on it, he heard Jimmy Mainelli frantically calling for help, issuing a Code 99 at their location. Kelly and Gray were already running for the door before the transmission ended.

All the detectives in the Homicide unit began clearing out. When a Code 99 came across, it was an all-hands-on-deck call to action. Kelly ran down the hallway, Gray close on his heels. As he ran down the stairs and out into the parking lot, Kelly realized they had a third member in their group, running along with them. It was none other than Sergeant Halstead.

Kelly was momentarily shocked. He had been conditioned by Sutherland's slow amble. Seeing his new supervisor keeping stride for stride with him was a nice change of pace.

Less than two minutes later, all three piled into Kelly's Caprice and tore off toward Connor Walsh's home.

The Caprice fishtailed slightly as it swerved onto the street. Kelly heard Barnes's voice on the radio, calmer than Mainelli's but equally chilling, telling them there were already two down. "DRT" was her acronym. Cop speak, meaning Dead Right There. Kelly knew it well. He didn't like it. And he knew Barnes well enough to know that she was already preparing to enter the fray, if she wasn't already in it.

Kelly floored the gas pedal. Even as the Caprice, with sirens wailing, raced forward, he felt as though no speed would be fast enough. Nothing would get him from downtown to Dorchester in time to save her and Mainelli.

Something was jammed against the door, making it nearly impossible to open. Barnes pushed against it with all her might, trying to force her way in. "I need a little help, Jimmy!"

The larger detective got low and leveled his thick shoulders against the heavy door, ramming into it again. He was met with resistance, but it started to give just a little.

Prying it open about six inches, Barnes quickly realized why they were having such difficulty. It wasn't barricaded. There was a body in front of it.

That brought the count to four. The killer inside that room had dispatched four of Walsh's best men in a matter of minutes, and he was likely still somewhere inside. That left only two of Walsh's security detail and Walsh himself.

Barnes pressed hard, and with Mainelli's support they were able to force the door open, shoving the body along the floor. The opening gave Barnes enough wiggle room to squeeze inside. Harder for Mainelli, who kept his expletives to himself.

When she wriggled her way in, Barnes took up a prone shooting position using the dead mobster's body as a human sandbag of protection.

She saw nothing, even though it was an open layout. Walsh's master bedroom and office were ahead to the right. The mobster had given them the layout when the security detail was assigned in the event something broke bad. Something definitely had.

There was a six-by-four marble pillar in the center of the room dividing the bar from the living room. Inside the pillared centerpiece was a fireplace with access points to both sides of the room.

Gunfire kicked up again before Barnes had a chance to formulate a plan. One of Walsh's men popped up from behind the bar and was firing wildly toward the pillar. His rounds skipped off, chipping away at the marble.

"He must have a visual on him," Barnes said just loud enough for Mainelli to hear.

She took aim where the mob man was firing but didn't see anything.

The mobster ran his weapon dry. In the split second it took him to drop the magazine and dig into his pockets for another, two muffled bangs came from the other side of the room.

The mirrored wall behind the bar was instantly painted in the mobster's blood and brain matter. He swayed for a moment as his body remained in a brief suspension, already dead before he hit the ground.

Barnes still couldn't see the shooter. She didn't want to take her eyes off the fireplace pillar, the direction of the gunfire.

Did he hear us enter? Does he know we're here? Her mind was racing. She knew the only chance she'd have would be the element of surprise. Barnes waited in the quiet seconds that followed the last shootout.

The bedroom and office doors were closed. It was like a game show. What's behind door number one, door number two? Except guessing wrong could end in death. *Where would the killer go? Where did Walsh run to?* Mainelli tried to squeeze himself next to Barnes, but she waved him back with her free hand.

"He's over there," she whispered. "I can't see him, but he's somewhere behind that fireplace wall."

Mainelli took a crouched firing position using the door as both brace and cover, while Barnes maintained her prone position.

She pulled slowly at the hip line of the dead man she was lying behind, trying to roll him up onto his side more. Barnes hoped the extra layer of flesh and bone would be enough to protect her.

And then the strangest thing happened. With the calm of somebody on a Sunday afternoon stroll through the park, the white jacket appeared as The Penitent One moved across the floor toward the closed door of Walsh's study. He didn't see her.

Barnes fired twice as she yelled, "Police, drop the gun!"

The impacts of her two rounds spun the killer in a wild pirouette.

His face, even after being shot, was dead calm as he turned toward Barnes. He raised his pistol and fired controlled bursts at her.

She ducked as low as humanly possible, shrinking herself as the mobster's body shook. His hip and belly were pelted with the silenced rounds of the gun.

Mainelli had fallen backward and was sprawled into the hallway.

Barnes tucked herself down as low as she physically could. Then, as quickly as the gunfire had started, it stopped.

She counted silently, "Three...two..." She willed herself to move. "One!"

Barnes raised herself up, preparing to face the threat, her gun pushed out in front of her. Looking down her sights, she realized he was gone.

It took half a second for her mind to play catch-up. The study door was now open.

Gunfire rang out from within. Six, maybe ten shots were fired, Barnes couldn't keep track. She quickly ran her hand over herself, ensuring none of the rounds he'd fired at her had found their mark. Although she was now covered in the blood of the man she'd used as a human shield, Barnes wasn't hit.

She rushed forward toward Walsh's study as she heard the loud crash of breaking glass. Mainelli huffed a curse from close behind.

Barnes didn't pause outside the door. She entered, button-hooking in and taking the room in a swift sweep of her weapon.

To her left, against a bookcase, was the last man in the mob security team. His body was riddled with bullets. Behind the overturned desk was

Connor Walsh. His hand was partially exposed, as was a bit of his face. He was covered in blood and didn't appear to be moving. No sign of The Penitent One.

Then she saw the source of the breaking glass. The back window had been shattered, spraying glass all over the floor. Barnes rushed to the window, her eyes following a bungee rope that led down the side of the house.

She looked out to the street just in time to see a gray Kawasaki motorcycle disappear down Harvest Street and out of sight.

Mainelli was standing in the doorway, taking in the scene and then Barnes, looking shocked. "That was some ballsy police work there."

"I think I got him," Barnes said. "Obviously I didn't stop him." The high and low in her voice was a side effect of the adrenaline coursing through her veins. She flexed her shaking hands and holstered her weapon.

A gasp and gurgling noise came from Connor Walsh as he rolled to his side and coughed blood. He looked bad. She couldn't tell how many times he had been hit from the amount of blood covering his clothing.

Watching the mob boss flail, Barnes paused, thinking of Mainelli's earlier conversation about killing two birds with one stone. *How hard would it be to not render aid? To let this pariah of a human being slip away into the abyss?*

She pushed back the thought. Not her call, not who she was.

Barnes moved over, pushing the table further out of the way so she could get a better look at the damage to the bleeding mob boss. She ripped open his button-down silk shirt and saw he had been wearing a bulletproof vest. It looked as though two of the rounds he'd taken had bypassed the Kevlar, leaving his upper chest and shoulder bleeding heavily.

She sank her finger deep into the bullet hole just beneath his clavicle. She could feel his pulse through the blood pushing against her finger.

"We've got six dead and one critical. Suspect on the loose. Gray motorcycle heading West on Harvest," Mainelli radioed in, and then knelt alongside Barnes, putting pressure on the other wound.

26

Kelly screeched the Caprice to a halt near the intersection of Dorchester Avenue and Harvest Street. Easy enough to find with the florist van fully engulfed in flames by the curb. Kelly passed the two dead mobsters with the green roses on their chests and ran into Connor Walsh's home. Kelly and his team weren't the first on scene. Patrol had already converged on location minutes before their arrival. He ran up the stairs to the third floor, Gray and Halstead close behind.

They entered Walsh's suite on the third level of the converted triple decker. Barnes was standing in the center of the room near a fireplace when Kelly entered.

He wanted to run to her, to step over the dead mobster and take her in his arms and hold her. But he resisted the urge, forcing himself to walk. A euphoric wave of relief washed over him upon seeing her unharmed.

He walked directly to Barnes and Mainelli. "You guys good?" He addressed both of them but was looking directly into Barnes's emerald green eyes.

She nodded but didn't speak.

He could see the look in her eyes, the distant stare. She was there, but she wasn't. Kelly had been in shootings himself and knew that everybody's brain reacted differently. There was a universal truth—nobody bounced back immediately. The brain had to process, and that process took time. Being on scene, covered in other people's blood, was not the place where that mental healing could begin. The brain needed distance from the causative event if it were to begin to repair itself from the trauma.

Halstead walked up. "I'm glad you two are all right. Now listen carefully, I don't want you to say anything to anybody here on scene. Do you understand me? We'll reconvene for a formal statement of what occurred here. We'll do it by the numbers when you're ready, and I'll make sure that you have union representation on hand when we do." He paused and looked down at her holstered weapon. "Detective Barnes, I'm going to need to take your duty weapon."

There was no feeling worse for a cop than having their gun removed. It made the officer involved feel like they'd done something wrong. Kelly knew this all too well. Halstead must've understood also after working in IA for eight plus years. As soon as he took her gun, he unholstered his and placed it into her holster.

"No good cop should be without. You two are going to be riding a desk for a bit until this gets sorted by the official channels, but let me say—you did a hell of a job here today. And you have my word, I'll back you all the way."

Kelly looked on as the medics prepared to move Walsh on the gurney.

The mob boss he'd recently discovered was his biological father was breathing from an oxygen mask, his eyelids fluttering, as they wheeled him by. Kelly felt a strange impassivity at seeing him in such a condition. He had no feelings for the man, even after learning their connection, other than knowing he was one of the city's biggest problems. His issues on that would have to wait. Because right now, the killer who had just executed six mobsters, and nearly Barnes and Mainelli, had just escaped capture once again.

The only difference was he was now wounded.

Kelly looked at the floor as the gurney was wheeled down the hallway and out of view. On the plush white carpeting, now smattered in various shades of red, were the remaining green roses. A total of seven in all, meaning their killer knew exactly the odds he was up against when he entered. Now, six of those seven were dead, and one was hanging on to life by a thread.

Dawes had been sent to process the scene while Charles continued to work on the evidence from the house in Agawam. The door to The Depot was closed as Halstead recounted the situation and the state of the case as it was. The three detectives, plus Gray, were present.

Mainelli couldn't stop rubbing his thick hands together, as if he couldn't get the sweat or Walsh's blood off his skin. He looked paler than usual. The olive-skinned Italian was as white as an Irishman in winter. Even though he hadn't fired his weapon, he was still involved, still there when the rounds flew, and it had obviously taken a toll. The mental strain was evident on the veteran detective's face.

Barnes, on the other hand, seemed to be making her way back. Pulling the trigger also had that effect; Kelly had seen it firsthand when he had been in a situation that called for him to take action. The other officer on scene didn't fire his gun, but the one who makes the decision to pull the trigger when it's justified or righteous can usually come to terms with it.

It's a much harder thing to grip when you didn't fire, when the enemy was downrange and presenting a threat but for some reason you couldn't pull the trigger. Mainelli fell into that category. He would be filled with the self-doubt and self-loathing that came from those rarer than rare moments in law enforcement where deadly force was necessary. Everybody thinks that when push comes to shove, when their life is on the line, they'll take the shot. But some don't. Some freeze. At least in this case, it didn't cost another cop her life. And maybe if Mainelli had fired, it would have stopped their killer. Maybe not. He would forever question that, and the answer would forever elude him.

"As far as field work, we're down to three, including me," Halstead said. "Mainelli and Barnes will assist from the desk. Just so you know, I've already given a quick debrief to Superintendent Acevedo. And he said, barring any new information, you guys should be good on the shoot. You know how these things go. It's going to take a little while to clear you, especially once press gets wind. I've put you both on light duty, effective immediately. Meaning you can come and go as you please in the building, regular shift stuff, and you can work the paper trail from inside the office. Just no field work. Kelly and

Gray, you guys will handle any of the field work required from this point forward, do you understand me?"

Both nodded.

"Try not to blow up any houses this time," Halstead added.

It was the first time Kelly had seen Halstead try to make a joke. If it was a joke. Impossible to tell from the man's flat inflection.

Kelly's phone vibrated with a text message from Charles that said, "Call ASAP."

"It's Charles," Kelly said, interrupting Halstead. He called the senior crime scene technician. "What do you got, Ray? I'm in a meeting."

"Well, put me on speaker."

Kelly did as he was told, placing his cell phone in the middle of the conference table.

"You've got everybody here. Sergeant Halstead, Mainelli, Barnes, myself, and Gray."

"Guys, you're going to want to hear this."

"We're all ears, Ray," Halstead said. "Go ahead."

"Well, I took that prayer kneeler from the Agawam house. I took the whole thing. I wasn't sure, but I just felt like there were such potential DNA points beyond the shackles that it was worth bringing it in and going over it with a fine-tooth comb."

"I thought you already sent those submissions off for analysis."

"I did, and we're still waiting."

"Then what's the news?" Halstead asked.

"I found something in the wood siding. I don't know what made me look there, but I was looking for some trace fibers along the seam of the wood, an opening at the joint. It was hollowed out. I pried it open and found something extremely interesting."

"Please tell me you're not going to make us guess," Halstead said.

"I know who our guy is." Everyone was silent, as if the air in the room had been sucked out.

Kelly sat forward, listening intently. "How'd you figure that out? We're still waiting on the DNA. Did you get a print?"

"Better. I got his ID. Well, it wasn't an ID per se. It was a newspaper clipping from some thirty years ago."

"A newspaper clipping?"

"In it, there was an article about a boy who'd been tortured and abused by his religious zealot parents. A boy who, at the age of thirteen, had set his house ablaze, killing both mom and dad."

Kelly edged forward, as if he could see whatever Charles was looking at.

"The boy's name was Christopher Vance."

"Do you have the address of the fire, where it took place, the house?"

"I just texted it to you." Kelly saw the alert, an icon indicating the message had been received.

"Amazing job, Charles," Halstead said.

"We owe you, buddy."

"I'll take my payment in the form of a Dunkin' cup of Joe," the technician said with a dry, raspy laugh before clicking off.

Kelly looked around the table, Gray's eyes catching his attention. He looked like he had just opened the biggest present under the tree on Christmas morning. He had a gleeful expression unlike any Kelly had seen since they'd met back in November. Kelly knew why. Gray finally had The Penitent One's name. He'd now be known as the agent who got further than anyone in fifteen years.

Gray almost leapt out of his seat and ran toward the cubicle station he'd turned into his temporary office space. He began typing away furiously at the computer keyboard.

Kelly followed but didn't interrupt. He could see that the FBI agent was totally focused on the task at hand, most likely looking up information on the name just provided by Charles. A few minutes later, he pushed himself back in the roller chair and around to Kelly's cubicle as the printer began to whir.

"I think you're going to like what I just put together."

"Can't wait," Kelly said.

A second later, Kelly held a single-page printout with the name and date of birth for one Christopher Vance. The Clint Vesper name used to purchase the Agawam house now made more sense. He had given a false name but used the same initials, probably out of some comfort or another one of his quirks. Apparently, Christopher Vance had many quirks and a penchant for violence.

"Not much, though, huh? Name and date of birth. I'm not seeing a driver's license or anything."

"I know. I've run it. It's not coming up."

"Then why is this sheet of paper interesting? It just looks like another dead end," Kelly said, almost crunching the paper in frustration.

"See that Y next to DD214?"

Kelly looked down at the paper again, then nodded.

"That's the military's discharge paperwork. I ran him through the military records database and found something. I've just got to place a call or two to get a little more information. But it looks like our guy has a military service record. And with that, there'll be a DA photo if I can track it down."

Gray picked up his cell phone, scrolled through his contacts, and placed the call.

"It's Sterling. I know, long time. Need that favor now. I've got a name and date of birth. I need everything you have on this person, and a photo would be helpful." Gray then relayed the information he had and hung up.

Kelly only heard one side of the conversation but could pick it apart enough to know Gray had just reached out to a source, most likely someone within the Department of Defense.

"You seem to know a lot about the military," Kelly said. "I mean, the inner workings of it."

"Well, that's because I spent eight years in it."

Kelly nodded, impressed on two fronts. One, because he served, and two, that he'd never felt the need to mention it until asked.

"Army?" Kelly asked.

"No, Air Force. Pararescue."

"That's like Special Forces stuff, right?" Kelly was reminded of a Discovery Channel video he had seen during one of his late-night insomnia-induced TV binges.

"It is."

"And the contact you reached out to?"

"A friend. Somebody who owes me, somebody who has the ability to get us what we need. Our Mr. Vance has a military record. But everything I've tried to pull up in the database has been redacted. Typically, that's done with either top secret or special operations. Either way, it would explain why he's been so effective at eluding us."

"And it further proves," Kelly offered, "your BAU guys were spot-on. The top of their analysis said ex-military/police." Kelly breathed a silent sigh of relief that the latter wasn't true. He'd already dealt with an undercover gone rogue and didn't have the stomach for dealing with another. Not that him being ex-military made it any better.

Gray's phone rang a minute later. The conversation was brief, less than ten seconds. All Gray said was, "I'll send you a fax number."

A few more minutes passed and the copier/fax machine whirred to life again. This time it printed several pages, the top one a black-and-white eight-by-ten of a young man in military uniform wearing wire-rimmed glasses.

Kelly picked it up, the paper still warm. He and Gray looked at the image and then at each other.

"I've waited a long time to see that face," Gray said. "And now we're going to put him behind bars."

"I like the sound of that," Kelly said. "Knowing who he is, knowing what he looks like is great, but we still don't know where he is."

"One thing for certain, he's not going to go to a hospital. But we know he's injured. Barnes was confident she hit him. And the blood spatter recovered on the wall of the fireplace was most likely his. But again, DNA confirmation isn't going to help us with the here and now."

Gray shuffled the papers and then found what he was looking for. He tapped it, directing Kelly's attention toward it. "Next of kin. Every service member has it in the event of their untimely death. A family member to whom their benefits would go and a point of contact if they were killed in action."

"I thought his parents were killed."

"It seems as though he had a sibling."

Kelly looked down at the name. "Marcy Vance, three years younger. Why was there no mention of her in that article about the fire?"

"Seems as though she was taken from the family on reports of abuse and put into the foster care system. But it looks like—and this is my guess, of course—that Vance making her his next of kin means he had reconnected with her, maybe after coming out of juvenile detention."

"I didn't think you could serve in the military after committing a crime, especially murder."

Gray shrugged. "His juvenile record was redacted, number one. And number two, maybe it was deemed some level of self-defense and expunged. Either way, whatever the loophole, he was able to get through and into the service and apparently was good at what he did."

"And what was that exactly?" Kelly asked.

"He spent ten years in the Army, with the last five being in Special Forces. Two tours of combat, one in Afghanistan and one in Iraq. So, we're dealing with a combat vet with Special Forces experience. No wonder he's been a ghost. His whole life has been preparing him for this."

Kelly looked down at the address on the information sheet forwarded from Gray's contact. "His sister lives in Sudbury?"

"I guess we know where we're going."

27

It was dark as they pulled down Lakewood Drive in Sudbury, darker still because Kelly had shut off the Caprice's headlights a few houses back. They crept along, slowing at the intersection with Basswood. Marcy Vance lived two houses up on the left on Lakewood. Kelly could fit ten triple decker homes in the space separating them from the target location.

He turned left onto Basswood and stopped out of view from the intersection.

Kelly had never been to Sudbury, but he understood why Christopher Vance would choose this as a place to hole up. It was rural and isolated. They'd done a Google Maps search and looked at it from the overhead satellite imagery before departing. Kelly had tried to get a ground-eye view, but apparently the mapping system hadn't gone down that road, or any of the others in this neighborhood.

The overhead showed it was surrounded by a dense forest. And it was no lie. Marcy Vance's home backed up to the Assabet River Wildlife Preserve. The house itself wasn't very big in comparison to its neighbors. The records online showed it to be two thousand square feet, but with the surrounding acreage, it would fetch a hefty price on the market.

It would also keep Marcy secluded from her neighbors and make it the perfect hiding spot for their killer while he healed from the gunshot wound, or wounds, gifted to him by Kristen Barnes.

"I know Halstead said to stay put and wait till they can come up with an attack plan, but I think it's in our best interest to see if we can get a visual before we blow up this spot and make it obvious that we're onto him. If he wasn't running before, the minute he knows that we know who he is, he'll be gone forever."

"Fair enough," Kelly said, not wanting to disobey his boss again, but knowing if they rolled in with SWAT and turned out to be wrong, then this would probably be their last chance at ever finding him. Kelly sided with Gray. He didn't want to ruin their best chance of catching the killer who'd eluded the FBI for fifteen years. The same killer who murdered Rourke, Kelly's partner, and had haunted him for almost nine years.

They exited the Caprice and made their way into the woods. When they looked at the topography, they saw a two-mile stretch of protected forestland that stretched toward Marcy Vance's property line.

The ground was still frozen solid. The high trees had shaded most of the winter's snow, leaving about five or six inches of iced-over, hard-packed snow. The benefit of it was that it brightened their walk, negating the need for them to use flashlights as they navigated the dense network of trees.

Kelly saw a light in the distance as they got closer to the property line, or what they assumed was the property line. It was a lot easier when looking at the overhead map versus tracking their way in through the icy, snowy woodland area.

Kelly paused and picked up his binoculars. "That's our house. It's got to be."

They were within visual range, at least through binoculars. Kelly spent the next several moments going from window to window. He was hoping to see their target pass by, but no such luck.

"Want to try moving a little closer?" Gray said. "I mean, it'd be great if we can get close and cover it from opposite corners of the house. We'd have a great vantage point for when tactical arrives. If he tries to evade, then we can cover pretty much the perimeter of the house visually with both of us."

"Okay, sounds fair enough. We'll break off when we get a little closer, and I'll work my way around to the other side unless you'd rather?" Kelly offered.

"Either's fine by me."

Kelly knew Gray was right about covering the perimeter. During his years on SWAT, he knew that a perimeter team, if you were short-handed, could be handled by posting two operators on opposite corners. Their visual periphery would effectively cover two sides of the house each, therefore making it possible for two men to hold all four. It wasn't ideal, but it was good enough for an overwatch while they waited for the tactical team to deploy.

SWAT wasn't here. Kelly knew the lag time from activation to deployment. He didn't want to miss an opportunity, however fleeting it might be, to ensure that their target didn't escape.

He wasn't completely disregarding his boss's order. They'd briefed him on Vance's military connection and his sister's address. It had been Halstead who approved them getting eyes on the target location while the tactical element mobilized. What he didn't approve was the two investigators getting out on foot and closing the distance to the house.

Kelly knew that by following along with Gray's plan, he was stepping beyond the gray area of his new boss's orders, and he wasn't sure how that was going to play out after Halstead had admonished him the other day for failing to keep him in the loop. But if it meant capturing Christopher Vance, The Penitent One, then he was willing to take the tongue lashing and any potential fallout.

They moved slowly, stopping every ten to fifteen steps and taking up a position near a tree. From there, they looked through their binoculars' scoped lenses and scanned the house. Still nothing. No new lights had been turned on since they'd first spotted the location. There was one on the upper floor of the two-story house, and it looked like two of the rooms on the bottom floor were illuminated. Otherwise, the house was dark.

Kelly got an incoming text alert from Barnes. "Arrest warrant a go. SWAT heading your way. Be safe."

"Goes without saying, we should be ready for anything," Gray said.

Kelly had held up the text to Gray as his radio chirped to life. The volume was as low as it could go without deactivating, but in the dark stillness of the forest, it echoed. Kelly panicked trying to turn it lower but almost turned it off.

It was Halstead. "Tactical en route. ETA twenty minutes."

Kelly responded, "Roger that. We have eyes on the house. Lights on, no visual of the suspect." He then clicked his radio off.

"We've got twenty minutes to work our way around this house before tactical lights it up and the show really begins. Think we can make it?"

"I don't see why not. Just keep a steady pace," Gray said, stepping off.

A few minutes later they were nearing the back of the house. They didn't need the binoculars at this point, although they continued to use them when they stopped.

The trees ran right up to the house, minus a twenty-foot open swath behind a patio.

"All right, this is where we should separate," Gray said. "I can cover the back corner if you want to work your way around."

"Maybe with your military background, you should be the one sneaking around back," Kelly said, thinking twice and defaulting to the man's special forces background.

"Fair enough." Gray peered out at the dense wood line.

Kelly took one step forward to better position himself behind a thick maple tree's knotted trunk when he felt something snag his foot. He instinctively bent and tugged at it, thinking it was a vine or a root. His fingers immediately registered the difference.

He looked down at what he was caught up in. A small orb planted in the ground only a few feet high bounced a barely visible green beam of light against the outside of his boot. "What the hell is this?" Kelly said in a hushed whisper.

Gray bent down, clearing away some snow and underbrush around his boot. He canted his head sideways, running his eyes up and down the path of the beam. "Shit," he said. "Motion sensor."

"Like the exploding kind?" Kelly asked, his heart racing as he remembered the fireball at the Agawam house.

"No. But it's tripped. If he's in there, he knows we're coming."

They both simultaneously looked toward the house. Kelly stepped over the wire and scanned with his binoculars. The light on the second floor went out.

"He's here. I'm going to be moving fast," Gray said. "If he pops up, cover me."

"Will do." Kelly shuffled further toward the house, watching where he stepped.

Gray was moving in a sweeping direction to flank around the back side of the house when he let out a blood-curdling scream.

Kelly left his position and sprinted over, trying to be as careful as possible, not sure where the threat was coming from. When he got to Gray, he was biting down hard on the sleeve of his heavy coat, muffling the screams of agony while gripping his right shin.

Kelly looked down and saw with dismay a bear trap had snapped shut against his shin bone. The teeth ripped through the jeans. Even in the poor light, Kelly could see the broken bone poking out of his skin. It was a devastating wound to behold. Warm blood melted the icy hardpack as tendrils of steam rose up around the injured leg.

This is bad. Kelly went for his radio.

Gray reached up and grabbed his arm. "He's going to be coming. No way he didn't hear that. This wood line is probably loaded with them." He grit his teeth in an effort to maintain composure. "There's no way around it. He's going to know where we are from the motion sensor. You've got to get ready."

"Your leg," Kelly said, looking down at it. "You're going to bleed out."

"I'll be okay." Gray immediately undid the belt from his pants and cinched a makeshift tourniquet just below his knee. "This will hold it. I'll be fine. Just make sure he doesn't get away. This is our only chance. Do you understand me? This is it."

Kelly nodded. "He's not going anywhere."

He moved out, disregarding the crunch of icy snow beneath his feet. Kelly was almost at a run when he slipped on a patch of ice. His feet shot out from under him and he landed flat on his back, knocking the wind out of himself momentarily. As he sat up, his face was peppered by fragmented wood chips, stinging his cold skin. Kelly looked up to see three holes punched in the bark of the tree in front of him.

He never heard the shots, even in the quiet, although the crunching and movement in the trees and the ice underneath didn't help. Kelly was being hunted.

He scrambled behind a nearby tree trunk. Pinned down, he reached for his radio as three more rounds hit a tree on the other side of him.

Kelly started backing up, working himself away from the kill zone in some poor attempt at a crab walk. Moving on all fours, staying low, he tried to keep as many trees as possible between himself and the killer stalking him.

His hand ran into something cold and sharp. Kelly turned. Just beneath a few ice-covered branches was the jagged, sharp teeth of an open bear trap. Just like the one that got Gray. And Kelly had almost put his hand inside it.

He was about to bypass it when he had a thought.

Kelly let out a scream rivaling Gray's. Possibly louder. "My leg!"

Gray was close, but not that close. He heard him call out in a hushed whisper, "Stay down, Kelly. I'll try to come to you."

Kelly responded, "Stay where you're at." He then screamed again for effect, but stayed tucked behind the tree, which was now shredded by bullets.

He worked his fingers around the base of the trap. It took a little effort, but he quickly released it from the frozen ground's icy grip.

Kelly waited in the dark. Every few seconds, he'd let out a wail or a curse, giving away his position time and time again.

Less than a minute later, he heard the crunch of approaching footsteps, still a short distance away but closing in. Kelly knew it could be only one person, and he was coming to finish the job.

Adding to his ruse, Kelly picked up his radio, still turned off, and relayed, "All units be advised, Gray and I are both down. I repeat—officers down! The place is booby trapped. All responding units, take caution. Target on scene!"

The crunching steps were closer now. Kelly rolled to his side and wailed, projecting his voice to one side of the tree just as he heard the killer step around the other.

Split seconds. That was all it took. Action versus reaction. Kelly rolled to his side, facing Vance, and flung the bear trap forward. Vance raised the gun to shoot as the trap struck his extended hand and slammed shut with a sickening crunch.

The pistol was knocked from his hand as Vance wailed like a siren. The damage from the steel trap's sharp teeth was readily apparent, nearly severing his hand clean off.

Not waiting for him to recover or react, Kelly launched himself off the icy ground and swung his right hand down harder than he'd ever thrown a punch. Kelly's legendary overhand right crashed into Vance's face. He felt the crunch of his nose and the snap of his glasses underneath his bare knuckles. A devastating blow in the ring. More so now, ungloved and unpadded, his cold, hard knuckles delivering justice a long time coming. And it felt good.

Vance staggered back on the uneven icy ground. Between the blow and the bear trap, he fell, slamming his head into an exposed tree root. Not waiting a second for him to recover, Kelly pounced on top of the man.

Vance's head bobbled loosely as Kelly rolled him over. The punch had rendered him unconscious, or close enough to it. He cuffed him, cinching the other cuff above the damaged arm ensnared by the trap, then did a rapid but thorough search of him, making sure he didn't have any other weapons.

Satisfied, Kelly dragged him and sat him a few feet away from the pistol he had used to try to kill him.

Keeping his gun on the killer, Kelly pulled his phone. "We got him."

"Wha—" Halstead started to say.

"Send medics. Gray got snagged by a bear trap. Vance is injured too. Tell the guys to be careful. He's got the surrounding woods rigged with traps." He hung up before giving his boss a chance to respond. Kelly knew there would be time for that later.

Kelly stared down the sight of his gun at the man who had killed his partner nearly nine years ago, the same man who had killed an undercover FBI agent and who had nearly killed his girlfriend and partner. A deep-rooted rage boiled inside him, and he fought to control it. He could pull the trigger now, end it, end this man who had caused so much misery.

Kelly's finger toggled the Glock's trigger, taking it to a fraction of an inch from the break point and holding it there. One micro squeeze, and the round would free itself from the chamber and end this man's life.

But Kelly wasn't an executioner.

With an exhale, he released his finger and indexed alongside the slide. He held steady as the sirens in the distance grew louder.

28

Halstead arrived on scene and took in the aftermath. Gray was already on his way to the hospital, and Christopher Vance was being stabilized and readied for transport. Two uniformed patrolmen accompanied him in the ambulance, and one followed behind. They were taking no chances with the killer, the trained assassin who had proven himself to be as dangerous and elusive as they came.

Halstead stared blankly at Kelly, the cobalt blue of his eyes betraying none of his thoughts. And then he opened his mouth to speak.

Kelly readied himself for whatever onslaught of expletives he had in store. He was prepared for the fallout. He deemed it worthy, whatever the cost. And then Halstead did something that surprised Kelly completely. He smiled and slapped him on the shoulder. Kelly shook himself, as if stuck in a dream.

"Good job. It's a hell of a thing you did here today."

Kelly continued shaking his head in disbelief.

"Didn't expect that?" Halstead asked.

"Didn't know you could smile."

Halstead laughed. And then, as if flipping a switch, his face was deadpan again. "You believe all that stuff you hear? The Iceman? You of all people,

Michael Kelly, should know better than to take anything at face value. Now, go get cleaned up and we'll meet back at the office for a debrief."

"I'd like to stop by the hospital first. Need to check on a friend."

Bobby McDonough had a bandage running across his face, covering most of it. The only thing visible was a corner of the left side of his face, including his eye. His hands and part of his midsection were also bandaged in white gauze. Monitors chirped and beeped in the backdrop. Kelly sat in the chair next to his lifelong friend, reached out, and gently grabbed his wrist.

McDonough stirred, and his one visible eye blinked open. It watered as the light struck it.

Kelly reached out and wiped his friend's cheek. "How you holding up, pal?"

"Like I passed out drunk at a beach and woke up with a third-degree sunburn. How do you think I feel?" McDonough snarked.

"Good to see you haven't lost your charming personality. No luck of that getting burned away, is it?" Kelly chuckled, giving his friend a dose of his own medicine.

"Thanks," Bobby said quietly.

"For what?"

"Oh, you going to get all humble on me now, Saint Mike?" McDonough said. "Look, I already heard one of the cops talking. You pulled me out. I would have been dead back there in that house. You saved my life."

"You act like that's such a bad thing," Kelly said.

"It is, if you're going to hold it over my damn head for the rest of my life."

"Nah," Kelly said, "I think we're even."

He knew McDonough understood exactly what he was talking about. The life debt had been repaid with a life, the only way to truly pay those kinds of debts.

"I don't know if they told you, but your boss is down the hallway," Kelly said, rolling his eyes slightly.

"We're hard men to kill."

"Guess so."

"Then I guess you also heard we got him."

McDonough nodded slightly and then winced at the pain of the movement. "I did hear that."

"You know, a lot of this could have been avoided had you just told me who the hell he was. You know that, right?" Kelly leveled a serious stare at his friend's one visible eye.

"I guess, although I didn't know his real name. We called him Gabriel, or that's what he told us to call him. Something about the archangel. Guy was a nutjob."

That made sense, Kelly thought. Fit his whole motif. He was sure the psychiatrists at the FBI were going to have a field day interviewing him post-arrest to dissect him like a guinea pig.

Serial killers of all kinds got a special place in the post-arrest arena. They were treated in an iconic fashion, separated from the general population and held in reverence by psychologists. And with everything Kelly had learned about Christopher Vance, AKA The Penitent One, he would no doubt fit the bill.

"You may not have known who he was, but you could have pointed me in his direction, given me his contact information. Like how you reached out to him for a job. We could have set something up. We could have done this years ago." Kelly was referencing Danny Rourke's case, and McDonough knew it.

McDonough coughed and then groaned in pain but didn't respond.

"Why Tomlin? Why Rourke?"

"Those are two entirely different questions," McDonough said. "And everything I tell you here now is because of what you did for me in that fire. But none of it, and I mean none of it, will ever go on record, because I'll never speak about it again. And I know you won't name me as your source."

Kelly knew he was right. "Then tell me."

"Tomlin was business. We got word that they had put somebody in play to eavesdrop on Walsh. We heard it was an agent, so we hired outside to take care of the problem. Gabriel was our handyman, our cleaner, when a job needed doing that we couldn't do ourselves."

"Then why did he come after you? Why did he come after Walsh?"

"O'Toole."

"O'Toole? What do you mean, O'Toole?"

"He wanted double because he was doing a fed. Walsh agreed, but O'Toole shorted him."

"I guess that wasn't a good idea," Kelly said.

McDonough nodded and then looked down at an IV drip extending from the line in his wrist. "I guess you could say that. But what's done is done."

"Okay. Why Rourke then?"

Bobby turned slightly away from Kelly. Every movement, no matter how subtle, seemed to cause his friend pain, and it hurt Kelly to watch. But he wasn't leaving this room without an answer, and Bobby knew it.

"You're not going to like what I have to say. Me holding this back from you was as much about protecting you and the memory of your friend and partner."

"Tell me," Kelly said.

"He was dirty, Mike."

Kelly sat back. He felt sick. *Danny Rourke, dirty?*

"I warned you it wasn't going to be something you wanted to hear. But it's the truth. He was on the take. He was in charge of making sure that certain businesses paid up. Problem was, what we paid him for his services wasn't good enough. He got greedy. Walsh didn't like it. Walsh doesn't like being stolen from. There's no coming back from it."

Kelly heard his friend's words, but they didn't make sense. Didn't match what he knew about Danny Rourke. But the more he thought about it, the more he knew that McDonough wasn't lying. The truth sometimes tasted funny, like day-old pizza. Rourke's memory soured in his mind.

Kelly stood. There was nothing left to say. He needed time to process everything. He'd risked his life tonight, and so had Barnes and everyone else in their unit, to bring to justice a person who had killed a cop. And he had just found out the reason why and couldn't tell a soul.

"I'll be seeing you, Bobby," Kelly said, turning and walking away.

"I'll be kicking your ass in that ring in no time," McDonough offered as the door closed behind him.

Kelly walked down the hallway toward the elevator.

Up ahead, two doors down, he saw the strangest sight. Under different circumstances it would have registered as comical.

On one side of a patient door was a uniformed Boston police officer. Sitting in a chair on the other side was one of Walsh's goons. Two polar opposites guarding the same man.

Kelly walked by the room. The door was open enough to see in. The legendary mob boss was surrounded by several of his closest friends. The doctor was fighting an uphill battle and wasn't faring well, evident as Walsh gave him the middle finger and then stuck a Tootsie Pop in his mouth.

Kelly walked by without stopping.

Kelly, exhausted, was sitting at his desk. Barnes and Mainelli had gone home two hours ago, and Gray was in the hospital recovering. His first visit tomorrow morning would be to the FBI agent.

Kelly stared at the murder board. He had already taken down Tomlin's card, switching it from red to blue. Same with O'Toole's. He stared at the last red one, the one that had topped his board since he came to Homicide.

Kelly stared at the card for what seemed like an eternity, then reached out to remove it. The red card seemed as distant as if reaching for the sun. The un-closable case was now shut forever. The card felt foreign in his hand, its value disintegrated with McDonough's words.

He pulled it off the board, holding it between his fingers before transferring the information to a blue one. When he was finished, he grabbed his coat and made his way to the door.

On the way, he tore Rourke's red card in half and dropped it in a trashcan.

Then Kelly walked out of the second-floor offices of Boston Homicide, leaving nearly a decade of emotional baggage behind him.

SIGN OF THE MAKER
A BOSTON CRIME THRILLER NOVEL

A serial bomber is on the loose in Boston.

If Kelly wants any chance of stopping the attacks, he must join forces with the most unlikely of partners.

Get your copy today at BrianChristopherShea.com

JOIN THE READER LIST

Never miss a new release! Sign up to receive exclusive updates from author Brian Shea.

Join today at
BrianChristopherShea.com/Boston

Sign up and receive a free copy of
Unkillable: A Nick Lawrence Short Story.

YOU MIGHT ALSO ENJOY...

The Nick Lawrence Series

Kill List

Pursuit of Justice

Burning Truth

Targeted Violence

Murder 8

The Boston Crime Thriller Series

Murder Board

Bleeding Blue

The Penitent One

Sign of the Maker

Never miss a new release! Sign up to receive exclusive updates from author Brian Shea.

BrianChristopherShea.com/Boston

Sign up and receive a free copy of

Unkillable: A Nick Lawrence Short Story

ABOUT THE AUTHOR

Brian Shea has spent most of his adult life in service to his country and local community. He honorably served as an officer in the U.S. Navy. In his civilian life, he reached the rank of Detective and accrued over eleven years of law enforcement experience between Texas and Connecticut. Somewhere in the mix he spent five years as a fifth-grade school teacher. Brian's myriad of life experience is woven into the tapestry of each character's design. He resides in New England and is blessed with an amazing wife and three beautiful daughters.

facebook.com/BrianChristopherShea

twitter.com/BrianCShea

instagram.com/BrianChristopherShea